P9-BYH-763

Fog of Doubt

Fog of Doubt

CHRISTIANNA BRAND

With a new introduction by

CHRISTIANNA BRAND

Carroll & Graf Publishers, Inc.
New York

Copyright, © 1952, 1953 by Christianna Brand.

Reprinted by arrangement with the author's agent.

Introduction copyright, © 1979, by Christianna Brand.

All rights reserved.

First Carroll & Graf edition 1984.

Carroll & Graf Publishers, Inc.
260 Fifth Avenue
New York, N.Y. 10001

ISBN: 0-88184-065-3

Manufactured in the United States of America

Introduction

I'M SURE IT'S MOST IMPROPER to say of ones own books that one likes them, but I must confess that I simply love mine. After all, if I didn't, I wouldn't publish them. And of them all, the one I love best is this book, *Fog of Doubt* (1953).

Just for fun, I set the scene in my own house. In the book, there's a desk in the hall and in our house, there's this desk in the hall. In the book, the curtains in the drawing room are coral-colored and the chair covers are the sort of green that would go with coral-color—and so they are in our house; (it has a 'drawing room' because it is that sort of house: a Regency house, left over from the elegent days when the mistress's carriage would drive into the cobbled yard and the horses be stabled where our garage now is—there are still cobblestones and you can see the stalls). In this house and in the same district, using the real street names, with the same accommodation and the same furniture and even much the same people and very much the same baby and the same poodle and the same Siamese cat, I placed my book; and people who have lived round here since long before the book was written, have told me that nowadays they never pass the bench outside the church without thinking 'That's where Melissa sat with Damien', or the telephone box on the corner without thinking, 'That's where Rosie called up from.' I suppose it does make for a sort of reality—using what you *know* about.

As far as I'm aware no murders ever took place in this house; but something rather odd did arise from the book. In the days when it was written, it was not yet fashionable to call girls by the simple old names, but I christened the two sisters-in-law who are major characters in the book, Matilda and Rosie. A neighbor, an old man who had lived a long time next door, asked me, "How could you have known that fifty years ago, there lived *in your house* two sisters called Matilda and Rose?" I knew nothing of the history of the house and certainly nothing of any Matilda and Rose; for a while I kept looking over my shoulder to see if they were there.

There is something I think of as "author's luck" and this plot arose from a bit of author's luck. I read a book and thought, "Oh, yes, I see what's coming—" (and I may say, I added, "What a marvellous idea for a plot!")—and in the end it wasn't that plot at all. So I used it for my own plot, and whatever its merits, it has this: the entire explanation is given in the last line. It has one other peculiarity too, but if I mention it here, I'm giving my own game away. The reader may like to work it out for himself; it's glaringly there, for all the world to see.

In England, the book was titled *London Particular*. Well, first it was titled *Kensington Gore*—there is a street in London called Kensington Gore and I wrote the whole thing round it, placing it, naturally, in Kensington—which, in turn, is a district of London. Then I discovered that someone else was using the title so I had to unravel it all and place it in Maida Vale and the new title, *London Particular*, was one I came to love. A London Particular was the old name for a London fog. We don't get them now, not the real fogs: we're obliged to use only smokeless fuels and it does keep the air cleaner. But up to 15 years ago, or so, we had them, sometimes for two or three days at a time, and it really was true that you "couldn't see your hand before your face". A pea-souper was another name for them and indeed they were actually thick, a sort of thick yellowy-greeny-grey, very fumey and horrible, and leaving a nasty taste in one's mouth. It was frightening because, entirely familiar with your surroundings, you could still be bewildered as to just where you were. There was a horrid fascination about them, but it was all pretty grim; the city would grind to a halt, traffic couldn't move (you could hardly see the glimmer of the street lights, let alone be lit by them) and one hardly dared to venture forth for fear of getting lost. It was all very dank and cold, and infiltrated into the house and made everything dirty. It is part of the absurdity of us who love London—"most kindly nurse" as Spencer called her—that in our secret hearts we were rather proud of our pea-soupers.

In such a fog, I set my book and called it *London Particular*. Naturally such a title meant nothing to most Americans, so it was entitled there, as it is now, *Fog of Doubt*.

As London districts go, Maida Vale, where the book is set, is not—by that name at any rate—particularly old; though through it runs one of the great, straight enduring roads that the Romans built, 2000 years ago, from their "Londinium", slowly developing from its huddle of huts on the banks of the river Thames. The long slope of the hill that runs down towards our part of the road, was densely covered with trees and called St. John's Wood. It was land which from the beginning of the 14th century had belonged to the order of the Knights of St. John of Jerusalem, and later was part of the royal hunting ground of Queen Elizabeth I. Gradually, as the city grew, the forest was cleared for farmland and by the beginning of the 19th century when it became Maida Vale, the area was famous for its gardens—we still go to a little old pub in a street called Violet Hill—and especially its fruit gardens. Our huge old mulberry tree—they are very rare in London now, and indeed in most of England—is clearly a hark-back to those days. Pineapples were coming into fashion and a few doors up from our house is one whose gates are still ornamented with plaster pineapples—there was a big pinery there. Gradually these houses were being built up along the old road—one of them being our house; and during a great revision of the paths, toll gates and so on, the district was rechristened Maida Vale, after the battle of Maida in southern Italy; there is a pub called the Hero of Maida (you could write a history of Europe round our old pub names, I sometimes think. Many of them have become confused over the ages; a famous one is the Elephant and Castle, which is believed to have been named originally after that Isabella—the "Infanta Castille"—who packed Columbus off to discover America).

So Maida Vale, and this house, where all the plot of *Fog of Doubt* takes place, is 150 years old, or thereabouts. There are no pineapples now, except those plaster ones on the gate along the street; and no fruit trees except for very old apple and pear trees keeping up the tradition in many of the gardens on either side of the house—and our own great mulberry. You will find the mulberry mentioned in the high-walled garden of the house in *Fog of Doubt*.

This book was of the genre of the "classic" detective story— Dorothy Sayers disapproved of their being called "thrillers" or indeed anything but "detective stories". The Detection Club over which she imposed her reign for so long, actually laid down certain rules. One of these was: "there shall be no Chinamen." By this was meant that scenes and characters should be "real"; the Mysterious East, unknown poisons, anything that was not possible, credible, acceptable to the standards of every day life—all that was out. Except for murder of course; but the murder had to be reasonably accounted for, in a recognizable setting, with a cast of comprehensible people; and there had to be a detective and detecting.

I think she would not have agreed with my word "fantasy" but in this kind of "entertainment literature" where, in those days especially, the characters were everyday people living in nice, everyday homes—I do think that the intrusion of murder is so unlikely as to amount to "fantasy". Personally, I accept it as such and then strive to make the unreality as real as possible. No people of this kind, I say to myself, living this kind of life, would ever get themselves into this sort of situation. But, confronted with such a situation after all, I then ask myself how, together and severally, these people would have behaved. I often use real people, people I know, and apply the same question—how would they have behaved? There are several characters in *Fog of Doubt* who are taken from people I know: they react to a situation which would in fact have been quite alien to them, exactly as those friends of mine would have reacted. But the whole basis of the story is—of course it is—a fantasy.

This is a very difficult kind of book to write. Because it's made (I hope) "easy to read" that doesn't mean that a huge amount of work and concentration doesn't go into the making of it. Just think of the complications. To build up a case against half a dozen people, each of which is absolutely water-tight except for one small point which destroys the theory—every facet dovetailing with all the facets of the *other* watertight cases against the *other* people—all the time concealing the real plot while at the same time placing every fact squarely before the reader: it takes a bit of doing! An enormous amount of sleight-of-hand is required to produce each necessary fact, disguising its importance, its real meaning—and *not* by mixing it up with a lot of facts not otherwise necessary to the story: I like to say that no two lines could be removed from any work of mine, whose removal would not leave somewhere else in the book, a gap, which those lines referred to. If I so much as say that a character "went wearily upstairs, cleaned his teeth and fell into bed"—you watch it! The "wearily" may catch your attention and so deflect from the apparently throwaway detail that he cleaned his teeth, which sounds like just a bit of "color". But no, no: the fact that his toothbrush is damp, and has evidently been recently used—that may be the important phrase, may be going to fit in somewhere later on. Nor will the "wearily" have been used only as a deflection of the reader's attention from the toothbrush; there will be a reason somewhere why the character was weary. You may even find that "he went upstairs" is the vital point: two pages ago he was in a ranch house—without your noticing it, he must have changed his scene, he was going to bed elsewhere. Three little, apparently unimportant phrases; but each of them germane to the plot, each of them possibly important to the plot and each of them—and for the author this is the tricky part—fitting in with *all* the actions of *all* the other people taking part in the plot.

Then again, we say lightly "all the other people". Just those six or seven people and no others? How exclude the gardener, possibly a burglar, the apparently casual passer-by? The reader must be protected from the trouble of suspecting outsiders who have no part in the story and yet in the ordinary way would be part of the scene. "Least likely person" must be one of a well-defined group. The writer leans over backwards to isolate this group—they are on an island, fenced in by some boundary, cut off by snow, flood, fire, fallen tree, what have you? But "what have you?" in this case is a by no means unlimited choice and the old ploys grow stale, at best are too often labored and obvious. For myself, when it has not worked out simply that the group falls into a natural isolation—my book, *Green for Danger* (1945) was a good example, the action taking place in an operating theatre where there were of necessity only a limited number of characters—where this doesn't happen, I adapt a simple solution. Beneath the title page, I list my cast of characters, leaving out, as I say, the gardeners and the burglars and the passers-by, and add: "within this group of people were found two victims and a murderer."

Within the small group of people who circled about the house in Maida Vale on that fog-bound night, were found two victims and a murderer. A little before the end, the reader will know the identity of the murderer: not until the last line—unless of course he has brilliantly deduced it all—I don't mean "guessed"; no crime writer is interested in peoples' guesses, he places his clues for the purpose of deduction—unless he has deduced the solution to it all, and heaven knows, it has been placed squarely in front of him all the way through, and I do mean all the way through—will he know how it was done.

I know who did it *and* how it was done; but I still read it over and over again. Like I said, I simply love it!

CHRISTIANNA BRAND
London, England

Fog of Doubt

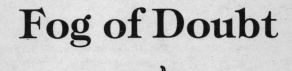

*

*To my
adopted daughter*
VICTORIA
'Emma for Love'

*

. . . I asked him whether there was a great fire anywhere? For the streets were so full of dense brown smoke that scarcely anything was to be seen. 'Oh, dear no, Miss,' he said, 'this is a London particular.' I had never heard of such a thing. 'A fog, Miss,' said the young gentleman. *Bleak House*

*

The scenes, characters and events portrayed in this novel are entirely imaginary and no reference whatsoever is intended to any living persons.

*

CHAPTER ONE

THE dank grey fog was like an army blanket, held pressed against the windows of the car. It seemed an age before Tedward returned from his reconnaissance, his yellow wash-leather glove looming up startlingly, a disembodied hand, knocking at the glass beside her with a terrifying little, muffled thud. Rosie lowered the window and poked out her lovely head. 'Any luck?'

'Yes, it's Sutherland Avenue we're in, not Elgin Avenue at all.' He flashed his torch and there, all the time, was the street name, just a few feet from them, a gleam of white along the low railing. The light went out and he melted back into the grey; she saw the flare of the torch again, dimly glowing, as he passed round the back of the car and climbed into the driving seat, settling himself beside her, stout, solid, comfortable old Tedward, with a reassuring pat upon her knee. 'Won't be long now, chicken. I know exactly where we are. Don't worry.'

'That's what you said before,' she complained, driven by shock and anxiety to an unwonted peevishness.

'Yes, but this time I really do; only we seem to have got back-to-front, God knows how, and I shall have to turn her round.' A bus crept by, a ghost bus, a-glimmer with eerie lights, with more lights making pin-points in the leaden dark where a line of lesser vehicles crawled in its broad wake. He swung round with infinite caution and for a minute or two they crept along in the queue before edging

9

off cautiously, hugging the gutter, to the left. 'Don't worry, pet! I really do know now.'

Rosie jerked impatiently. 'How *can* I not worry? We've been hours already.'

'A quarter of an hour at most, Rosie. I couldn't have driven an inch faster, darling—pea soup isn't *in* it.'

'No, but losing the way like this—you surely ought to know it by now.'

'I do, when I can see an inch in front of me.'

'If only we'd rung up the police before we started,' she said, fretfully.

'I know,' he admitted. 'That was my fault; I ought to have thought of it. But there it is—it's usually only about five minutes from my place to yours, and one's instinct was to leap into the car and dash round. I'd no idea the fog was anything like this.'

Her round young face was white with anxiety, her long legs twisted about one another, muscles tight with nervous strain. 'Tedward—you don't think he's dead, do you?'

'How the hell do *I* know?' he said, losing patience a little in his own acute nervousness.

'Well, you're a doctor, aren't you?'

He leaned out of the window to watch the kerb as they crept round to the left again. 'Just because I'm a doctor, it doesn't mean I can diagnose a message over the telephone. Tell me again just what happened. . . .'

'I've *told* you, Tedward. The telephone rang and I thought it might be a patient for you, so I picked it up, just like I would at home for Thomas. And the voice said in this frightful sort of croak, "Come quick!" and I said, "Who is it?" and he said, "Tell the doctor to come quick," and then he said, "Someone came in and hit me with a mastoid mallet," and then he said, "I'm dying." So of course I was utterly bewildered, but I still thought he was just a patient and I said, "Well, tell me where to come to," and he gave our address. *Our* address!'

'You're sure it was your address?'

'Well, I suppose I know where I live, don't I?' said Rosie, querulously.

'And he definitely said "a mastoid mallet"?'

'Thomas must have left one lying around somewhere and the burglar just picked it up and hit poor Raoul with it. There's a lot of old instruments stuck away all over the place.'

'You're sure it *was* this Raoul Vernet?'

'Well, the voice said our address and Raoul was having dinner there to-night, and there wouldn't be anyone else there with a foreign accent. Oh, Tedward—do you think he could be really dying? Of course Frenchmen do make a fuss.'

'You could judge better than I could, Rosie. I didn't hear him.'

'He sounded frightfully faint and then there was a clonk as though he'd dropped the receiver. . . .'

'Well, we'll soon be there,' he said. They swung round once more, hugging the kerb. 'This is Maida Vale now: we shan't be long.'

They drove on in silence, the little car stealing through the muffled murmur of the fog-blanketed city like a marauding cat—creeping along on its belly, grey body melting into the grey, only its two bright eyes round and agleam in the night. The man's heavy, middle-aged face, usually so jocund and smiling, was lined with anxiety and as leaden and grey as the fog outside; the girl sat with plump, tapering fingers locked tautly about a nyloned knee. He, whose whole training had been in the preservation of life, told himself stoutly that anyway all vile, seducing rats like this creature Raoul Vernet were a great deal better dead; she, young, anxious, over-excited, gave herself up to the contemplation of her delectable sins and cudgelled her foolish wits to decide whether, from her own point of view, it was a Good Thing or a Bad Thing if poor Raoul proved to have pipped off. And what, if he *had* pipped off, he had said to Matilda before he pipped.

CHAPTER TWO

IT was just a week since Rosie had told Matilda. 'I say, Tilda, I wanted to ask you something. I'm afraid I've got myself into a most frightful muddle. In fact I think I may be going to have a baby.'

Tilda sat staring at her, struck motionless, one hand grasping the tail of Emma's nightdress. Emma, straining against white Dayella like a dog on a leash, postured with great silliness before Adorabella, the copy-cat baby in the glass who obligingly postured back; such sycophancy suddenly palling, gave up and stuck out her tongue. This strictly forbidden gesture brought Tilda back to life. She hauled her child on to her knee and, automatically beating its round, pink mushroom of a behind, said with a sort of despairing resignation: 'Oh, *Rosie!*'

'Well, there's no use being horrified,' said Rosie. 'It's done now, and that's all there is to it.'

'It's not all there is to it, I assure you,' said Matilda, restoring the blithely uncaring Emma to an upright position and undoing her own good work by responding to craven caresses. 'Having an illegitimate child's no joke, my dear, especially at the ripe age of eighteen years.'

'Good gracious, you don't think I'm going to *have* it, do you?'

'What else do you propose to do about it?'

'Oh, well, my dear, there are thousands of ways. I mean, dreary old women in back streets with hot water bottles, though what they do with them one never can imagine. But still *I* needn't worry; I can always go to Tedward.'

Tedward was Thomas Evans' partner in medical practice. 'Tedward wouldn't touch a thing like that.'

'He might not for other people, but he would for me. I mean, he's frightfully soppy about me, isn't he?'

'I think he is, rather, God help him!—but all the more reason why he shouldn't help you under these circumstances. And what on earth,' said Tilda, miserably, 'what on earth is Thomas going to say?'

'I thought perhaps we needn't tell Thomas,' said Rosie, quickly.

'Oh, don't be silly, child; living here in the house with him—*and* being a doctor. . . .'

Rosie was Thomas's sister, thought she was less than half his age. She had been left a burden on him, while he still fought his way through the years of his medical training and he, since the burden was rounded of face and limb with warm, amber eyes and foolish curly yellow hair, and had, moreover, grown up gay and easy tempered and not more incredibly silly than the next pretty girl, had conceived an idealistic passion for it, had exalted the burden in his otherwise eminently cool and sensible mind, into a treasure of infinite virtue and charm. Matilda, in the twelve years of their marriage, had tried diffidently to suggest to him now and then that so much physical allurement allied to so much careless generosity and a skull of purest ivory through and through, might be pregnant of future danger—and pregnant, it now seemed, had been just the word. But Thomas, in all other matters quite aridly rational, was a damn fool about Rosie and that was all there was to it. He had reiterated indulgently that she was a perfect bloody idiot, of course, like all girls of her age; but, *un*like the rest, as good as gold. And he had completed his folly by packing her off, all on her own, to a finishing school in Switzerland, still with a beautiful faith in the armour of a round felt hat with a crested school hatband, and a uniform overcoat. Rosie had, of course, pitched the hat out on to the line, the moment her train steamed out of Victoria station, and sought a compartment not reserved like her own, 'for ladies only'; and even an old school hat might have some virtue in it, it seemed, if virtue was quite the word for it: for its flight past the window had provided an opening for conversation with her first pick-up, a young dog who had subsequently proved to be up to some very old tricks. So that now, despite the kind help and chaperonage in Geneva of Matilda's own one-time flame, Raoul Vernet, here she was back on the family's hands, not to say in the family way.

Raoul Vernet! Tucking up the sleepy baby into its white blankets, putting out the nursery gas fire, feeling her way across the darkened room, Tilda smiled reminiscently and was back again with Raoul under the trees outside the little pub in Carouge, a tram ride from Geneva; with a carafe of red wine between them on the white tablecloth and Raoul murmuring that to-night, now really to-night, at last they would go to some place and be alone together. . . . 'Eh, Mathilde? Ah, Mathilde—dites oui; dites oui!' A fine one *I* am, she thought, to be preaching morality to poor, fallen Rosie.

Rosie, fallen perhaps but not noticeably crestfallen, was curled up in the firelight on the shabby sofa-bed in Thomas's 'office'. 'Well, now, Rosie—you had better tell me all about it. . . .'

And, damn it!—there she was, back in Carouge again; sitting under the trees with the fairy lights, seeing again the table before her as bold and clear as a Van Gogh painting, white rolls broken on a white cloth and a bottle of rough red wine. . . . 'Of course you wouldn't know about it, Tilda,

15

it's a little place outside Geneva, "our pub" we used to call it, and it was most terribly romantic and I suppose we were young and idiotic, of course I'd be more experienced now. . . . But we used to go out there evening after evening and have dinner and sit under the trees and hold hands. I think we were quite dotty for a little while; you wouldn't understand, but one gets into a sort of a state where one just doesn't think that anything else exists or matters in the whole world. And he—he had a little flat that somebody had lent him, because of course he was only a student, he hadn't a sou, right up on top of the hill, you went up a heavenly crooked little street to it, and it was too heavenly there and—well, in the end I just sort of gave up even trying to be good and we used to go up there for days and days together and nights too of course, and we were so madly in love it wasn't *true!*'

'What on earth was the school doing, Rosie, all this time, to let you behave like this?'

'Oh, well of course I told them a whole lot of lies and then I finally pretended that you'd come to Geneva to find out what I was up to, and I used to put on a funny voice and pretend to be you on the telephone talking to Madame, and we used to nearly die with laughter because of course she got frightfully confidential about how awful I was and of course I used to agree like mad. . . .'

'Why on earth couldn't the damn woman write to me?' said Matilda angrily.

'Well, I'm telling you—she thought she was practically in daily communication with you over the 'phone, only you had la grippe or something or other madly infectious, so you couldn't actually meet her because of course she was petrified of getting it. And then of course you were most frightfully considerate and were afraid I might carry the infection back to the school so I had to stay away for more and more days and nights, and in the end I think she just gave us all up; but anyway by that time he'd gone home so it didn't matter anyway.'

'Well, where *was* home—I mean who *is* this man?'

'Oh, don't get excited, Tilda and think I can marry him or anything of that sort, because I can't. His people were farmers or something, miles away in the mountains—you can't see me spending my life on an alp for the sake of my Littel One, *can* you?—yodelling away at goats or whatever they do.'

'I gather that you have recovered from your grande passion?' said Matilda dryly.

'I meant it at the time,' said Rosie, a little shame-faced. 'It was—I don't know, it was simply tremendous.' She added with an air of experience that it had been too tremendous to last, that was the trouble; and it just hadn't. These things simply couldn't last for ever.

'Not even three months, in fact.'

'Oh, well, if you're going to be stuffy about it, I wish I hadn't told you. I mean, I did think *you'd* be a bit more broadminded, Tilda. You usually are.'

Matilda's heart smote her; beneath the airy confidence, she knew there must shelter a sick anxiety, she saw that there was an added whiteness, a paper whiteness, under the pink and white skin, a hint of desperation in the indignant amber-coloured eyes. If only the young could make their demands upon one's pity and affection without feeling compelled to assume an air of such contemptuous superiority. However. . . . 'I don't think you can accuse me of a Victorian scene, exactly, Rosie,' she said. 'I'll help you in every possible, conceivable way I can; only I can't help you to get rid of it, because first of all I think it's horrible in itself; secondly if anything goes wrong it's too dangerous to every-one concerned, including you, and incredibly sordid to

17

boot; and thirdly, I'm married to a doctor, and you're the sister of a doctor, and it would be ghastly for Thomas if either of us got involved in a thing like that. Anything else. . . .'

'Well, I shall have to go to Tedward, that's all,' said Rosie.

So Rosie told Tedward. He sat at his desk in the surgery at his house on the canal bank, ceaselessly tapping with the point of a dark green Venus pencil. 'Do you mean, Rosie, that the man got you drunk?'

'He was so much older than me, Tedward,' insisted Rosie, gabbling it all out again as she had earnestly gabbled it to him three times already. 'And he—he took me to this wonderful restaurant, I mean the most frightfully grand place right on the Jardin des Anglais, and—well, *I* don't know, the lime trees were in flower, you know, and it all smelt too heavenly and he was so terrifically sort of sophisticated and all that and I suppose I tried to be sophisticated too. . . .' She looked up at him piteously, poor little wronged, broken-hearted, disillusioned flower who didn't seem, somehow, to have caught what the gentleman said. . . . 'And we had a terrific dinner and simply thousands of wines. . . .'

'I'll bet,' said Tedward, dryly.

'I know it was silly of me, Tedward, but he was so much older than me, I mean really quite old, but really very handsome and terrifically well-dressed and of course terribly experienced and all that. Actually, I suppose he was what you might call a roué.'

'I wouldn't be surprised.'

'And then he asked me if I'd like to go back to his appartement and have a cup of real English tea. . . .'

'What, no etchings?'

18

'No, English tea seems to have been his line,' said Rosie, simply. 'I suppose it's more original in Switzerland. And he had a wonderful flat, looking out over the bay, because he's quite rich and all that; and then he—he sort of began to make love to me and I felt so stupid and sleepy and I suppose I was sort of flattered. . . .' She burst into tears again.

He looked at her wretchedly. His kind, round, friendly face seemed quite altered all of a sudden, she thought, covertly watching him through her highly becoming tears; with sagging white cheeks and jaw. She scrubbed her nose to an endearing pink shininess with her silly little handkerchief and went and perched herself on the arm of his chair. 'Don't take on so, pet. It isn't the end of the world, I suppose.'

'I just can't believe it, Rosie,' he said. 'Not about you.'

'That's because you still persist in looking on me as a little girl.'

'Don't you believe it,' he said, ruefully. He took up her plump white hand and held it for a moment against his cheek; but immediately released it, rose, and went and stood staring out of the window. He said at last: 'Rosie—I suppose it wouldn't do if . . .?' But he broke off. 'No, never mind. I'm a fool.'

'Yes, but what were you going to say?'

'I had a vague idea that I might help you out by making an honest woman of you,' he said. He waited for not more than half a second. 'But never mind, skip it.' He came back to her and took her chin in his hand, looking down, smiling, into her tear-bright eyes. 'I don't think we need resort to such desperate measures as that! We'll get round it some-how; I'll stand by you, I'll do everything in the world I can to help.'

But there was one thing, it seemed, that Tedward would

by no means consider doing after all; the one thing, said Rosie, when at last it dawned on her that he was adamant, that she had come to see him about. 'I don't see *why*, Tedward. Because of the risk?'

'Because of the ethics. But that's something you just wouldn't understand, my little mutton-head, would you?'

'But Tedward—as it's me?'

'Put it out of your mind, Rosie. Anything else in the wide world I'll do for you—but not that. After all, we can find a place for you to go to, the baby can be adopted afterwards.'

'I won't have any damn baby,' said Rosie, 'and that's flat.'

'Rosie, I can't help you in that way; you least of everybody in the world.'

'But, Tedward . . .'

'Once and for all, darling—no.'

'All right, then,' said Rosie. 'I'll find someone else. There are thousands of people.'

'Not available to young ladies with medical backgrounds, my pet.'

'Anything's available to anyone if they've got enough money,' said Rosie, tossing her head.

So Rosie told Gran. 'I say, Gran—if I tell you something you won't be shocked, will you?'

Mrs. Evans, like her grand-daughter-in-law, Matilda, was incapable of being shocked by anything other than cruelty or vulgarity. She had been a Victorian beauty, successful and gay, and now was heartily bored with her quiet life in the big, first-floor room in her grandson's home in Maida Vale, looking out over the charming gardens that meet the gardens of Hamilton Terrace and stretch away on either side, concealing the houses in front and to right and left of them. 'Almost like being in the country,' Matilda would say, advancing the virtues of the quiet room. 'Well, but who wants to be in the country, anyway?' Mrs. Evans would reply. 'Not you, for one, my dear; and not me either. Nasty grass and mud and leaves and nothing else—it's just like that awful American song says, "God can only make a tree".' And she would suddenly go gaily off her head, and, rushing to the window, hurl out whatever came first to hand, crying loudly, 'Fire! Fire! Fire!' 'Throw them further out, beyond the greenhouse,' Matilda would say mildly, knowing it useless to resist and concerned only to save the conservatory roof. 'Throw them across on to the lawn. The flames are coming up through the greenhouse, can't you see?' Mrs. Evans, who often saw a great deal more than she let on, would obediently fling cushions and tea cosy and combs and brushes out on to the grass and even the smaller bits of furniture. It was remarkable that she never threw books, which she loved; and that a certain rather valuable china tea service was also, apparently, invulnerable to the flames.

Rosie, without a tenth of her grandmother's essential beauty, had yet inherited much of her one-time charm: a freshness, a radiance, a look of health and vitality, of generous good-nature, that saved her soft, round face and big round eyes and little round mouth and rounded button of a nose, from insipidity. She settled herself comfortably down on the hearthrug, one arm hung confidingly across the old woman's bony, bird-like knee. 'It's the most awful thing, Gran, but I know you'll help me. Nobody could possibly understand except you, but even if you *are* old, you're broadminded Gran, aren't you?'

'It's because I'm old,' said Mrs. Evans. 'Not in spite of it. What's the matter—you've met some man, eh?'

'Yes, pet.'

'When you say a man—do you mean a man? Or a gentleman? Or merely a gent.?'

It had obviously better not be merely a gent, but Rosie was at a loss to know which of the other two would best please Granny in her present mood; Mrs. Evans was an ardent reader of romance and vacillated a good deal between Gentlemen and Rough Diamonds—not to say Black Diamonds, for at the moment she was in the throes of a rediscovery of the works of Robert Hichens. Rosie cast her mind back among her admirers in Geneva; the best of having been really a *bit* of a basket there, was that one didn't have to make up, one could just choose. With the unerring cunning of the intensely stupid, she selected the one best calculated to appeal, even right down to the little dash of colour. . . . 'He was so sort of—well, sort of strong, Gran, and of course people in the East have a different idea of how to treat women, that's all, and he just—well, he didn't bother about whether I wanted to be made love to or not, he just swept me off my feet, he didn't give me time to think, I couldn't have resisted even if I'd wanted to and I must say, when people are so sort of strong and sweeping, one doesn't seem to want to very much. He had a boat there and he just took me by the hand and said, "Come with me," or something like that, because of not speaking English very well, and I was sort of compelled like a rabbit, or a bird with a snake or whatever it is and I just went with him and he carried me down to the water's edge and lifted me into the boat and we sailed out on to the lake in the moonlight. . . . And the thing is, it's too frightening, but I think I may be going to have His Child.'

'Then he must marry you,' said Mrs. Evans at once.

'How can he, darling? He's—well, I mean, he's only a fisherman,' said Rosie, hurriedly improvising.

'There's as many good fishermen in the sea as ever came out of it,' said Mrs. Evans vaguely. 'And he must marry you.'

'Yes, but he can't, Gran, you see, he's—well, he's gone back to the East with his fish by now.'

'Then he must be brought back from the East. Your father must seek him out and drag him back here; by the scruff of the neck, if need be.'

'But Granny, darling, don't be silly—how can he? He's dead.'

'Dead?' said Mrs. Evans. 'Nonsense! Why should a man die all of a sudden like that? It's a ruse to get himself out of this mess, depend upon it.'

'I don't mean him, Granny. I mean my father.'

'Who's talking about your father? I know *he's* dead—bother it all, he was my own son, wasn't he?'

'But you said . . . Well, never mind, Gran, but the point is that I simply can't marry this chap because he's—well, you see, he's really got a girl of his own already, a gorgeous ranee or sari or whatever they call it, back home in where-ever-it-is. So you see, I thought,' said Rosie desperately, 'that perhaps you might possibly lend me a hundred pounds or so and then I could get something—well, some sort of pills or something, only they're frightfully expensive, and then I needn't have the baby at all. . . .'

But a terrible storm had suddenly blown up and the waves in the garden were lashed to fury by the whistling wind blowing down from the Swiss Alps, and it was necessary to jettison the contents of Mrs. Evans' room immediately—out of the front window, this time, on to the garage drive. The neighbours, who were used to a sudden descent of household linen and infrangible objets d'art, took it all in good part and merely remarked that old Mrs. Evans was having one of her turns again; but a gathering crowd of passers-by remained to stare and a small boy improvised a commando raid. Rosie, flying downstairs to rouse the household and warn off the marauders, sadly acknowledged that she was a fool to have forgotten that one could never get anywhere positive with Gran before flood or fire or earthquake intervened; and that it would be useless to try again. Only one chance remained to her and a pitifully small one it was likely to turn out to be. But he *had* got a couple of hundred pounds in the bank, she knew, and he *had* been in love with her for years and years. . . . She must tell Damien.

So Rosie told Damien.

Damien lived with his mother who kept a terribly superior sort of lodging house somewhere off behind Kilburn, almost far enough up to be called St. John's Wood, and not very far from the Evans menage in Maida Vale which, unlike Damien's mother, they frankly called Maida Vale. He had been on and off in love with Rosie since she had been a tiny thing with yellow pigtails in the kindergarten of his little-boy school in the country, years ago. More off than on, of course, since he had become a serious, though not very well-informed, Communist, and realized how deeply involved her family was in bloated capitalism. Old Twm, Thomas Evans' grandfather, had had interests in coal, grinding the blackened faces of the miners, though from a decent distance which did seem to make a difference when one remembered—and couldn't help loving the memory of—Old Twm. But Twm had died years ago, and then what had happened to the money? Passed on by inheritance, by inheritance, mark you, and not a hand's turn done to earn it, except of course by Old

Twm who, having so earned it, had had the idiotic idea that he might use it as he would, even to the education and advancement of his only son, young Twm. But young Twm, had not lived to enjoy it, but very deservedly had been killed off during the first world war; leaving it all to his own son Thomas who had invested it in a medical training and was now living very comfortably on the proceeds. It was true that Thomas Evans had never 'gone on and specialized' because the famous fortune had, in fact, been less than enough when it came to providing a home for his sister and for his widowed grandmother who was slowly and delightfully going off her nut; but there it was, they all lived in comfort and happiness; founded upon—what? That sorry old story of laugh, clown, laugh, smiling nigger-minstrel faces that had concealed exploited and aching hearts. Damien's mother, upon attaining widowhood had not, it was true, immediately distributed *her* legacy among the workers whose horny hands had accumulated it for her; but then she had not let it just lie fallow in the bank but had sunk it (and sunk was right!) in her 'house' and now worked herself to skin and bone, lying on a sofa directing the activities of a host of little old women who came in at odd hours of the day and were referred to collectively as 'my wretched staff'. Moreover, it had not been a success. They didn't live in comfort (and neither did their lodgers) like the family in the shabby, but indisputably Regency house in Maida Vale, careless about money and, if not actually extravagant, at least not saving of pennies and tuppences and cockle-edged threepenny bits. . . . Somehow, even where principle was involved, it did make a difference to right and wrong—whether the result were failure or success.

But as for Rosie, petted and spoiled and entirely dependent upon the shameful inheritance. . . . 'What have *you* ever done, Rosie, for the Community, that entitles you to all this gadding about with a whole lot of worthless Frenchmen in France?'

'Geneva's in Switzerland, ackcherly,' said Rosie. 'Not France.'

'Well, I don't think you knew even that before you went Abroad,' said Damien, 'so you've learnt something, even if it's only a bit of geography.'

Rosie replied with truth that she had learnt a great deal, most of it unconnected with geography.

'Anyway, that's not the point. The point is that you contribute absolutely nothing to the State as a whole.' Damien contributed to the State as a whole from a desk in a city office where all day long he jotted down and totted up figures in the shifting columns of wealth in the despised capitalist country which so patiently suffered him.

'Well, it's not my fault if I haven't got a job. Damn it all, I've only this minute left school.'

'Many girls in this country leave school at the age of fourteen.'

'I wish I could have,' said Rosie. 'I simply loathed that old St. Hilda's.'

'God knows they didn't teach you anything worth learning.'

'They didn't teach me anything at all,' said Rosie. 'They couldn't, poor things, I was too dumb.'

'Well, there's no room in the world to-day for helpless drones.'

Rosie didn't want to be a drone at all, she was simply dying, ackcherly, to get a job as a model at Paquin or somewhere like that. But if she couldn't, well, what could they do about it? They couldn't just have her painlessly destroyed, now could they? She wondered if, as a drone mother-to-be, she might fit in more comfortably with

Damien's uncomfortable ideas. 'I say, Day—I wanted to talk to you about something. Well, I mean it's about—better say a *friend* of mine, and the thing is, she's—well, matter of fact, she's going to have a baby.'

'Ah—Unmarried Mother?' said Damien with a brightening eye.

'Well, yes, she certainly isn't married, but if she could help it, she would like not to be a mother either.'

'Nonsense,' said Damien. 'Women have a right to motherhood if they want it. You tell her to stick to her guns.'

'The trouble is, they're not so much her guns,' said Rosie, uneasily, 'as more of a sort of pistol to her head. I mean, she believes madly in marriage and all those—um—outworn shibboleths, Damien, because if you don't well—well, you never *get* married, *do* you?'

'Then I've got no patience with her,' said Damien. 'She shouldn't have given herself to her man, if she was unprepared for the burden—as things now are—of single parenthood.'

'He wasn't her man, exactly. He was someone she—well, he was in a train, ackcherly, and there she was, she was absolutely terrified, she was young and unsophisticated and all that, and she just got scared and lost her head. . . .'

'All the better. Those are the children we want, children not born into the shackles of the old conventions, children who can start out from the very beginning free to believe in the—er—the freedoms; I mean free to believe in equality—and—and tolerance and—well, all those things,' said Damien, running out of freedoms; he was not a quick study, poor boy, and all too frequently fluffed or forgot his lines; nor was he adept at striking out on his own.

'Oh, *lor'!*' said Rosie, gloomily.

'So give your friend a jolly good pat on the back from

Us, and tell her to come along to a meeting we're having at my place next Thursday. After all, one never knows,' said Damien, waxing enthusiastic upon visions, 'what her Unborn Child may yet turn out to be. But she isn't one of your French friends, is she?' he added, breaking off a little anxiously. Everybody knew what those French girls were!

'No, no, she's English. *Ack*cherly,' said Rosie, nervously, 'you know her quite well.' She added that her—er—lover had been French. In fact, he was still on the continent now, which was one of the troubles. . . .

'You'd think these Frogs would be up to all the dodges and not land themselves in these messes, wouldn't you?' said the advocate for unmarried motherhood.

So there was nothing left for it. Rosie told Melissa.

Melissa was the daughter of a rather old old girl at Matilda's convent school; and Matilda, who was habitually more kind than she was sensible, gave her a small salary and the use of the flat in the basement of the house in Maida Vale, in consideration of some help in the kitchen and attendance upon old Mrs. Evans. She was a thin, nervous girl with a crowning glory of curly nut-brown hair, of which one lock was for ever falling forward over her right eye to the infinite irritation of all beholders and the great satisfaction of Melissa herself, who practised in the looking-glass tossing her head back and immediately letting the lock fall forward again. At twenty-two, she remained an adolescent; unloving and unloved, introspective, dissatisfied, tortured with uncertainty about her future should she fail to 'get married'. Men and marriage were indeed, and rightly, all she ever thought about, and she was consumed with envy for the careless rapture of Rosie's easy-going carryings-on;

28

so much so that even the guilelessly unsuspecting heart of Miss Evans had been vaguely aware that all between them was not entirely well. Now, however, bereft of other friends, she was forced back upon Melissa's mercy, and she curled herself up on the rather grubby off-white cushions on the divan in the basement flat and asked with elaborate carelessness if Melissa happened to know of a nice, cheap, quackified abortionist. 'Because it's too boring, but I seem to have gone and got myself in the family way. These Continentals are so ardent, *aren't* they? There's no resisting them.'

Melissa had spent a couple of terms at a convent in Brussels and on the strength of it wrote her sevens with little dashes through them and was frequently at a loss for the English word; but her experience with 'Continentals' was absolutely nil, as indeed—though not for want of increasingly desperate trying as she approached her twenty-third year and began to fear 'the shelf'—was her experience of any other breed of men. She produced a little notebook, however, and riffled through the pages, in search of the numerous abortionists whom she and her friends purported to patronize. The names appeared to have got themselves mixed up with those of more innocent entries, however, and, after much searching, she still could not lay her finger upon one working practitioner to whom Rosie, in her extremity, might resort. They fell to boasting to each other of their conquests instead; and which was the more to be pitied might be in doubt—she who had already had too many, or she who had had none.

And yet, that last was not strictly true; for some weeks ago, while Rosie was still in Switzerland, Melissa, having read in a woman's magazine that the way to make new friends was to go in for indoor skating and contrive to take a tumble (thus figuratively at any rate breaking the ice) had duly skated and duly fallen, though only in the literal sense; but literally and figuratively both, had duly been 'picked up'. She, too, had led her victim home for a nice cup of tea, but unlike Rosie had emerged unscathed; for despite the great nonsense she talked Melissa was the soul and body of respectability. She had, however, clung tightly to the young man, intriguing him with a wealth of phoney mystery, 'playing hard to get', hinting at depthless passions, reverting before his very eyes to an icy chill. He, older and far the more experienced of the two, played the same game and beat her at it hollow, and enjoyed himself enormously.

'He sounds too divine,' said Rosie. 'What's his name?'

His name was Stanislas—just Stanislas. They had agreed to call him—simply that. No surname, no address; just a telephone number, and 'Stanislas'. 'He's probably a prince or a count or something,' said Rosie, much impressed. 'Is he foreign?'

Melissa, uneasily aware that Stanislas had in all probability been christened plain Stanley, said hurriedly that his accent was perfect (which was not entirely true) so that one couldn't quite tell. In return for Rosie's interest, however, she asked kindly what *her* chap had been like?

'Which one?' said Rosie. 'There were such a lot.'

'Well, er—the Father of the Child.'

'My dear, I haven't a clue,' said Rosie, astonished that anyone could be so dense. 'I thought I told you.'

'You mean all those people were your real—well, I mean your real *lovers?* And you don't *know* which?'

'No, of course not,' said Rosie. 'That's just what I've been saying. And that's why I can't sort of get married or anything or do anything about it. There was—well, let's see, first there was a chap I met in a train and then there was rather a poor one but with a heavenly little flat right up on a hill and that went on for quite a long time, I mean weeks; and then there was a terrifically rich one, only I think I was rather tight at the time, and then there was one with a boat only the boat kept rocking about and I got the giggles, and then—oh, well, I don't know, simply dozens . . .'

'But no princes or counts or anything like that?' said Melissa, clinging jealously to quality in face of all this incontestable quantity.

'No, not like your Stanislas. I think he sounds *much* nicer than any of mine,' said Rosie, generously; and since her mind ran in simple circles, never inclusive of more than two ideas at once, she added, hopefully: 'I suppose he wouldn't know of a nice cheap foreign abortionist?'

'I don't think I'd quite like to ask him,' said Melissa, with no less than the truth.

And so Rosie had told Matilda and Tedward and Granny and Damien and Melissa. And she couldn't tell Thomas. And there was nobody else.

CHAPTER THREE

O N the morning of the following Thursday, a voice
rang up and said, 'Mathilde?' and Tilda said, 'My
God! *No?*' because only one person in the world
would ring up and say, 'Mathilde?'. And, sure enough, it
was Raoul.

'But Raoul, what on earth are you doing in London?'

'I flew here yesterday evening, by air. I have some
business in Bruxelles and on the way I thought I might also
do a little business in London. And I wished to see you,
Mathilde, and have some talk with you.'

'Well, yes, Raoul, how lovely! When could we meet?
Any time suits *me*.'

'This morning I have business and then business lunch
and in the afternoon more business: this leaves only this
evening because to-morrow morning I fly by air to Bruxelles.
You come then and dine with me here at the Ritzotel?'

Matilda, having assured him that any time would suit
her, now found that in fact there was no time at all that
would. 'The hell of it is, Raoul, that it's the girl's day out
and there's no one to leave in the house. Come to dinner
here?' (My God, though, what on earth could I give the
man?)

'I wish to talk alone with you, Mathilde. Come to my
suite here.'

But Tilda was having no more of that Carouge nonsense!
And, anyway, there was the baby and Gran and you could

never count on Thomas being in. 'Hang on for a minute and I'll see.' She called down to the basement to know if Melissa could possibly change her day but Melissa had a date with Stanislas and Matilda believed passionately that if one's employees had arrangements, they shouldn't be asked to alter them. 'I'm terribly sorry, Raoul, but I simply can't.'

'If you think I shall make love to you, Mathilde, it is not this.'

'How disappointing!' said Matilda, laughing.

'Perhaps that a little too. But it is of something else I must speak.'

'It's something to do with Rosie!' said Tilda, tumbling to it at last.

'Well, perhaps; but I cannot speak of it on the telephone. Already I have the idea that someone listens.' There was a click on the line and he said: 'There!—you see.'

'How very peculiar,' said Matilda.

'Well, never mind. I said nothing. Now, to-night—can I see you alone?'

'Well, yes, all right. You can have dinner here and we'll talk afterwards. I'll arrange it.'

'Alors—bien! I come to your house this evening. A quelle heure?'

'Make it half-past seven, will you Raoul? I'll have to cope with dinner and then there's the baby to put to bed. You remember I have a daughter now? She's two and a half.'

'Ma foi!' said Raoul. The things attractive women did to themselves! She would appear, untying a white flannel apron, holding out hands red from washing little garments, her lap all spread from sitting on a low chair for hours with a baby sprawled across it; when he had known her three or four years ago, already she had been putting on weight. But she had been—très gai! *Très* gai, toujours gai! And some-

33

thing a little more. That evening under the trees out at Carouge. . . . A pity that at the last moment . . . But all English women were virgins at heart. 'Alors, ma chère—à bientôt!'

Matilda put down the receiver, looking ruefully at her ruined hands; such good hands before Emma had arrived, not small, but white and always well-manicured, with the oval nails impeccably varnished. It was her one gesture to vanity, to any maintained preoccupation with her appearance. In the old days it had been different, the gay old, racketting-round old days of her working life in London; she had earned good money and spent it too, on clothes and hair-do's and what the French so impressively call one's maquillage. There had been nothing else to spend it on. But now . . . Oh, well—one couldn't have all this and Thomas and Emma too, and one wouldn't swap, not in a thousand years. She got up and shook herself back into the frame of mind that copes with dust and dinners and nurseries, but still she glanced at herself with reawakened eyes as she passed the looking-glass. My *God* I'm getting fat! Oh, well, she thought again—what the hell? If I look thirty-eight it's because I *am* thirty-eight; and she was not so vast that a good black dress couldn't still do wonders for her. For the rest—if one had never had beauty, one had worked all the harder at the other thing—and she knew that she still could whistle a tune that would bring the little birds fluttering down off their branches, cocks and hens and fledglings and eggs and all!

Except perhaps Raoul. Raoul was a Latin, and almost frighteningly cool and appraising and faintly cynical. He divided his relations with women into three pigeon-holes—devotion, a sort of flirtatious friendship, and something that he referred to as 'eroteek leuve'. Matilda since her abortive adventure in Geneva into eroteek leuve had been relegated to the second category; but their desultory friendship had continued sufficiently over the years, to permit of her writing at once when Rosie was sent to Switzerland, to beg him to keep an avuncular eye on her. Poor man, he was doubtless now hastening to apologize for having failed in this unexpectedly arduous duty. Geneva was a little place and probably humming by now with the doings of the English Miss.

Melissa was in her little basement kitchen making some pastry with thumpings and bangings and rollings that went to Matilda's heart. No wonder she suffers from backaches, she thought; not to mention indigestion. She stood on the stairs and called down to her. 'Melissa—have you been up to Mrs. Evans yet?'

'No I haven't, Mrs. Evans,' said Melissa, thumping away.

'Well, could you go soon? She must be wondering what's happening.'

'I can't go yet,' said Melissa. 'I'm making some pastry.'

'Couldn't you make your pastry later on?'

'No, I'm afraid I couldn't,' said Melissa. 'It has to stand. You have to leave pastry standing, you see,' she added kindly; Melissa was past-master at teaching her grandmother to suck eggs.

'Not that kind you don't,' said Matilda. 'Only puff.'

Melissa looked at her pityingly and immediately she was assailed by doubts. 'In any case, Melissa, I really don't think you can start making pastry before you've even been upstairs. Why must you have it to-day?'

'Well, it's my afternoon out,' said Melissa, as though that explained everything. She took the war into the enemy's camp by adding that she was very sorry but really she could not go changing her plans at the last minute and start cancelling dates and things, one had to consider other people too, and she was frightfully sorry but at the eleventh hour like this one couldn't get out of one's arrangements. . . .

'Nobody's asked you to,' said Tilda, reasonably.

'Oh? I thought you called downstairs. As the gentleman's coming to dinner. . . .'

'How do you know the gentleman's coming to dinner?'

'I thought you called downstairs,' repeated Melissa, hastily.

'It's Monsieur Raoul Vernet,' said Matilda, to cover her acute embarrassment at having caught Melissa out in listening on the office extension of the telephone. 'He's a Frenchman; at least he's a Belgian actually. He knew Rosie in Geneva.'

'Ah—quelle domage!' said Melissa, shrugging in an excessively Gallic way. 'Mais je suis. . . .' She fumbled for the word and at last was obliged to resort to a literal translation. 'To-night I am occupied.'

'Oh, but I would not dream of inconveniencing you,' said Matilda in inaccurate but tremendously rapid French. 'It was merely that this very old friend of mine was on his way to Belgium by air and it would have been nice if I had been free to go out with him on the one night he was here; but of course if you're occupied, you're occupied, and I would not lower myself to ask favours of you and you don't understand a single word of what I'm saying, *do* you, my precious French scholar?'

'Of course, of course,' said Melissa, smiling valiantly.

'Well, please do go up now and help Mrs Evans get dressed.' Granny, despite the exercise she got throwing things out of windows, could not raise her arthritic right arm sufficiently to do her hair; which, strictly speaking, was not her hair at all, but Thomas's, since he had paid a great deal for it in a Bond Street shop. (If Damien could have seen how little remained of old Twm's ill-gotten Capitalist gains, he would doubtless have despised the old gentleman heartily for having, out of so much opportunity, made so little disgraceful profit.)

Thomas was out in the garden with Emma who had discovered a filthy old bundle of rags which had somehow got itself launched in a neighbouring tree, and, determined that it was a birdie, was hurt in her feelings because it would not fly away. He was a small, slight man; the autumn of life had got into his hair transmuting its sovereign gold to the dead brown colour of the falling leaves; his face was creased into a foolish smile and his fine, white, spatulate doctor's hands encouraged the birdie to fly with a flurry of unavailing gesture. Tilda joined them. 'Thomas—will you be in to dinner to-night?'

'Why?' said Thomas warily.

'Raoul Vernet's coming; that Frenchman from Geneva, you know.'

'People from Geneva are Swiss,' said Thomas.

'Well, as a matter of fact he's actually a Belge, so there. And don't you be trying too. Except for trying to get home for dinner in time. He's coming at half-past seven.'

'What time's he going?' said Thomas.

'How do I know when he's going, darling? But if you're bored,' said Matilda, very offhand, 'you can always pretend you've got a case and slope off into the office.'

'Oh, can I? Good,' said Thomas, innocently.

'Well, then, look—I'll start a build-up when he comes about how you will have to leave us after dinner; and then you can make an excuse and hop off. Only, don't let me down; don't forget to hop.'

'I may be late, anyway,' he said. 'It looks as if there's going to be a fog. If so, I'll just have dinner on a tray in the office and not appear at all. Where's Rosie?'

'I don't know—still hogging it in bed I expect.'

Thomas picked up a ball and threw it for the poodle. 'She doesn't seem very well since she came back from Thingamajig.'

'It's the change of food, I suppose,' said Tilda, quickly. 'And Damien *will* take her out drinking beer at the Hammer and Sickle or whatever his pub is.'

'On the contrary, she's gone off alcohol altogether, she doesn't even have a drink before dinner now. And that's funny too,' he said, thoughtfully; adding, suddenly: 'Who did you say was coming to dinner to-night?'

'Raoul Vernet, darling; that chap I had a flirtation with once, in Geneva.'

'Oh yes, in Geneva,' said Thomas, vaguely. 'What's he doing in London, all of a sudden?'

'How do *I* know?—some business meeting or other.'

'I see. And he's coming here to dinner and you want me tactfully to leave you alone together afterwards.' There was a strange light about the garden as though one were looking at the high brick walls and the narrow path and the pear trees and the mulberry tree, through clouded spectacles. 'Anyway, if this fog gets going, I shall probably reach home after he's gone and not even meet the gent.' He gave her a brief smile; but he did not look much amused as he walked away into the house.

'Well, what a bloody day!' said Tilda to herself, following him. With this fog coming down, should she leave Emma in the garden, or make up her mind to a morning in the nursery? And had Melissa gone up to Granny yet? And what on earth could one give a fastidious Frenchman for dinner? And Rosie? She went upstairs to the little attic room with its frilly curtains and patchwork counterpane. 'Rosie! Aren't you getting up?'

'I've been up,' said Rosie, coming to the surface and

38

poking out a round face unattractively covered with nourishing cream. 'I got back.'

'Are you feeling rotten?'

'Morning sickness,' said Rosie. 'Me! Morning sickness!'

'You haven't been going and taking pills and things?'

'No, I haven't. Tedward won't give me a thing and then he just pretends that they wouldn't do me any good anyway, and only make me feel worse. As if I could!'

'Well, *I* don't know what to do, Rosie,' said Matilda, moving round the little room and automatically picking up and tidying away the scattered things. 'Thomas has noticed that you aren't well and now *he's* getting worried.'

'You don't think he's guessed?'

'Well, he's a doctor,' said Matilda, shrugging hopelessly. 'Honestly, darling, I don't know whether we ought not to tell him.' And yet she was desperately reluctant to do so. Thomas's heart was buried so deep, under so many layers of reserve and detachment and astringent unsentimentality, that if he broke it over this affair of his precious Rosie, there was no knowing how to apply the balms that might help to mend the heart of an easier man. 'Oh, by the way, I don't know how you'll feel about this, but Raoul Vernet's in London. He's coming to dinner to-night.'

Rosie sat bolt upright in bed and her jaw dropped. '*Raoul?*'

Yes, I expect Raoul knows a thing or two about you, my puss! thought Matilda. Though what he could have to tell more shattering than Rosie's own blithely shameless confession, it was difficult to imagine. Poor man, she thought, now that one comes to consider it, he's probably coming here, trembling, to warn us of her affair with her student, never dreaming that she's already quite gaily informed us herself. She said: 'You needn't see him if you don't want to.'

'I don't want to see anyone,' said Rosie. She sat up in

bed hugging herself and looking very white. 'I've got a frightful pain.'

'A pain? Where? What kind of pain?'

'Well, just a *pain*, Tilda, all over. I mean, sort of all over here,' said Rosie, making a circular movement with one hand in the general area of her stomach.

Matilda looked at her dubiously. 'What—all of a sudden, like this?'

'Sudden! I like that,' said Rosie. 'I've been dashing back and forth to the huh-ha all morning.'

'Well, stay where you are for a bit,' said Matilda, not very sympathetically. She went down to the telephone with Gabriel, the poodle, at her heels, and rang up Thomas's partner. 'I say, Tedward, I'm terribly sorry to worry you, but Rosie doesn't seem too well. You wouldn't be passing this way, would you? Thomas has gone.'

'I'll drop in this morning, Tilda,' said Tedward immediately.

'Oh, bless your little cotton socks, Tedward, *could* you?'

'I'll be round,' said Tedward, cheerfully.

Melissa was coming downstairs from Granny's room. 'Is Mrs. Evans all right?'

'Yes, she's fine,' said Melissa. 'She's in the desert to-day— I think she's in an old silent film or something, ackcherly, The Shake or something.' She added with a rare gleam of humour that that was rather a comfort because there was no chance of a flood in the desert and very little of earthquake or fire so they ought to have a quiet morning.

Matilda sent her out shopping for to-night's dinner, and lugged the baby in from the deepening fog. Tedward arrived and was closeted with Rosie. He came downstairs and accepted a cup of coffee in the office. 'I don't think it's anything out of the way. What brought on this pain, do you know?'

40

'I think it was the mention of a gentleman called Monsieur Raoul Vernet from Geneva. He's coming to dinner to-night.'

'From Geneva?' said Tedward.

'Yes, he's suddenly turned up and says he wants to talk to me. I suppose she's scared of him spilling the beans—though I should have thought she'd spilt enough herself, already.'

'She's told you everything has she?'

'Yes, she's perfectly frank about it; she doesn't seem in the least ashamed.'

'They aren't these days,' said Tedward, tolerantly. 'Who is this Raoul Vernet?'

'Well, he's a chap I did a bit of bundling with myself four years ago; I met him when Thomas was at some conference at Lucerne or somewhere and I couldn't bear the other wives and stopped off in Geneva. I sent Rosie over with an introduction to him and I suppose now he feels bad about what's happened and he wants to talk it over.'

'Well, that's something,' said Tedward.

'To tell you the truth, my dear, I think Rosie was heading for this kind of thing anyway, whatever anyone did. However, I shall have a talk to him this evening; I'll get Thomas to push off in here and leave us alone.'

'He doesn't know yet?'

'I'm terribly afraid he's beginning to suspect. He's noticed her always being off-colour.'

'Well, tell him I saw her this morning and I thought she'd had a touch of gastritis, probably due to food poisoning of some kind; that'll put him off the scent; and meanwhile we'll get cracking on it and think up something or other to do with her. We must fix her up in some job abroad or something; a year in Italy next time, learning Italian.'

'I'm afraid Rosie's going to talk the same language wherever we send her,' said Matilda. 'And we'll have to think up somewhere further—Thomas would always be popping over to Rome or wherever it was, on visits.' Upstairs, Emma started yelling and she got up and said, 'I must go, pet.'

He rose too, putting down his coffee cup on the mantelpiece, looking about for his coat and gloves. 'I must go too; I shall take twice as long on my rounds with this bloody fog. It's a filthy day out.'

'It's a filthy day in,' said Matilda, holding his coat, with one ear cocked for real desperation to enter into the baby's cries and force her immediate attention. 'The poor wretched child's been hoicked in and out of the garden like a jack-in-the-box, Melissa was making pastry at nine o'clock this morning, apparently on the general grounds that it was her afternoon off, though what that can have to do with it I simply can't see; and Granny's galloping about the desert in a Rudolph Valentino film. The din overhead is the sofa flat out under whip and spur. But I wish she'd let him catch up with her now; a long, long, silent kiss, the silenter the better, would suit my headache fine.' There was a crash overhead. 'Oh, *now* what? Either Adbul the Disgusting has fallen over the trip-wire outside her tent, or the Sheik has felled him to the ground, not a moment too soon.' She went to the top of the basement stairs and yelled for Melissa to go up for goodness sake and see what was happening. Melissa yelled back that, sorry, Mrs. Evans, she couldn't come now, she was just taking her pastry out of the oven.

Tedward strolled out after her, laughing. 'Never mind, Til! You cope with the old girl, I'll see myself out.' Gabriel followed him barking gaily, under the chronic delusion that anyone in an overcoat was necessarily about to take him walkie-palkies, and Annaran, the Siamese cat, who was very sillily called after the film Annaran the King of Siam, poised ready to dart out to certain death under the traffic wheels of Maida Vale. '*Gab*riel! *An*naran!' shouted Matilda, in despair, above the din. The telephone rang, Emma reached boiling-point, Rosie screamed out from her attic that if that was Damien on the 'phone she would come down and speak to him, and out of a first-floor window flew a long-sleeved woollen nightie. A strong smell of burning pastry arose from the basement. 'My *God*, what a house!' said Tilda. From the hall came a last shrill yelp of disappointment as Tedward shut the door in Gabriel's face; followed by a squall as it closed upon Annaran's shining tail. The fall of the night-gown had been followed by a heavy silence in Mrs. Evans' room. To-day of all days!—Granny was always at her most impossible, after Worse than Death.

CHAPTER FOUR

Sure enough, it was Damien on the telephone. Matilda caught snatches of Rosie's end of a long and intensely boring quarrel culminating in a slammed-down receiver, more telephone calls, and a return to bed. She called up to the attic to know what Rosie wanted to do about dinner to-night.

'I shall be out,' said Rosie.

'Out? I thought you were supposed to be so ill?'

'Well, I am, but I shall be better by this evening and I'm going out.'

'If it's because of Raoul, you needn't see him, darling,' said Matilda, repenting of having been impatient and unkind when, after all, the poor child was worried and unwell; but people were so hopeless, they got themselves into muddles and then sat back and were aggrieved with everyone but themselves.

'I just don't want to see anyone—it's not especially him.'

'But there's going to be an awful fog, Rosie, it's as black as pitch already. Stay in bed, darling, and I'll bring you up some dinner on a tray . . .' (in the intervals of cooking a Ritzotel dinner for Raoul, putting the baby to bed, dealing with Gran's post-seduction remorse and steering a safe course between concealing from Thomas that she wanted to be alone with Raoul for the purpose of discussing Rosie, and encouraging him to believe that it was from her own desire to be false to her marriage vow. . . .)

But Rosie, muttering darkly about the general rottenness of men, insisted that, fog or no fog, she would get up and go out; meanwhile, could she have her lunch in bed please, now.

'No, I'm damned if you can,' said Tilda. 'If you're well enough to go gallivanting—with Damien Jones, I suppose? —you're well enough to have lunch in the dining-room.'

'Well, if you want to know,' said Rosie, 'I am not going gallivanting with Damien, so there; for the simple reason that Damien has a Meeting to-night, and would he leave his precious Meeting for me, oh, no of course not!—much as I might need his sort of support and things . . . I should think it would be better to do something about just the dull, ordinary person that you saw every day and who ackcherly needed your help, than sit around incessantly discussing a whole lot of people that you never set eyes on, who only might.'

This accorded so closely with Tilda's own conception of helping one's neighbour, that she refrained from remarking that she, personally, had so far received little thanks for trying to help the one, dull, everyday person who actually needed it. She contented herself with saying that Rosie could come down to lunch in her jenking-gowns but to hurry up. Melissa produced the more ruined remnants of her scorched pastry and generously handed them round. 'Who're you going out with this afternoon—Stanislas?' said Rosie, making civil conversation. Melissa gave her a warning grimace. 'My dear child, if it's me you're worrying about, please don't,' said Matilda irritably. 'If you were going out with the King of *Greece*, I couldn't care less.' Though why the poor King of Greece, she could not imagine. My God, what a day, she thought again.

At six o'clock Damien presented himself at the door, the thick, grey fog swirling in with him as she opened it. He looked rather pink and white, and carried a small, crushed bunch of flowers in a paper cornet. 'Could I see Rosie, Mrs. Evans, please?'

For all he was such an ass, Matilda couldn't help being fond of Damien Jones. He was a nice-looking boy, with a handsome, sullen face and forward-curling hair, and as long as he treated only his equals as Comrades and didn't drag her up into it, she respected the honest idealism which drove him to improving a world in which he, himself, had not yet learned to live. 'She is, Damien, dear, but I don't know whether she's see-able. I think she's going out.'

'Who with?' said Damien, blurting it out before he could stop himself.

'I don't know, my dear. Go and wait in the office and I'll call her.' (Blast the boy!—with Melissa off duty, Emma half-undressed for bed, probably by now sailing her bed-room slippers in the bath, and the animals singing lustily for their supper . . .) But she toiled upstairs and called up to the attic that Damien was here and Rosie called back that Damien could go to hell and Matilda replied that Rosie could tell him so herself, then, because she was not going to, and went into the nursery. She heard Rosie thump down the little attic stair and duly lean over the banister and call out to Damien that he could go to hell. Damien apparently came out into the hall and said something in reply, for Rosie called back that she couldn't, she was in her pants and bra, and that anyway, if she had been as fully dressed as an esquimo or an igloo or whoever those people were, she wouldn't, so he might just as well fuss off because there was no point in his staying. He evidently hung about for a little while; just as Tilda, unable to bear the thought of his hurt young face, was about to abandon the baby once more and go down and administer comfort, the front door banged. Oh, well, she thought; I really didn't have time!

46

She dumped the baby in its cot, where it stood looking over the high railed side with a trembling lower lip; in its white woolly sleeping-bag, with its halo of red-gold hair, it looked as though it were about to enter a sack-race in some celestial school-sports. She caught it up and kissed it, besought it not to add to the complications of life by weeping, and hurried away, thankfully closing one door at least behind her. Emma gave a couple of dismal yells, changed her mind and broke, instead, into loud singing. Outside, the fog was like a blank grey face peering in through the window-panes. Pray heaven, she thought, that it means that Raoul will be late.

Thomas came in. He was bleary-eyed and coughing. 'Tilda?'

'In the kitchen, darling.'

Thomas appeared at the kitchen door. 'Is he here yet?'

'No, thank goodness. I'm praying he'll be late. I'm not nearly ready.'

'Perhaps he won't come,' said Thomas, hopefully. 'The fog's frightful. I almost thought I might have to leave the car.'

'You're not late, though.'

'I skipped all but the positively dying. I'll make a round of 'phone calls. Any messages?' He drifted off towards the office and came back a moment later with a small piece of paper. 'What's this about Harrow Gardens?'

'I don't know, darling,' said Tilda, straining potatoes, her head held back to protect her make-up from the clouds of steam. 'Harrow Gardens?'

'Yes, it looks as if I shall have to sweat out again—and in this fog. Oh, blast! "Ten weeks. D. and V. Three days." Who took it?—Melissa, I suppose?'

'I suppose so, but she's out,' said Matilda, pushing past his

47

unyielding form to get at the cooker again. 'Do *move*, sweetie, how can anybody get round you?'

'What the hell does she mean, "Ten weeks. D. and V. Three days"?'

'I suppose she means that a ten-weeks-old baby has had diarrhœa and vomiting for three days: what else? Thomas, I shall go mad if you don't move, darling.'

'Oh, hell!' he said, looking savagely at the note on the paper and very slightly shifting his position to let her get past, immediately resuming it again. 'I shall have to go.'

'My poor *pet*,' said Matilda absently, straining frozen peas.

'Where on earth's Harrow Gardens? Somewhere round the Harrow Road, I expect, *miles* from here, of course, and off any known map route, nobody to ask the way of, and the fog like a sort of veil of wet Jaeger coms all over one's face.' Cheered by this vivid metaphor, he went through to the drawing-room and crashed about among Matilda's carefully arranged bottles, mixing himself a drink He came back with it in his hand. 'When did this message come, do you know?'

'Darling, I tell you I don't know anything about it; but if Melissa took it, it must have been before one, because she wasn't on duty after that.'

'Well, I think I ought to eat something now and do my 'phone calls and go. If I hang about for this French chap of yours, it'll be a couple of hours before I see the child.'

'If it's had its D. and V. for three days, would that make much difference?'

'It might,' he said. 'Anyway, they must be getting worried, waiting all this time. No telephone number of course, so I can't ring them up. *And* no name. Trust Melissa!'

'Harrow Gardens off the Harrow Road doesn't sound very private-telephoney,' said Matilda.

Rosie's voice called softly on the stairs in an unwontedly melodious pipe. 'Tilda! Anyone here yet?'

'No, come on down,' called Matilda. She added, warningly, however, 'Only Thomas.'

Rosie appeared in the kitchen doorway. She looked excessively smart in a gay little hat and bright scarlet coat and a pair of very high heels held on by a sliver of sole and a couple of thin leather straps. 'Well, hallo and good-bye, chaps. I'm off.'

'What, in this fog?' said Thomas. 'Where to?'

'Just—out,' said Rosie, shrugging.

'Aren't you staying in to see this wonderful Frenchman?'

'No, thanks very much,' said Rosie. 'I'm *not*.'

Thomas raised his eyebrows. 'Aren't you? Why?'

'Oh, lor,' said Rosie, impatiently. 'Because I don't want to, that's why.'

'As it's *my* hand he's coming to hold, why should she?' said Tilda quickly. 'Look, you two, how do you think anyone can cook a dinner in a kitchen this size with three people milling around in it? Rosie, if you're going out, darling, go; and Thomas, you'd better have something on a plate now, because he'll be here any minute and then it'll be sauve qui peut, as far as I'm concerned.'

Rosie started off with alacrity but Thomas, unusually persistent, followed her out into the hall. 'It doesn't seem very polite.'

'Well, *I* can't help it if I've got an appointment, Thomas.'

'You did know this man in Geneva?'

'Yes, I *knew* him,' acknowledged Rosie, reluctantly.

'But not very well?'

'If you want to know, I knew him a great deal too well,' said Rosie, bursting out with it, irritably. 'Now may I go, please, as I happen to have an appointment and I'm late for it already.' Tilda heard the bang of the front door as she flounced off down the steps. Thomas opened it again to call out after her: was it she who had taken this message about a case in Harrow Gardens? Her denials floated back to them, muffled already by the fog. There was a rattle as she struggled with the little gate. The faint clip-clop of her high heels whispered of her uncertain progress through the impenetrable grey. Thomas wandered back into the kitchen looking thoughtfully into the glass in his hand, apparently not much edified by what he saw there. Matilda, glancing anxiously at his face, served some food from the saucepans on to a plate with a great banging of spoons against china, and put it on a corner of the kitchen table. 'Eat this, darling, and I'll just run upstairs and take Gran hers.' Mrs. Evans usually ate with the rest of the family but she was too unpredictable a member to be trusted when there were guests. This evening, anyway, she was mourning her lost virtue, and refused all food and drink. 'Sand, sand, sand!' she said to Matilda, looking about her close-carpeted room with a delirious brightness in her eyes. 'Nothing but sand! I don't think I shall ever see anything again, Matilda, my dear, but all these wastes and wastes of golden sand; and not so much as a camel galloping towards me with my Sheik aboard!'

'Aboard?' said Matilda.

'The Ship of the Desert,' said Mrs. Evans, fixing her with an eye that dared her to say, Here, Gran—come off it!

'Well, darling, try and eat your supper. It's very special, all hashed up by me out of Tante Marie, for my Frenchman.'

'Frenchman? What Frenchman?'

'Granny, I told you this morning—a man I used to know in Geneva.'

'What's he coming here for?' said Mrs. Evans, sharply. 'From Geneva.'

'Well, he wants to see me, that's all.'

'I shall come down,' said Mrs. Evans, scrambling up off the sofa which earlier in the day had carried her so bravely in her vain dash across the burning sands, and beginning to hunt through her wardrobe for an appropriate change of dress.

'No, you can't,' said Matilda, a little too quickly. 'He—well, he wants to see me alone, Gran. He wants to talk to me.'

'How can he see you alone? What about Thomas; and Rosie?'

'Rosie's gone out to avoid him, and Thomas has to go on a case. Darling, do eat your supper. You must keep up your strength, you know,' said Tilda, resorting to a rather low trick, 'if you've got any more dashing about the desert to do.'

'Not much use dashing once they've caught up with you,' said Granny, shaking her head. 'And he caught up with me all right.' She smiled reminiscently, but after a while her thin old hands shook so that the knife and fork clattered against her plate. 'Tell him I won't see him any more,' she said. 'Never again! He has broken his English Lily, he has deserted her for another and left her there, weeping among the golden sands; but let him beware, for Madonna Lily is a Tiger Lily now.' She declaimed it again, more dramatically, in a high, cracked voice. 'Let him beware—Madonna Lily is a Tiger Lily now!' And she put her knife and fork together and lifted a lid to see what there was for a pud. 'These Frenchified Arabs are always the worst,' she said.

Thomas was still making telephone calls when Tilda got back downstairs, jotting down appointments for the morrow in his little book, advising, explaining, insisting or soothing, as he spoke to homes where he would have "dropped in" if the fog had not been so bad. 'Your boy friend's late.'

It was getting on for eight. 'That sounds like a taxi now.'

'I'll go into the kitchen,' said Thomas, 'and nip out when you've got him into the drawing-room. I don't want to see him.'

Really, thought Tilda, if poor Raoul knew how many people in this house did not want to see him, his self-esteem, which was ordinarily considerable, would suffer a mortal blow. She called out from the front door, directing him up the unfamiliar steps; she could not see him until he was almost inside the door and upon her, a large bouquet wrapped in cellophane held carefully in his gloved hand (she thought of Damien's poor, squashed little bunch of flowers and felt a pang of affection for his clumsy old Englishness).

'Mathilde! At last I am here. Did you despair? Very sorry to be late, but you British are so generous with your fogs, you assure us that you have them only occasionally but every time a poor foreigner arrives in London, you kindly lay one at his feet like a red carpet; or shall we say a grey carpet . . .?' He kissed her hand and handed her the bouquet followed by a selection of hideous woollen mufflers unwound from his neck as he anxiously sniffed and cleared his throat, testing for incipient signs of le rheum. She hung up his belted overcoat, which had apparently been run up out of some mottled underfelting, predominantly green, and hung the scarves over the radiator. 'It was terribly good of you to have made the effort at all. I really thought that you wouldn't risk starting out.'

'By the Ritzotel it is not so bad,' said Raoul. He kindly explained to the Londoner born and bred that this was because the Ritzotel was quite close to Saint James Park and that London fogs were always less dense near an open space. 'But from the Marble Arch down to this Maida Vale—phoo!'

'Well, come into the drawing-room and get warm,' said Matilda, feeling more and more large and English-rosey beneath his uncompromisingly appraising gaze. Not that he was so excessively beautiful himself. He was a tall man; the face that under the influence of the fairy lights in the trees at Carouge had seemed pale and interesting and rather sad, was really just a long, sallow, blandly self-satisfied face, with bright, dark eyes and a little black moustache; his hair was black too and rather fuzzy—at the back, the head sloped away, leaving a round bald patch, very clean and yet covered with infinitesimal little black dots as though the hairs had not so much fallen out as come to the surface of the scalp and just stopped growing, in despair. Really, she thought, he is *not* very attractive when you get him home, as it were; and she felt thankful now that Thomas would not be meeting him. Thomas would refer to him for ever as that frightful Raoul of yours, and she did not want a too constant reminder that her beautiful memories had turned out rather shame-making delusions after all.

She poured him out a sherry. Upstairs, the baby slept, lying like a pearl in the oyster shell of its soft, white, woolly shawl. In the kitchen, Thomas listened to hear that all was quiet, before slipping through the hall and out to his car. In his empty surgery, Dr. Ted Edwards glanced at the clock, glanced at the telephone-pad which had written on it, 'Rosie—eight o'clock', glanced across anxiously at the fog-muffled window and returned to his perusal of the *B.M.J.* In the house in Kilburn, Damien Jones sat restlessly with two enthusiastic but non-English-speaking Austrian refugees, one vaguely sexed Welsh intellectual and five assorted adolescents of non-British origin, and thought bitterly that when one had made such terrific sacrifices to

53

be present at the Meeting oneself, it was a bit thick that so few should brave a bit of a fog to turn up; and out in the bit of a fog, Melissa paced like a tigress baulked of its prey, up and down, up and down, up and down. . . . Upstairs on her sofa in the house in Maida Vale, old Mrs. Evans sat quietly nursing her arthritic right arm, staring into the fire and thinking of many, many things; and in a fog-dimmed telephone booth not fifty yards away, Rosie came up for air and coughed a bit with the fog and was caught and held again, close in a young man's arms. Zero hour minus—X. In the long, white, firelit drawing-room, the victim bowed and smiled and reeled off his devoirs before the serious work of the evening should begin; within the radius of one fog-bound mile, were these seven people, one of whom was very shortly going to murder him.

CHAPTER FIVE

A T nine o'clock, Edward was still sitting by the surgery fire but he was no longer reading the *Medical Journal*. When the bell rang, he jumped to his feet and almost ran to the door. 'Rosie! My dear girl, where on earth have you been?'

'I got held up,' said Rosie vaguely, coming in out of the dank grey fog in her gay red coat and her funny little hat, all lit with youth and freshness and vitality and—had he but known it, poor man—by a new and secret joy.

He led her into the sitting-room and lit the gas for her and drew the curtains and lifted the cat off the chair. 'I've been worried to death about you; I thought you'd got lost in the fog or fallen into the canal or something. Frightful visions have been flashing through my mind; I didn't like to go out and look for you in case, meanwhile, you turned up and couldn't get in. I kept telling myself you hadn't started out, because of the fog.'

'It's frantic,' said Rosie. 'Like walking through grey cotton wool.' She pulled off her gloves and threw them on the table, took off her little hat and ran her fingers through her bright, fair hair. 'Why didn't you ring up?'

'My dear Rosie!—after the fuss you made about not saying you were coming here?'

'Oh, well, that was only for Tilda,' said Rosie, comfortably. 'I had to pretend you were a proper date, or she'd

55

never have let me come out, just for the sake of avoiding Raoul.'

So that puts me where *I* belong, thought Tedward, ruefully: not even a sufficient excuse to Matilda for going out into a fog! (Dear Tilda!—would *she* have understood, if he had ever dared to confide in her, the secret sickness that night and day was eating away his heart?) He stood warming the broad seat of his trousers before the fire, praying like any adolescent calf-lover that Rosie would kiss him before she sat down—just one of the sexless pecks, cheek banged against cheek, that now and again she so meaninglessly bestowed upon dear, fat old Tedward, who had family doctored her since before she was born. But she did not. She flung herself into the armchair, curled up her long legs to make a lap for the dispossessed cat, and said could she possibly have a cup of coffee or something?—she hadn't eaten anything since lunch (except tea), and jolly little then because the family had all been at their worst and too *aw*ful. . . . While he made it on the kitchen stove, his housekeeper being away on one of her periodic visits to a sister conveniently neurotic, she yelled through the intervening doors a few cheerful commentaries on the awfulness of families in general, culminating in a vivid account of Granny's latest adventure with the Sheik of Araby. 'Tilda says it's some film star, Rupert Valentino or something, but *I've* never heard of him. Anyway, he seems to have given dear old Gran the time of her life, ackcherly, so God bless him who*ever* he is!'

He came back with the tray of tea things and a plate of biscuits and cakes. 'I hope this'll do? I don't know what else I could raise. The old girl's away, as usual. Do you think it's enough?'

'I don't know,' said Rosie frankly. She added that they mustn't forget she was 'feeding two'.

Tedward went back to the surgery and returned with a sheet of headed writing paper in his hand. 'Well, Rosie— here's the prescription. I said I would and I have, but I'm not very keen on it.'

'Oh, Tedward, you angel! Now it'll be all right, *won't* it?'

'Well, I don't know,' he said. 'We'll hope so.'

She looked with dawning suspicion at the paper in her hand. 'It really is something? You're not just pulling a fast one on me?'

'No, no,' he promised, 'you can ask the chemist when you get it made up. Which, by the way, I should *not* get done with your regular man.'

'Oh, no,' said Rosie, 'I'd never have thought of that.' She added, hopefully: 'Because it's illegal?'

He laughed. 'No, it's not illegal; I've tried to explain to you that I don't do illegal things—not professionally, any-way. But you don't want it known all over Maida Vale that Dr. Thomas's sister is taking abortifacients.'

'Good lord, what a heavenly word!' But she was mildly alarmed by it. 'It won't do me any harm, will it?'

It would not have done a kitten the slightest harm—or the slightest good either; but at least it would stop her from going where harm might be done. To make doubly sure he insisted: 'You're not to take the second dose till three days after the first; promise?' That would give them a breathing space while they made some arrangements for her. 'I'm going to see Tilda to-morrow, and really talk over what we're to do.'

'Now you've given me this, we won't have to do anything, *will* we?'

'Well, no, perhaps not,' he said. He changed the direction of the subject. 'How did you feel this morning, after I left?'

'Well, of course I was really skrimshanking a bit because

of getting out of seeing Raoul. But still I did feel grim, and then I had this fuss with Damien on the telephone and I felt grimmer still. Tilda wanted me to stay in bed all day but I wouldn't, so then of course she was cross because I didn't get up that *min*ute and whizz round doing my stuff. That's the worst of Tilda—you must be ill or well with her, you can't be just sort of grey.'

'She's probably worried to death about you, out in this fog.'

'Not she,' said Rosie. 'She's sitting listening to lies about me from Raoul.'

'He'll have gone by now.'

'Good lord, no, it's only about eight o'clock.'

'It's a quarter past nine,' said Tedward.

'No, is it really? I must have taken hours getting here,' said Rosie, with not even the grace to blush.

'You must be worn out,' said Tedward.

'No, I'm not. After all, it's no actual distance, and it was quite fun, really, I mean one foot in the gutter, and chains of hands with strangers across the roads.'

But she was tired. The unexplained exhilaration was dying away, leaving her very pale; there were shadows under the amber eyes and her round face had a suddenly peaky look. 'I'll get the car out,' he said, 'while you finish your tea. You ought to be in bed.'

'But if he's still there. . . .'

'It'll take me half an hour to manœuvre the car out of the garage in this; he may be gone by then, but anyway, we can ring up and ask Matilda, before we start. You get on with your tea.'

'Oh, *cat*,' said Rosie, 'do shift over a bit, I can't reach anything. . . .'

But when he came back to the sitting-room, five minutes later, leaving the car ticking over in the little drive outside his front door, she was standing in the middle of the room and the cat had gone. 'Tedward! The most frightful thing's happened. I—I think it must be Raoul.'

'What do you mean? What's happened?'

'The telephone,' said Rosie, sweeping her hand vaguely towards the little table where it stood. 'Somebody rang up. Tedward, I think it was Raoul and I think he's been hurt.'

'He rang up *here?*'

'Well, the bell rang and I picked up the receiver and a voice said, "Come quick!" in a sort of a peculiar hoarse kind of a whisper as though they could hardly breathe, and then he said, "Tell the doctor to come quick," and then I began to think that his voice sounded rather foreign. So then I said, "Well, who is it? Where are you?" Just thinking it was a patient, of course, and he said, "A man came in and hit me with a mastoid mallet," and then he said—oh, Tedward, he said, "I'm dying".' She bit her lower lip and two tears tumbled slowly down her round white young face.

'A *mas*toid mallet?' he said incredulously.

'Well, that's what it sounded like, but of course I may not have heard properly. Only how could anybody have come in and hit Raoul with a mastoid mallet? It's simply mad!'

'But, do you mean this Raoul Vernet? Why on earth should you think it was him?'

'Well, he sounded foreign, Tedward, and of course I went on and on saying, "Tell me where you are," and at last he sort of gasped it out and it was our address. *Our address!*'

'Come on!' said Tedward. He caught up her hat and coat from the chair and thrust them into her arms and ran out with her through the hall and into the warmly purring car. She tumbled in beside him and he let in the clutch. 'And then, Tedward, it was too awful, but there was a sort of bonk, and nothing more.'

'You mean as if he'd dropped the receiver?'

'Well, *I* don't know; just a bonk and then nothing.'

A bumper scraped against wood as the car crept out of the gate and into the street that ran along the side of the canal. He said: 'My God, this fog's worse than I thought. I wonder if we ought to ring up the house, first, and see.'

'Well, it did come into my head but then I thought that if he'd dropped the receiver, it wouldn't be any good.'

'Well, I think we'd just better get there as quick as we can.'

But as quick as they could was still not very quick. Muttering curses, he steered the car through the network of streets that in the daytime he knew so well. Rosie sat huddled beside him in the scarlet coat. *Could* it be Raoul, Tedward. . . .? But Tedward, how could Raoul have known to ring up your number. . . .? And what about Tilda. . . .? And what about Granny . . .? And why didn't Tilda ring up? and, don't you think that surely Thomas would be back by now. . . .? 'Rosie, darling, how on earth can *I* know?' he said, nervously irritable; making good headway here, creeping at snail's pace there, finally giving up and confessing that he had hopelessly lost the way, climbing out to reconnoitre, coming back, shivering—for he had not waited even to snatch up his overcoat—having discovered that they were in Sutherland Avenue after all. 'Won't be long now, chicken. I know exactly where we are, don't worry.'

'That's what you said before. . . .'

'Yes, but this time I really do. . . .'

Until at last he said: 'This is Maida Vale now—we shan't be long,' and edged the car round a corner, hugging the kerb, and crept along the broad, straight level of the main road, and, after a little while, pulled up. 'It must be somewhere just here, Rosie; I'll edge her across the road.' She got out and stood on the step, directing him, looking over the roof of the car at the row of houses on the other side of the street. Not even an outline, not even the outline of the familiar, rather lumpy gateposts, but—dimly, dimly glowing through the thick veils of the fog, lights where lights should be at this hour if this was home: a light in the ground-floor right-hand window, a light in the hall, a light on the first floor, in the nursery. . . . (Goodness knew, Tilda was a maniac about the baby's routine, but surely to heavens she wasn't serenely potting Emma while Raoul lay slain with a mastoid mallet on the floor below?)

The gateposts loomed suddenly up before them. 'Yes, this is us—whoa! Well, you've overshot it a bit, but never mind. . . .' She leapt off the running-board and scrambled round, with a hand for a moment on the warm bonnet, fumbling, almost before the car had stopped, at the handle of his door. He got out, thrusting the ignition key into his pocket. 'Steady on now!' He held her for a moment, quietening her; and up in the nursery, the light went out.

Up in the nursery, the light went out. By the little car at the gates, Tedward held Rosie, for a brief second, trembling in his arms; half a mile away, Thomas Evans crawled homewards again, blear-eyed and sick at heart, a moment away Damien Jones leaned against the solid comfort of a rough brick wall and vomited up his panic-stricken little soul; down in her basement room, Melissa stared into a mirror that reflected back a terrified, sick white face, and, up on the first floor, old Mrs. Evans leaned back panting against her pillows, her wig awry. In the nursery, Matilda Evans put out the light and went softly out and started down the stairs.

At the turn, she stopped. Ted Edwards was standing in the open doorway, staring up at her, Rosie at his shoulder, the curls of the grey fog eddying about them, like smoke. And, between stairs and door, pitched face-downwards on the floor of the hall, lay Raoul—Raoul Vernet who, two brief hours before, had arrived with his bouquets and his speeches at her door; lying there on the floor of the hall one hand still clutching the receiver of the telephone, with the sloping, round bald patch at the back of his head, smashed in. No little black dots now, but a lake of hideous red. . . .

CHAPTER SIX

So Rosie told Inspector Cockrill.

Cockie was sitting with his feet up on the mantelpiece—which fortunately was a low one, or his short legs would have been practically vertical and his behind in the fire—languidly reading the *Kentish Mercury*. It was a strange occupation for the Inspector at ten o'clock in the morning; but Cockie was on a holiday-at-home—and all he could say was that if this were a foretaste of what retirement was going to be like, he had better invest in a couple of disguises forthwith and set up in a private detective agency, to give himself something to do. Not that, down here in Heronsford, concealment would be of much use: no density of beard and whisker could long conceal *him* from the sheep, black and white, among whom he had moved, the Terror of Kent, for so long; no upturned collar and down-pulled hat disguise the sparse grey hair, the splendid head, the beaky nose, the bird-like bright brown eye. He would have to set up somewhere else, and London, of course, was the place. But Cockie had had his bellyful of London, last time he came up. That Jezebel case—and that maddening young, cock-a-hoop chap, Detective Inspector Charlesworth, forsooth, of Scotland Yard. . . . Oh, well, he thought; no more of *him!*

The telephone rang. A feminine voice concluded what had evidently been a mildly flirtatious skirmish with the male voice of TOL., and asked for Inspector Cockrill.

'Cockie? Oh, Cockie, it's Rosie—*you* know, Rosie Evans. Cockie, we're in such a *thing* up here, do come and get us all out of it, I can't tell you how awful it is.'

'What are you talking about?'

'Well, I'm just telling you. Cockie, dear, I'm most terribly sorry to bother you about it, and especially when you're so busy and terrifically important and everything, but you're the only person in the police that we can turn to. . . .'

Cockie reflected briefly that a great many people prefaced an appeal for help with the not very flattering confession that he was the only person they were able to turn to; still, Rosie at any rate added that he was terrifically important— and, what was more, confidently believed it. 'Now start at the beginning, my dear child. What's happened?'

'Well, Cockie; it seems quite incredible but a chap's been killed, I mean a friend of ours, killed here in our house. I mean murdered. Some horrible burglar or somebody came in and blipped him on the head and killed him.'

'You've called in the police?' said Cockrill, quickly.

'Oh, good lord yes, at least they've called themselves in, hundreds of them, milling all over the place. But they're no good, they're only making it worse. I mean, Cockie, it's too incredible for words, but I don't believe they think it was a burglar at all. They think it was one of us.'

'Oh, dear!' said Cockie. That was different.

'I mean, Cockie, *you* know Thomas, you've known him for ever, *can* you imagine him hitting somebody over the head and killing them?'

'They suspect *Thomas?*' Cockie, as it happened, could well imagine Thomas hitting somebody over the head and killing them. He was a quiet man: a man of few words, but those words pungent and to the point; he looked frail but he had been a great little fly-half in his day. Yes, Thomas might kill a man: not impulsively, not in a fit of temper, not, as it were, "lightly"—but in a cold, white, deep, indignant rage. Because of injustice, because of cruelty, because of betrayal of the innocent. . . . 'Who was this man, Rosie?'

'He was a Frenchman. . . .'

'Oh, a Frenchman,' said Cockie. Really then, it hardly counted, after all.

'He came from Geneva; you know I've just come back from Geneva, Cockie? I was at a sort of frightful school there, only I simply never went near the school and I'm afraid I was a bit of a basket. But anyway, he came over here and he came to dinner and Thomas went out and got lost in the fog and the police think he came back and came into the house and killed Raoul while Tilda was upstairs in the nursery. You know what she is about "routine", Cockie, I mean if the *Queen* came to dinner, she'd still walk out backwards or whatever it is you have to do, at exactly half-past nine, and go up and do the baby. . . .'

Cockie gave it as his opinion that the Queen, being a mother herself, would perfectly understand Matilda's walking out backwards at half-past nine to do the baby. 'Well, then?'

'Well, then, they just think he killed Raoul and then went away and drove about in the fog again and only pretended to be surprised. At least we're sure they do.'

'They haven't charged him yet, then?'

'Charged him? Good lord, no, Cockie, what for? They only sort of hint and ask peculiar questions and don't believe a word any of us says.'

Cockie considered. 'Well, Rosie my dear, I'm very sorry about it, very sorry indeed, and you must tell Matilda and Thomas that I said so. But *I* can't do anything about it, my dear child, can I? *I* can't come up interfering with Scotland

Yard. They have to ask questions, but if Thomas is innocent the whole thing will fizzle out—you needn't be frightened, the police don't make mistakes.'

'But suppose they did? Matilda's simply petrified—you know what she is about Thomas; and I do sort of vaguely feel that it's all my fault—so I thought I ought to try and do something, so that's why I rang you up. No one else dared.'

'Well, you must just trust the police that's all; they don't make mistakes.'

'They seem very nice,' admitted Rosie, doubtfully. 'There's a young man called Charlesworth who I must say is perfect heaven. . . .'

'Called what?' said Cockie.

'Called Detective Inspector Charlesworth.'

'Oh, well,' said Cockie. 'That's different. I'll be up this afternoon.'

And that afternoon he arrived (Detective Inspector Charlesworth, indeed!), a small, shabby country sparrow, come to visit his cousins caged up in their terrible town; cheap suitcase in hand, mackintosh trailing over one shoulder (yesterday's fog had gone, leaving a bright, warm day), battered felt hat perched all anyhow on his fine head with its halo of prematurely whitening hair. 'Excuse the hat,' he said to Rosie, who was hanging about waiting to meet him at the gate. 'I can't think whose it is. I must have picked it up somewhere. However, exchange is no robbery and it's quite a good fit.' Anything which did not actually deafen and blind him was quite a good fit to Inspector Cockrill.

'I was waiting here to try and catch you before you went in, Cockie,' said Rosie, hooking a hand into his arm in her own confiding, absurdly endearing way, urging him a little way down the road past the gate. 'I wanted to say something to you before you saw Thomas.'

'Well, say it,' said Cockie.

Practice had made Rosie fairly fluent in her recitation. 'Well, Cockie, I told you I'd been a bit of a basket in Geneva, and the truth is, I'm afraid I was. And buns in the oven is the net result.' She looked at him in bright-eyed expectancy.

'Baskets? Buns? What are you talking about?'

'Well, I mean I'm going to have a baby. I suppose now,' said Rosie, 'you'll be shocked?'

'My dear child, you should come to the Heronsford police court some time. I'm sorry it should be you, but that's all. Then this dead man . . .?'

She poured it all out to him and it was worse, much worse, than he had supposed. If Thomas knew that Rosie had been seduced, deserted, with a baby on the way . . . 'Well, but Cockie, Thomas didn't know. He knows now and he's a bit sick about it, only nobody can think of anything but the murder; but up till then we'd all been working like mad to keep it from him.'

'He's a doctor. And he was here in the house with you.'

'But then, wouldn't he have said?'

'Who—Thomas?' said Cockie. How much more likely that Thomas, heart hot, head icy cold, would not have 'said'; would have bided his time, saying nothing, and when the opportunity suddenly presented itself, struck and struck hard, in two senses at once, and so dealt with a vile offender, unpunishable by law. 'But anyway, why should he have thought it was Raoul?' said Rosie. 'He didn't know anything about him.'

'You say it quite definitely wasn't this Raoul?'

'What, *Raoul?*' Rosie spewed up laughter into her hand. 'That stuffy old thing! He was as bald as a coot.'

'Why else should he have come over here?'

'Well, you know what these businessmen are, they fly all

over the place at the drop of a hat. It all goes down in expenses, so what do they care? He probably had to come, anyway. Not just because of me.'

The rest of the family were waiting for them in the house, gathered unhappily about the office fire. Mrs. Evans seemed quite restored to her predominant mood which was one of mischievous sanity, Thomas had retreated into the inarticulate resentment which was his customary defence against the intrusions of personal drama into his busy, anxious professional life; Tedward was civilly striving to disguise the fact that he had returned, perennially resilient, to his everyday buoyancy; Melissa sat looking very white in a big armchair, her lock of hair dangling, as usual, over her eyes; Matilda—Matilda was cold with horror, sick and cold with the horror of it all, the ugliness and the dread, the memory of Raoul lying there in the hall, in their own, dear, shabby, untidy, familiar hall—Raoul, the too-suave, the invulnerable, the didactic, the smug, who now had been hauled off to lie among strangers here in this strange land, until his poor, dissected, degutted, cobbled-up body could be shipped home to the very few people who had loved him there. . . . 'Oh, Cockie—it was naughty of Rosie, but I *am* so glad you've come!'

Inspector Cockrill dutifully embarked upon a speech about the impossibility of interfering with the activities of the police on the spot, but she did not listen to him, she did not care. She poured it all out to him, heaped facts and figures at his feet. 'So there you are, Cockie, how could it have been anybody but a burglar, how could Thomas have had anything to do with it. . . .?'

'Nobody says I have, Tilda,' said Thomas, crossly. 'Except you.'

'I only say that the police . . .'

'Never mind, never mind,' said Cockie. 'Just keep quiet

and let me get this straight. Now, Matilda—this man, Vernet, rang you from the Ritz yesterday morning and arranged to come to dinner at half-past seven—right? He was late, he arrived about a quarter to eight. Melissa was out for the afternoon and evening; Rosie had gone out just before he arrived; Thomas went off directly after, without seeing him; Mrs. Evans was upstairs in her room, ditto the baby; so you were to all intents and purposes alone with him. You had dinner and, at a quarter past nine, you went upstairs to do the baby, etcetera, leaving him in the drawing-room. Two minutes later, he was ringing up Dr. Edwards' house saying that he had been attacked with a mastoid mallet, whatever that may be. Rosie was there and she took the message. She and Dr. Edwards rushed round as fast as the fog would let them, and got here at about twenty-five to ten, just as you were coming downstairs again. Vernet was lying dead in the hall, with his head caved in and Dr. Edwards says he had only been dead a few minutes; the telephone receiver was still in his hand, and the wire had been yanked right out, as though by the fall. At this time, Melissa had been in quite a while, but downstairs in her flat, and Thomas was driving about in the fog, trying to find a patient's address. He got in ten minutes later. Is that all correct?'

'Yes, it is, Cockie; so there you are, how could Thomas possibly . . .?'

'All right, Matilda, don't go *on* about it,' said Thomas.

It was a comfortable room; a rather shabby, very untidy, unselfconscious, comfortable room, with ugly, fat, comfortable old armchairs regrettably out of keeping with its high, moulded Regency ceiling; with Thomas's all-important desk poked away into an unconsidered corner, Thomas's appointment pads and books and a litter of pencils and scraps of paper on the wide marble mantelpiece; the screen behind which he must modestly conceal his female patients in their process of disrobing before they appeared stark naked before his professional eye, was now folded away against the wall (in fact he saw the vast majority of his patients in their outside surgery in St. John's Wood); and on the examination couch, Rosie was curled up in one of her lovely, curving poses, with Annaran, the Siamese cat, stretched out ecstatically on her lap, having his velvet stomach rubbed up the wrong way. 'Now, Rosie—stop messing about with that cat and listen to me: this telephone call you took——?'

'Well, Tedward was getting out the car, Cockie, and I simply took it, in case it was a patient or something, just like I would here.'

'Yes, all right. What time did you arrive there?'

'It was nine o'clock,' said Tedward, 'or very nearly. I know because I was watching the time—I expected her about eight.'

'But you left here at half-past seven, Rosie,' said Tilda.

'Yes, I know, but the fog was simply *frantic*,' said Rosie, walking pink-tipped fingers up and down Annaran's arched back.

'You made her some tea and then went out to get your car?'

Tedward sat forward in his chair, his hands between his knees; his trousers were extended, tight and wrinkled across his heavy thighs. 'Yes. I didn't like the look of her, I thought she looked white and tired and I wanted to get her home.'

'But she'd only just arrived.'

Couldn't the silly old fool realize that Rosie had struggled for more than an hour through the fog, baby and all? 'I thought she was over-tired,' repeated Tedward, crossly.

'All right, all right. Well, then—how long getting out your car?'

Tedward shrugged. 'I wouldn't know exactly. Three or four minutes Rosie? It was a hell of a job because the fog by the canal was as thick as cotton wool, and my garage is tricky, anyway. Does it matter?'

'I wanted to try and time the telephone call. Matilda left Raoul Vernet at exactly a quarter past nine.'

'Well, the 'phone rang almost directly after Tedward went to get the car.'

'Now tell me again exactly what was said.'

Rosie was busy making herself a Mandarin moustache with the end of Annaran's dark tail, but she desisted long enough to recite in a parrot gabble the gist of the telephone message, which she was by now heartily sick of repeating. 'He definitely said, Rosie, "A *man* came in and hit me with a mastoid mallet"?'

'Oh, I don't know about "a *man*", said Rosie, tucking Annaran's tail back around him. 'Mr. Charlesworth keeps asking me, too. Either "a man" or "someone" or something like that. But he did say about the mastoid mallet.'

'You're sure of that at least?'

'Well, yes, of course; because otherwise how could I have known about the mastoid mallet?'

'There was a mastoid mallet thrown down beside him in the hall,' said Thomas. 'It had obviously been used on him. It was mine.'

'Yes, I want to come to that now. You kept this mastoid mallet in the hall?'

It sounded very peculiar, it sounded as though one kept mastoid mallets tidied away in a corner with croquet and other mallets of that *ilk*, as Thomas would have said to annoy Matilda, who went nearly mad when people misused words. 'Yes. At least I think it would be there, though some of the stuff's in the old chest of drawers on the landing upstairs. My old Uncle Huw left me his instruments—

71

Doctor Evans Pink Medicine, he used to be called back home in Wales, to distinguish him from Doctor Evans Little Pills. The ones I had no use for I stowed away upstairs, or in the drawer of that bureau in the hall where the telephone stands.'

'And this mastoid mallet's missing from either upstairs or downstairs, wherever it was?'

'It's not exactly missing,' said Thomas. 'The police have got it, duly covered with blood and hairs and what not. But there's no mallet now in either of the drawers, and anyway, it's mine all right. I know the look of it.'

'What *is* the look of it?' said Cockrill. 'I mean what are these things like?'

'Well, they're just miniature mallets, like little steel croquet mallets or like those things you knock pegs in with; only the handle's much shorter by comparison. The business end's about as big as . . . As big as . . .' He looked about him for a comparison. 'Well, as big as an ordinary tumbler, if a tumbler was a lot smaller than it usually is; or as big as a tin of baked beans, though why baked beans, I don't know.'

'Very handy for killing a man with?' suggested Cockie.

'So a good many ear, nose and throat surgeons have discovered,' said Thomas, dryly.

'What precisely is the thing used for in the ordinary way?'

Thomas put two fingers behind his ear. 'Chipping away diseased bone in the mastoid region, here. You hold a sort of chisel in your left hand, and hammer away at it with the mallet.'

'It would be pretty heavy?'

'Heavy-ish,' said Thomas. 'But well-balanced.'

'As far as killing this man was concerned—anyone could have used the thing? A woman could have used it?'

portant. 'Thanks very much; what does that make *me?*' said old Mrs. Evans, laughing.

'You didn't think of running down, half-way through, and reassuring him?'

'Well, time passes so quickly when you're busy and in a hurry. I did call over the banisters once, but he didn't answer so I thought he hadn't heard.' She put her hand to her mouth in a gesture of dismay. 'Oh, heavens! You don't think . . .?'

'He didn't answer because he was lying there dead.'

'Oh, *Cock*ie!'

'You couldn't see down into the hall?'

'No, you can't from the landing; not unless you go down the stairs a little way.'

'And you didn't hear anything, Matilda?'

'No, Cockie, absolutely nothing. At the time of the 'phone call, I'd have been in my room doing my face, and you couldn't hear anything from there, even quite a row. We've tested it. And Gran says she heard nothing.'

'I daresay I'm getting a bit deaf,' said old Mrs. Evans—a most rare confession of weakness.

'Not even the ting of the 'phone when the receiver was put back?'

'Yes, but it wasn't put back,' said Tedward. 'He fell with the receiver still in his hand, *did*n't he? In fact, Rosie heard him fall.'

'Yes, his voice got fainter and fainter and then there was a sort of bonk.'

'Rosie heard the bonk over the telephone half a mile away, but you two good ladies, in your rooms one floor above—you heard nothing?'

Mrs. Evans gave a loud, suspicious sniff. 'Do I smell burning?'

'No, darling, you don't,' said Matilda. Granny's diver-

'You mean to say, Matilda, that you never did discuss whatever it was that he had come to say?'

'My dear, nothing would induce him to disturb his digestion with a painful discussion, that was the truth of it; and I just *had* to do my chores at a quarter past nine—and then, after that, well, he was dead.'

'How long were you away from him?'

'I've worked it all out about a million times for Mr. Charlesworth,' said Matilda, 'so I can tell you exactly. At a quarter past, I went to Granny's room and unhooked her wig for her, didn't I, Gran?—and undid the back of her dress, and then I went to my own room and tidied myself up for about five minutes, and then by that time she was undressed and I helped her into bed and gave her her Horlicks. And then I went into the nursery, and I know it was half-past nine then, because I always do Emma at half-past nine, though I'll spare you my well-known speech about the importance of regularity in bringing up children. So if I was five or six minutes with Emma, it must have been twenty-five to, or a bit later, when I came downstairs and saw Rosie and Tedward coming into the hall.'

'And that fits,' said Rosie, 'because if she left him at a quarter past nine and the 'phone call was just after that, then Tedward and I took about fifteen minutes in the fog, and we arrived between twenty-five to and twenty to ten. We've been over and over and over it all with Charlesworth.'

'You mean to say, Matilda, that you left your guest all alone for a whole twenty minutes?'

'Well, I couldn't help it, Cockie. These things had to be done.' She added that it was like being a farmer, if they knew what she meant; animals had to be fed and milked and things, and other things just couldn't be more im-

'Man, woman or child,' agreed Thomas, readily. 'Just the job.'

'How long have you had it? Who knew it was here?'

'We all knew,' said Matilda. 'We all helped to sort out Uncle Huw's legacy. Tedward, you were here that day, and one of Rosie's boy friends was here too—would it be Damien Jones?'

'Yes,' said Rosie. 'It was just before I went to Switzerland.'

'Well, all right. Now, Matilda—it looks as if this man was attacked almost directly you left him and went upstairs?'

Matilda, who thought in pictures, saw Raoul sitting as she had left him, bald head thrown back against the coral-coloured cushion in the big, pale green armchair, long legs crossed, the pointed toe of a too-ornate brown shoe, gently swinging. 'I'm terribly sorry, Raoul, but I must just go upstairs and fix up the old lady for the night and pot the baby; and then we can settle down and really talk. . . .' 'Mais, ma chère,' he had said, 'one hour and a half already I have been here and so far not one word of what I wish to say. Le cocktail, la cuisine, le café—et maintenant les vielles, les enfants. . . .' She had sworn that she would not be long, at least not *very* long—uneasily conscious that what she had to do must take her at least twenty minutes. 'Anyway, it's your fault, Raoul, for refusing to discuss things at dinner.' He had replied with ill-concealed impatience that what he had to say was extremely distasteful, that Mathilde would not like it any better than he did, and he preferred to dine before he was thrown out of the house, 'Alors, Mathilde—allez, allez, depêchez-vous, s'il vous plait. In one minute your husband will return and then . . .' He gave the sort of shrug with which the British caricature all Frenchmen on every stage. 'It will be I, ma chère, who depêche myself!'

73

sions had now and again come in handy with Mr. Charlesworth, but Cockie was 'on their side'; at least she hoped he was.

Melissa sat staring down at her hands and in all her life she had never been so much afraid. Now he's coming to me. Now he'll start asking me! Her head swam, her mind was a blank. What had she said to Inspector Charlesworth, what lies had she told that must be adhered to now? And if she contradicted herself, would this dreadful little fierce old man compare notes with the others—and find out the whole appalling truth? She bent her head still lower over the clenched hands so that her hair hung like a curtain over her face. She had said that. . . . She had said that she had been with Stanislas. And that had been all right because she could honestly say that she didn't know his name or where he lived or anything about him, as Rosie could testify; as to the telephone number, it had been too well-remembered to need writing down in the little book with the dearth of abortionists and one must just deny that one had ever known it. Mr. Charlesworth had said that no doubt the police would have very little difficulty in tracing him, and one could only hope and pray that that was not true. It had occurred to her to get in touch with Stanislas and beg him to keep silent; but all things considered. . . . No; she would not do that. And when he saw in the papers that she was mixed up in murder, he, who had to be so 'careful', would almost certainly stay away, slip away out of the whole thing, and for ever.

So she trotted out her story once again. She had met her Friend and they had started off to a cinema, had lost their way in the fog and just been—well, just walking about. And she had got back about half-past nine (or had she said to Inspector Charlesworth that it was a quarter to ten? It was so important, so ghastly-ly important and now she had gone and forgotten . . .), and had been in her flat, and heard nothing until there was a commotion in the hall, people talking and things, and she had gone up and found them all leaning over the body; they must have turned him over on his back by then because his two pointed toes were sticking up into the air. . . .

A little fish of doubt swam into Cockie's consciousness and hung about there for a moment waggling its fins at him; but he was more interested in Thomas than in Melissa Weeks and so he passed on and never knew how much trouble and tragedy might have been saved if he had noticed it. 'Now Thomas—let's hear from *you*.'

Thomas sat, looking rather lost in the big armchair. His short legs would not, comfortably, reach the ground and he had tucked them up under him, like a child. It gave him an oddly defenceless air, curled up there, with his pale face and untidy fair hair and the little bumps that came up under his eyes when he was tired or anxious or unwell. 'Nothing to tell you. I went out to see a case, I couldn't find the address, I milled about for hours in the fog looking for it, and finally I came home. By that time, this ruddy fellow was lying there dead, cluttering up my hall. That's all I know.'

'You never *saw* the case?' said Cockie, anxiously.

'I tell you, I couldn't find the address. I don't know that part very well, it's outside my usual territory, I lost my way about forty times and there was nobody about in the fog to ask. And in the end I may have got it wrong, because when I did get there the house was all shut up and there was nobody there. It was in a little back street, a sort of mews thing, called Harrow Gardens—too small to be in the London Guide.'

'Well, but Thomas, that didn't take you over two hours?'

'You don't know what the fog was like, Cockie; damn it,

it took Tedward twenty minutes to get from his place to here, and that's not half as far, not a quarter as far, and what's more, he knows the road, which I don't round that Harrow Road part. But apart from that, when I found the house empty, I thought I might have mistaken the address so, having gone so far, I looked round a bit more. I found a Harrow Place and a Harrow Street and a few more Harrows, but none of them went up to the number I'd got, so I gave the whole thing up and came home.'

'You didn't think of ringing up here?'

'I did, later, but by that time the line here was dead. Anyway, it was a forlorn chance; I thought Melissa had taken the message, and she'd still be out, so what could they tell me? I just went on searching.'

'Was it a serious case, that you took so much trouble?'

'It was a case,' said Thomas, briefly.

'Oh, Thomas, now don't get all cross and shut-up,' implored Matilda. 'This is what he does with Mr. Charlesworth, Cockie, when Mr. Charlesworth seems to think it's fishy. It *was* a serious case, at least it might have been; it was a baby and it could easily have died. Couldn't it, Thomas?'

'Were they private patients? Or would they be on your panel or whatever they call it with this National Health thing?'

'How do *I* know?' said Thomas. 'I haven't got their name. But it was unlikely they'd be paying patients coming from that particular district.'

'Would it be in your area?'

'I haven't got an area,' said Thomas, increasingly cross. 'I let my patients live where they like.'

'I'm merely putting it to you as the police on the job will put it, Thomas. You had an address and the fact that a child was ill. Out you went into practically impassable fog and spent over two hours searching for them. Wouldn't they meanwhile have taken the child to hospital?'

'That's what they probably did as the house was empty. But I couldn't count on it. Once patients have rung up for the doctor, they just fold their hands and wait patiently in sublime confidence that sooner or later he'll appear. And they wouldn't want to take a sick child out into the fog. Anyway, there's nothing wrong, I suppose, in a doctor going out to see a case? For Pete's sake. . . .'

'Now, hold your horses, son: nobody's accusing you of anything.'

'Don't you believe it,' said Thomas. 'Wait till you hear! *Where* did I find the message?—written on a scrap of paper lying on the appointments pad, here on the mantelpiece in this room, beside the telephone. *Where* is it now?—I tore it up; I copied the address into my little book in the usual way, and chucked the paper into the fire. Wasn't that rather a silly thing to do?—Well, yes, perhaps it was, in case I got the address copied down wrong, but there it was, I just did it. And, *why* is that rather a pity?—Because, my dear Inspector, I now can't show the scrap of paper to prove that it ever existed. *And nobody in the house ever saw it.* Nobody took the message, nobody wrote it down. Matilda didn't, Rosie didn't, Granny didn't, and now Melissa tells us that she didn't; and there's nobody else.'

'M'm,' said Cockie. 'It doesn't sound too good.'

'It sounds pretty good to Inspector Charlesworth,' said Thomas. 'It sounds just the job to *him*. I waved a blank paper under Matilda's nose, told her it was a case and I'd have to go out, skipped off without seeing the victim, presumably so that I wouldn't have as an excuse for killing him that I didn't like his face, hung about in the fog till I saw by the lights in the house that Matilda had gone upstairs and left him alone, whizzed into the hall, got my little hatchet out of the drawer, whistled him to come out of the drawing-room and be killed, and blipped him on the head. Then, not being a good enough doctor to know whether or not a man's dead, I went off into the fog again, leaving him to hop up and ring round telling everybody all about it before he passed away.' He looked Cockrill in the eye. 'And the hell of it is, that it hangs together you know; it sounds damn silly, and yet it's watertight. Charlesworth's not quite such a bloody fool as he looks.'

' 'Ere, 'ere, 'ere, 'ere, wot's all this?' said Detective Inspector Charlesworth, coming in at the door.

CHAPTER SEVEN

Rosie privately thought Mr. Charlesworth was simply *heaven!* Fancy a detective being so *young*, and then so frantically good-looking with his hair brushed up into divine little sort of moustaches over his ears; and lovely long legs and nice grey eyes and a *gent!* Even if he was rather beastly and suspicious about poor Thomas. I expect I could get round him, though, she thought; not to fuss any more but just say it was a burglar and be done with it. Getting round Mr. Charlesworth would in itself be quite fun.

Mr. Charlesworth was perfectly (and genuinely) enchanted to see Inspector Cockrill; no suspicion of unfriendly feeling, no slightest intention of giving offence lurked, or ever had lurked, in his guileless heart. He wrung the old man's hand, asked after Crime in Kent, rather as though it were the routine of general misdemeanour in a minor preparatory school, and referred with great jocularity to that Jezebel case, when they had worked together—apparently blissfully forgetful of where the ultimate credit for its solution had lain. Cockie, who had so recently adjured the Evans family to be of good behaviour with the police, set them but a poor example of frankness and honesty. He just happened to be in London. . . . And just happening to drop in on his friends, the Evans's. . . . 'I find them in rather an unfortunate situation; and I thought that perhaps . . .'

'We thought that perhaps Cockie could just explain to you how idiotic it was to think that Thomas could possibly have wanted to kill Raoul,' said Rosie, 'and then he could help you to find out who it really was.'

Cockie passionately disclaimed. Charlesworth declared that he would be only too happy to talk things over with the Inspector; but it was apparent that Rosie's words had brought him back to earth with a nasty bump. They strolled into the garden together. 'To be honest, Inspector, I don't like this case one bit.'

'Nor do I,' said Cockie.

'He seems such a nice chap,' said Charlesworth. 'And yet . . .'

There was a dank stone bench beyond the mulberry tree and they sat down there on Cockrill's mackintosh and offered one another cigarettes. 'You must say the thing about the message is pretty fishy.'

'I don't see how you can base a whole case on it. Accidents happen. That ass of a secretary girl, Melissa—she may easily have forgotten writing it down, or she's got in a flap and just blankly denies it; perhaps she knows she got it down wrong or something.'

'She seems rather a peculiar wench,' said Charlesworth, thoughtfully. 'I wish to hell she'd put a Kirbigrip in her hair.'

'Inferiority complex,' said Cockrill. 'When girls wear their hair draped over their faces, it's always a sign.'

'There was a girl called Veronica Lake who started off under the same disability,' said Charlesworth. If the dear old boy were going to begin delving into psychology. . . .!

Sergeant Bedd came out to meet them, moving quickly and quietly on his large feet up the overgrown garden path, as an elephant passes silently through the jungle. Like the elephant, he too wore a baggy, dark grey suit. His square brown face broke into a thousand delighted wrinkles at sight of Inspector Cockrill and he sat down before them, perched at their feet like a small boy, on the stump of a tree. 'What do *you* think of this business, Sergeant?' said Cockie. 'By the way, Thomas Evans is a friend of mine.'

'Well, it certainly looks a bit sticky for your friend, Inspector, but as I tell Mr. Charlesworth, there's no use in rushing things. If it was an inside job, it must have been either Dr. Evans, or his lady—after all, she was here in the house with the chap. The great question is—was it really an inside job?'

'What about the front door?'

'Just pushed to,' said Charlesworth. 'They're the scattiest family I ever came across. Everybody always forgets their latch key. . . .'

' "Everybody" means Rosie,' said Cockrill.

'I daresay. Anyway, the front door sticks just enough to keep it shut without the latch being down, and during the daytime, that's what they do with it.'

'But this was the night-time,' said Cockie.

'Yes, but Rosie was still out.'

'So that an intruder could just have pushed the door open and walked in?'

'Yep. And just the night for it, fog and all.'

'If the house had been watched at all, they'd know about the front door,' said Bedd. 'There's a lot of that stuff around Maida Vale. And seeing the doctor go out . . .'

'They may even have sent a fake message to get him out,' suggested Cockrill, a trifle too eagerly.

'Well, they might,' acknowledged Charlesworth.

Sergeant Bedd sat on his ricketty stump, looking up at them like an overgrown child with his elders, and thought his thoughts aloud. 'They've been watching the house. They know Mrs. Evans goes upstairs for quite a while every evening. They've seen the others go out—they believe she's alone. As soon as the lights go on upstairs, they push open the front door and go in. The Frenchie comes out to see what the noise is and they hit him over the head with the first thing handy and clear out.' He shrugged. 'We haven't found any signs of them,' he said.

'They'd have gloves and sneakers and all the rest of it.'

'Yes, it doesn't count much, one way or the other.' But there was a snag to it. Mr. Charlesworth and Inspector Cockrill sat eyeing one another warily. If the old boy didn't tumble to it. . . . If the young jackanapes couldn't see it. . . .

'But the snag is,' said Sergeant Bedd in his deep, slow rumble, 'that the mastoid mallet *was*n't handy, *was* it?'

Messrs. Charlesworth and Cockrill said that that was just what they had been going to say.

Back in the house, Matilda was sitting in front of the high chair, pushing bits of nourishing biscuit into Emma's reluctant mouth, with Gabriel at their feet in eager expectation of crumbs from the rich man's table. Emma had reverted as, when life became too complicated, she often did, to her earlier babyhood and kept up a monotonous bow-wow, chuck-chuck, quack-quack, most trying to the nerves. Thomas sat with his behind perched on the high nursery fender, earnestly fishing with a hair-pin for the hook and band which held in place two curved, fat celluloid arms. 'Don't you think that that child might be happier in a zoo?'

'I think we'd all be happier in a zoo,' said Matilda, with a sigh. 'Then at least we could be red in tooth and claw and it would only be our natures.'

The elastic slid off the hair-pin for the hundredth time. 'What I *can*not make out, Tilda, is why or how he rang up Tedward's number. He knew nothing about him.'

'Oh, I forgot; it's all been worked out. It's written in huge numbers over every extension to the telephone in the house, and DOCTOR in huge letters too, in case of you being out and Melissa alone in the house, and anything happening to Emma. It would be the first thing to catch his eye.'

'Yes, but you were upstairs. Why not just call out?'

'He may have tried,' said Matilda, going a little white at the thought of it.

'Of course his voice was very faint,' said Thomas. 'Or so Rosie says. I suppose if he couldn't make anyone hear. . . .'

'He'd see "Doctor" written there and the telephone right in front of him. And after all, when I did hear, the first thing I would do would be to ring a doctor. . . . (Come on Emma, if you don't want it, Gabriel does. . . .) No, it seems quite reasonable that he should have done it, Thomas; but the thing is how could he have done it with his head all—all bashed in like that?'

Thomas had caught the elusive hook and triumphantly slid the elastic over it and started on the legs. 'You only saw it when it was covered in blood and what-not, darling; you don't know how much or how little it was bashed in, under all that.'

'Well enough to kill him, damn it,' said Matilda, shuddering.

'Yes, but these head cases are funny. They often do all sorts of things after injury that you wouldn't dream they could. They're like Charles the Whatsaname, they walk and talk half an hour after their heads are cut off; they get what are called "lucid periods", or they may just do things, quite sensible things, not knowing what they're doing. It doesn't mean that they're not going to die in the end.'

'And it does seem as if poor Raoul took a long time to die. . . . (Emma, come *on*, darling! My God, I shall brain this child one day.).'

Thomas fished about blindly for the elastic hook. 'Perhaps you might settle for some other form of outlet? I feel that one braining may be enough for the moment.' He lifted his head from his absorption with the celluloid doll and smiled at her across the room. 'Don't let it get you down, darling. I know he was a friend of yours, but . . .'

She yanked the baby out of its chair and, sitting it on her her knee, began to wipe its grubby face. 'Oh, Thomas, for goodness sake don't start being kind and make me burst into tears. Raoul wasn't a friend of mine, at least not really—he used to be, but I'd quite got over him. Of course I'm sorry he's dead, I'm sorry for anyone if they're dead, but all I can actually feel is that I wish he hadn't got himself killed in our house. Which does seem ungrateful, I know, because after all he was our guest. . . . Well, you know what I mean!' She broke off, half laughing, half in tears.

'Yes, I know what you mean,' said Thomas.

'(Emma have milko now, lovely, heavenly milko!) But, Thomas, about him dying—it's definitely established that he didn't actually die for about ten minutes?'

'It may have been even longer. Tedward was about twenty minutes getting here after the 'phone call, and *he* says he thought when he saw him that he'd only been dead a very few minutes. The police surgeon confirmed that when he saw the body.'

'If only I'd gone down, between doing Granny and baby!'

'You couldn't have done anything, Tilda. He was going to die anyway, and after the telephone call he was almost certainly unconscious. You could see how he'd sort of clung on to the bureau with the receiver in his hand, and got weaker and weaker and fuzzier and fuzzier, I suppose, poor chap, and just passed into unconsciousness and slid down the front of the bureau and lain there with the thing still in his hand. What does it matter whether he was actually alive or dead? *He* didn't know anything about it; don't you worry.' He smiled at her again, briefly, and bent over the doll.

What goes on inside you? thought Matilda. What's in your head now?—being able to give your attention to that damn doll, and yet thinking so clearly and carefully. What do you know? What had you guessed?—about me, and about Raoul; and about Rosie. And if you suspected that I'd been unfaithful to you with that creature, would you—would you go out and bat him on the head, would you even mind enough to do that? As for Rosie . . . She remembered how sharply Thomas had questioned her about this sudden descent of Raoul Vernet upon them, how he had pounced upon the fact that she wanted to be alone with Raoul, how he had followed Rosie out into the hall. 'Aren't you staying to see this wonderful Frenchman?', and 'You did know this man in Geneva, didn't you?' 'If you want to know, I knew him a great deal too well,' Rosie had said, bursting out with it, irritably. He had come back into the kitchen, staring down into his glass with troubled eyes; though when, after the murder, she had broken to him the news about Rosie— knowing that in the subsequent investigations it must almost certainly come out—he had protested that he had had no suspicion, none. And yet . . . Could anybody stand there, could even Thomas, the quiet, the unfathomable, the unpredictable, could even Thomas stand there so nonchalantly, his mind apparently altogether intent upon linking up the arms and legs of a celluloid doll, while all the time murder was hot in his heart and head? She took the empty mug away from the baby, and holding it on her lap again, its red head leaning against her shoulder, wiped its sticky, rose-leaf hands. 'But *Thomas*,' she said, after a minute, 'you've put the legs and arms on back to front. It looks most *odd!*'

Damien Jones enjoyed little sympathy at home over his political views. 'What on earth were you doing at your meeting last night, Damien, with those nasty foreigners of yours? You've been as white as a sheet all day and I'm sure you're up to no good. You're not planning some sort of Attack, Damien, are you?' Mrs. Jones lived in terror of violence to members of His Majesty's Government at the hands of Damien's Branch—which, however, was so much more nearly a twig that the Home Secretary might be considered justified in sleeping soundly o' nights as far as that particular threat was concerned. '*And* you came home from the office to-day, limping, Damien.'

'Well, you don't think I've been out kicking the Prime Minister, Mother, do you?'

'If there's anything wrong with your foot . . .?'

'There isn't anything wrong, Mother, do stop fussing.'

'Then it must be your shoes,' said Mrs. Jones, fretfully. 'Your new shoes, Damien, and we paid such a lot for them. I don't know why they should suddenly start pinching you, they've been perfectly comfortable on you up to now, and Mr. Harvey's worn that kind for years and he's never had a minute's trouble with them, that's why we got them. . . .' Mr. Harvey was Mrs. Jones' pet lodger, a subdued little man who collected subscriptions for an insurance firm, and who now had weathered three years of the storms of what Mrs. Jones was pleased to call Liberty Hall.

Damien thumped on the table with a shaking hand. 'Mother, I tell you, there's nothing wrong with my feet. And there's nothing wrong with my shoes and I—*am—not*—*limping*. So please don't go on and and on about it, please *don't*, *please* DON'T!' Oh, God! he thought, if she goes and babbles all this out when the police come . . . *If* the police come . . .

'Well, all right, dear, don't shout. Oh, and some girl has been ringing you up all day.'

'A girl?' faltered Damien.

'Well, anyway, she's rung up twice in the last half hour.'

'I expect it was Rosie?' said Damien, all offhand.

'No, it wasn't—do you think I don't know Rosie Evans's voice? It was from a call-box. One of your Reds, I suppose, she sounded all whispering and mysterious like they always do.'

'What did she say?'

'Oh, lord, what did she say now? The usual thing, I've no doubt. "I'll meet him at the usual place only a bit further up, same day but not the time he arranged but an hour later," and not to tell a soul. Honestly, Damien dear, I have no patience. . . .'

If his mother knew, if she but knew the sick terror in his inside, the swirly-whirly terror heaving up and down in his stomach, the hot mist of fear that seemed to beat against his aching eyes, turning everything to grey despair . . . 'Mother, please don't go on and on, please give me the message and be done with it.'

'Damien, you're not well, child,' said his mother, looking at his white face with renewed anxiety.

'Yes, I am, mother, I'm fine; please, please don't go saying around that I'm not well, please don't go—don't go telling people that I wasn't well to-day, don't say I was limping, don't say anything *about* me. . . .'

'People? What people?'

'Oh, any people, anybody that—that just asks.' But now when they did ask she would remember this, she would know that something had happened last night. 'It's—something to do with the Party,' he blurted out wretchedly. 'You'll only get me into trouble if you go talking.' But that wasn't wise either; for when it came she would know that it was nothing to do with the Party at all. 'Anyway, Mother—this telephone call: what did she really say?'

'She just said she'd ring again at seven,' said Mrs. Jones, subdued.

And she rang at seven. 'Damien? It's me. Look, I must see you. . . .'

'No, no, Melissa, I think it's much better to—just to keep apart.'

'Has anything happened—to you, I mean? The police or anything?'

'Look here, do be careful, this thing may be tapped or something.'

'I know, that's why I think we ought to *meet* and talk. I'll be at the corner of Elgin Avenue, at eight.'

'Won't you be followed?' said Damien. Mr. Hervey passed him and stumped up the narrow staircase rather wearily after his heavy round of insurance collecting. 'Look, I'm standing in the hall with half the world listening-in. All right, I'll be there, if you think it's safe.' It sounded like a boy scout game, it sounded like a gangster film, and yet it was all true enough, real enough, horrible enough—he, Damien, who yesterday had been just an ordinary person, afraid now to go out and meet a girl 'on the corner' lest they be dogged by the police.

'I've been out to this call-box three times and nobody's followed me. Nobody suspects me or anything, it'll be all right. I'll say I'm taking Gabriel for his walk.'

So he crept out after supper, limping along in the just-too-tight shoes and there she was, waiting for him on the corner, with the little black poodle dancing about her, her eyes huge, her face pale, the hair with its threads of pure gold in the lamplight, falling forward over her cheek. They walked up the little rise into Hamilton Terrace and sat on the wooden bench outside the church. They talked in half whispers. It was very dark and still. 'Haven't the police been to your house at all, Damien?' 'No, why should they—unless you went and said . . .' 'I haven't mentioned your name, Damien, I haven't breathed to a soul that you were there at all, last night.' 'What did they say to you, Melissa, about yourself?' 'They just asked me where I'd spent the evening and I said I was with a—a friend of mine.' 'Won't they try to find the friend?' 'No, I—I told them I didn't know his name, I said he was kind of a pick-up and I had no idea where he lived and all that, and not even his surname. I said I came in—some time, I couldn't remember when, I got muddled up, but finally I just said "some time"; and that after a bit I heard a noise in the hall—and that was the first I knew about it.' She pushed her lock of hair back and, in the pale lamplight, looked him in the eyes. 'You do know that I—well, that I went up before that, Damien?'

'Yes, yes,' he said, hurriedly. 'Better not say anything about it, don't even put it into words; not now, not ever.'

Silence fell. Their white young faces stared through the lamplit darkness, they sat, tense and immobile, except for the nervous restlessness of their hands. All her silliness and affectation had fallen away from her, she was afraid, and in the reality of her stark fear, the reality of herself shone through. 'What shall I do now, Damien? Anything?'

'No, don't do anything, just keep quiet, just say nothing. Why do anything if they don't suspect?'

'But if they ask me any more questions?'

'Stick to what you've said. Be as vague as you can, so that they can't pin you down, like saying that you came in "some time", that was fine. But anything you do say, stick to it, that's all.'

'It seems simple when you're here,' said Melissa, wistfully. 'But things crop up out of the blue. And it does sound fishy to say I was walking about with—with my friend—all that time in the fog.'

'Millions of people were walking about in the fog; once you'd started you got lost and just sort of crept around trying to find the way. Couldn't you have said that you went to a cinema?'

'I nearly did, but then I thought they'd ask me what film I saw and I might get caught out. As you say, it's better to just be vague. Nobody can prove that we weren't just walking about in a fog.'

'Unless this friend turns up,' said Damien, uneasily.

'He won't,' said Melissa, more or less assured.

People drifted past, exercising dogs, to the great chagrin of Gabriel, pulling excitedly on his lead. 'I'd better go now, Damien; I could have walked round the block by now.' She stood up and shook back her lock of hair. 'You'd better not even come back down the hill with me, in case.' She said, abruptly: 'Good-bye.'

'Good-bye,' said Damien, standing with his hands in his overcoat pockets. He turned and started off at once, limping along Hamilton Terrace, shoulders hunched. After a minute she came running after him, the poodle towing her along gaily, on its scarlet lead. 'Damien! Half a minute!' She caught up with him. 'I just wanted to say—thank you, Damien.' She touched him humbly on the sleeve and turned and was towed away off down the hill; her hair gleamed gold for a moment as she passed under the corner lamp.

Ye Gods! 'Thank you,' thought Damien, bitterly. Talk about understatements!

Sergeant Bedd picked up the receiver in Thomas's office. 'Yes?'

'Could I speak to Miss Rosie Evans, please?'

' 'Oo is it speaking?' said Bedd, in a butlerish voice.

'Oh, er—just say John Brown, will you?'

'A Mr. John Brown is a-mouldering on the telephone for you, Miss,' said Bedd, ushering Rosie into the office and returning quietly to lift the receiver of the extension in the hall.

Rosie rushed all excited to the telephone. 'Hallo? Oh, gosh, Stanislas—I thought it might be you.'

'Can you meet me again, Rosie—round by the telephone box, eh?'

'My dear, I don't think I can. Haven't you seen the papers?'

'The papers?' said the disembodied voice, blankly.

'Good lord, it's in all the evening papers, the place has been absolutely swarming with reporters and things. Well, while we were—you know, round by the telephone box last night, a chap got killed here, in our house, somebody came in and hit him with a mastoid mallet. . . .'

'With a *what?* What on earth are you talking about?'

'It's in the *Evening Standard*, you can look for yourself. It was while I was at Tedward's, well, that's where I was going when I ran into you in the fog; well, while I was there a man rang up and said somebody had killed him and, my dear, when we came rushing round, sure enough there he was, lying dead on the floor in our hall.'

'My dear girl, have you been having one over the eight?'

'You just look in the papers, that's all. I expect the morning ones will be *frantic*. But, I say, Stanislas, the peculiar thing is that when the police asked Melissa where she'd spent the evening, she told them she'd been out all the time with you.'

'With me?' said the voice, alarmed.

'Yes, with you. Of course I haven't told her about you and me running into each other like that and being so silly and naughty, because my dear you must admit we *were* most terribly silly and naughty, and then discovering that all the time you were Melissa's famous Stanislas. But then to my utter astonishment, she trotted forth that she'd spent the whole evening till half-past nine wandering about in the fog with you. What a liar, isn't she?'

'How very queer,' said the voice, obviously not liking it one bit. There was a pause. 'I say, Rosie—did she give my name?'

'Only "Stanislas". None of us knows the rest.'

'No, so you don't, do you?' said Stanislas, much relieved. There was a further short pause. 'Well, good-bye, Rosie; thanks for the buggy ride—it was wonderful as long as it lasted.' The line went dead and in the hall Sergeant Bedd softly put the receiver back. 'Well, gosh!—what a so-and-so,' said Rosie—not referring to Sergeant Bedd.

And upstairs in the big bed-sitting-room with the dear old, stuffy, stodgy Victorian furniture from home, and the high brass double bedstead and the lovely bits of old china and glass, Tedward sat with old Mrs. Evans sipping a cup of after-dinner coffee and watching her steadily from under his bushy eyebrows. Mrs. Evans was in tremendous fettle. Seduced and deserted, Madonna Lily was now galloping back across the desert in pursuit of her errant knight ('Black but comely, dear Tedward, black but comely!'), hotly pursued in her turn by yet another Sheik, obviously up to no good. 'He's gaining on us, he's gaining on us!' cried Mrs. Evans, applying jewelled spurs to the sofa, flaying the air with an ebony and ivory whip. 'We must abandon the caravan, leave a few trusted men with the camel train and press on, press on! Jettison the jewels, the spices, leave my carved rosewood palanquin by the bleak wayside to be silted over by the silver sand. . . .' She paused for a moment, struck by this impromptu gem of alliteration and Tedward could almost have sworn that she winked at him; but in a moment she was at the window, jettisoning jewels and spices till the whole room was denuded of cushions. Tedward helpfully passed over his coffee cup, but this nice little piece of Limoges china was evidently too insignificant to hamper flight very seriously and she ignored it. 'He's catching up with us, he's gaining on us!' Madonna Lily was obviously marked up for a double dose of Worse than Death and Tedward, waiting a little apprehensively for his sedative to work, reflected that perhaps with luck it might be followed by another day of tranquil remorse which, in the shock and strain of their present regime, would be all to the good all round. But the pursuer caught up with Madonna Lily and— swept past. 'It's Edwin!' cried Mrs. Evans, falling on her knees with clasped hands, without troubling first to dismount from her Arab steed. 'It's Edwin who has loved me so steadily for so long. He has drawn his burnous across his face, but I know that brow, I know those eyes.' She found herself back in the saddle again and her thin old fingers, noded like bamboo stems, were clasped low on the flowing mane as she set off again at the heels of her avenger. 'Edwin! Edwin!' But the dose was beginning to take effect at last. The sofa began to slow down, she dropped her hands heavily into her lap, her eyelids began to droop. 'I must let him go on alone. I know the end. He will overtake my betrayer and there, alone in the desert, with the great storm of sand blowing up about them. . . .' She began to nod; straightened up with a jerk; drooped again. 'I'm so sorry, Tedward, dear. I feel so stupid and sleepy, I wonder if you would excuse me now. I think I'll go to bed. It was very nice of you to come and spend half an hour with a dotty old woman like me.' She jerked back her head once more and looked at him beadily. 'I hope I haven't been talking too much nonsense? I read so much, I sometimes get mixed up in my books, and all my ideas go skew-wiff.'

'It's only your wig that's skew-wiff this time,' said Tedward; his big, kind hands gently put it straight for her and he went out on to the lawn to pick up the cushions.

And next morning one, Stanley Breeks, a young gentleman, with too few hairs in his little moustache and too many spots on the back of his little neck, slipped over the channel (his passport was all quite in order) there to hang about rather bored and miserable in spite of being Abroad, till his mingy allowance should be all gone. Best to keep out of the way, thought Stan Breeks, sicking up dreadfully into the heaving sea; a woman scorned was indeed a terrible thing—

and then, damn it all, getting mixed up in a murder. . . . ! But the truth was that though one's family might have educated one to be a gent, thus breeding in one a magnificent contempt for one's origins, there they were still in the background all the time, and one had to put up with them because of cheques and things. And really one could not stand the thought of their ignorant mockery, their robustious 'teasing', their crude, vulgar laughter (for one's sisters had not benefited from a similar education) when it should be discovered that one had posed 'in the West End' as 'just Stanislas': Stanislas the exciting, the mysterious, the elusive, the highly born. 'Count Stanislas Breeks' his old dad would call him, banging him lustily upon the shoulder with an odorous hand—for Breeks senior had made, and still made, his pile in fish, and was not so ashamed of it as to be very particular about removing its unattractive trademark; and 'Stan, Stan, the flash in the pan' his common, bouncing, insensitive sisters would cry, dancing round the breakfast table 'jollying him along'—before he had even had his cup of tea and slice of lemon and his 'special' bit of toast. No thank you! That little ass, Melissa, had been quite fun, impressed and admiring, and Rosie had been a gorgeous armful and goodness knew, not backward in coming forward considering that they'd never set eyes on one another before they collided in the fog, night before last; but it wasn't worth it, there were lots more girls in France and Dad, who was so naïvely proud of his roving, imperious son, was quite ready to cough up the dibs so that he might (with one of his sudden strokes of swift decision) go off to complete his education 'on the Continong'. So Stan departed by the afternoon boat and Mr. Charlesworth's easy assurance of soon laying hands on him, did not come off; and Rosie and Melissa were left to their indignation and their memories. Their memories, at least, were pleasant. Melissa had not been in a position to be choosey and Rosie, in the fog, had never observed the scantiness of whisker or the profusion of spots. The mysterious Stanislas threw his dark cloak about him and melted back into the nothingness from which he had come; and that was that.

There had been another murder and the forfeit for both murders had been paid, before Stan Breeks showed his horrid little face in England again.

CHAPTER EIGHT

MR. CHARLESWORTH thought that one might as well trundle down and have a chat with Littlejohn, the path. man, over the post-mortem and, like one small boy inviting another to a party, suggested that Inspector Cockrill might like to come too. Cockie agreed without enthusiasm and, nursing his enormous hat on his knees, sat back in the little black police car and was duly trundled down to the mortuary. Raoul Vernet had been degutted and was now lying, looking rather like an outsize tin soldier except that he was stark naked, in a sort of very shallow, grooved porcelain bath, his toes turned up, his hands tumbled loosely at his sides; he looked a little grey and there were ugly blue bulges beneath his shoulders and thighs where the blood had slowly collected after death, but otherwise he looked peaceful and at rest, lying serenely to attention there. A straight line of large black stitches ran up his stomach and chest but his rather fuzzy, sparse black hair had been carefully arranged, with the mortuary brush and comb, to cover his broken skull. Dr. Littlejohn had his liver and lights in enamel trays and was fastidiously turning them over with a forceps point. 'Nothing here, of course. He died from the fracture of the skull, resultant cerebral lacerations, etcetera, etcetera.' He went off into a highly technical description of the wounds and what might be deduced from them. 'O.K., O.K.,' said Charlesworth. '*We* get you. He died from a single whack over the coconut probably while he was leaning forward a bit, or at any rate with his head bent forward; and his assailant was standing behind him, a little to his right. Yep?'

'That's about the size of it,' said Littlejohn. 'I'll get it all nicely written down on a form for you and of course the high ding-a-dings will want to pronounce, but that's what it amounts to.'

'Said assailant being either man, woman or child?'

'Well, not a *tot*. Said assailant would have to be fairly tall to get a good swing on said instrument; unless of course the tot were standing on a chair.'

'The only tot in the picture so far is aged about two, so we're not seriously exercised about that. How tall, actually, to do the job?'

'Oh, any reasonable talth,' said Littlejohn. 'It depends whether he leant forward or only bent his head a bit, and I don't think we shall be able to give a ruling on that. For the rest, the mallet's so heavy, and yet so easy to handle, that it wouldn't take an awful lot of strength. Just pick up the thing and put all you've got behind it and— whacko! Of course they were lucky to hit him just where they did.'

'Or clever,' suggested Cockie, sombrely.

'Well, yes, or clever. Only they must have been super-clever to persuade him to adjust his head so accommodatingly.'

'Yes, indeed,' said Cockie, standing there in the dreadful antiseptic green and white room, all polished and shining and shadowless and stinking of formaldehyde; his hands thrust into the pockets of his droopy, untidy old mackintosh, hat perched on the back of his head. 'Yes, indeed.' And he suddenly lifted his head and his bright brown bird-like eyes were a-shine with excitement. 'Yes, in*deed!*'

' "*Most* illuminating," ' quoted Charlesworth to himself.

Charlesworth had suffered before from Inspector Cockrill's flashes of inspiration.

Two mortuary attendants lifted Raoul's lank figure and wrapped him up in a vast linen sheet. Looking like nothing so much as an oddly-shaped bundle of laundry, he was wheeled away to cold storage. Cockrill had an unsolicited glimpse of other large laundry bundles as the great refrigerator doors were lugged open and Raoul slid, feet first, on to his slatted, metal bunk; three large white bundles and one much smaller one. On a blackboard outside the doors was chalked: 'One female leg for Prof. Prout.' He thought to himself that indeed beauty vanishes, beauty passes; one female leg: with a pretty ankle, perhaps, once much admired, with a nimble foot that had stepped lightly, danced charmingly, that had loved the feel of warm, golden sand trickling between the toes—one female leg, lying wrapped up in a frig., like a butcher's joint, ready for Prof. Prout to practise on. . . .

'Well, what do you think of all that?' said Charlesworth, climbing back into the little car.

'I think you should find out if one of the suspects possesses a gun,' said Inspector Cockrill.

Most illuminating.

There was a gun knocking about most gaily somewhere in the big, untidy house in Maida Vale: Melissa was sure of that, but she couldn't think where. Somebody would probably know, but they were all out at the moment. 'You yourself haven't seen it recently?' suggested Cockie, fixing her with his bright eye.

'No, I haven't, not for ages,' said Melissa, readily. 'But anyway, he was hit with a mastoid mallet, wasn't he? Not shot?'

'That's right,' said Cockie. 'He was standing turned a little away from his assailant with his head bent forward, presenting just the right part of his head as a target. Wasn't it nice of him?'

'You don't by any chance suggest,' said Charlesworth, seeing the light, 'that the attacker forced him into that position at pistol point? No man in his senses would obey; gun or no gun, he'd put up a fight, he wouldn't just tamely turn round and offer his head to be bashed. I mean, what had he got to lose?—he was going to die, anyway. There'd have to be some reason given, other than the bashing.'

'Yes,' said Cockie, 'there would, wouldn't there?' He said to Melissa: '*Where* do you say you were then?'

The bureau had been taken away from the hall, the telephone that had been there, had been replaced by another; desk and telephone would figure as Exhibits 1 and 2, no doubt, at the Central Criminal Court, one of these days. Meanwhile the hall was narrowed down by the barriers the police had put round the spot where Raoul Vernet had lain; Melissa had had to squiggle round to let them in, and now they stood bunched up round the door, uncomfortably close. The more uncomfortable they were, however, thought Melissa, the sooner they would stop asking her questions and let her go. 'I told you I was out in the fog: we were wandering about, trying to find the way to a cinema, and then trying to find the way back home.'

'You and "Stanislas"?'

'Have you found him yet?' said Melissa, quickly.

'No, we haven't,' said Charlesworth. 'Nobody else here ever knew him, you see, and your own description wasn't too marvellously helpful, *was* it?'

'I can't do more than tell you that he's sort of middling tall and middling dark-haired. . . .'

'Unfortunately he's so exceedingly middling all round,'

said Charlesworth. It suddenly struck him that perhaps excessively middling would be more the word. Considering that this Stanislas was her sole alibi, she didn't seem to be passionately anxious to lay hands on him. What if . . .? 'At nine fifteen when Raoul Vernet made the 'phone call, you were wandering about in the fog? You got in some time after nine thirty and you didn't know anything was wrong until you heard a commotion in the hall and found them all standing round X-marks-the-spot?'

'That's right,' said Melissa. (A glimpse of clay-white fingers still clutching the telephone receiver, smears of blood on the parquet floor, socks with rings going round and round them, two pointed brown shoes with their toes sticking up in the air. . . .) 'It makes me feel sick,' she said. 'Could I go now, please?'

There's something or other she's afraid of saying, thought Cockie; he had a vague impression that she had said it once and he should have observed it then, but had let it go. On the other hand . . . 'There's no evidence that she'd ever set eyes on the man,' he said to Charlesworth, rather uneasily.

'None to the contrary, of course. I wonder. . . . If Rosie Evans had confided in her. . . .'

'I don't quite see Melissa avenging a girl-friend's dishonour with a blunt instrument,' said Cockie. 'More likely to blip the girl-friend, I'd have said, out of green-eyed envy.' He added that apparently Melissa had known of a gun being available. Thomas Evans possessed one.

'If you set such store by this gun idea, we could get busy right away and search the house.'

'Perhaps it would be more simple to ask the owner first where it is,' suggested Cockie, sweetly.

Thomas Evans, coming up the steps at about this moment, replied at once that yes, he had got a gun, if you could call it a gun. It was about a million years old, a sort of species of blunderbuss, and most of the guts were missing. It had belonged to the same Uncle Huw Evans the Pink, who had provided what he supposed must henceforth be referred to as Ther Weapon. Where was it? Well, it must be in the bureau drawer, he supposed, with the other things—where Ther Weapon had been. 'Get on to the Yard, will you, Bedd?' said Charlesworth.

'Or on the landing,' said Thomas. 'In the chest.'

But it was not on the landing, in the chest. 'Said assailant seems to have been quite a guy,' said Charlesworth, to Cockie. 'In the space of roughly two minutes, i.e. between Mrs. Evans going upstairs and Vernet making the call, he's rootled the gun out of the drawer, selected the mastoid mallet as being handy for the job, enticed the victim out into the hall, threatened him into assuming an accommodating attitude for slaughter and'—Sergeant Bedd at the telephone made a thumbs-up sign and went on talking—'returned the gun to the drawer and closed it, as we found it.' Bedd put down the receiver. 'Any prints?'

'Nothing positive, sir; but they wouldn't be astonished if they was told that it had been recently handled; nothing to produce in court, they say, but it's just got that sort of *look:* these chaps get to know, sir, don't they? Handled with a handkerchief or gloves or something, of course. And what's interesting—it was just slid down inside the front of the drawer on top of the other things.'

'Might easily have slipped in there with the drawer only a little open?'

'That's what they reckon, sir,' said Sergeant Bedd; and one up to the old man, thought Inspector Cockrill grimly to himself.

Charlesworth thought so too; but it cut both ways. 'We haven't abandoned the burglar theory, Inspector, of course, and we're still working hard along those lines; but this does seem to strengthen the idea of an inside job. Suppose for some inexplicable reason the burglar did go to the drawer and get the mallet and the gun (and, incidentally, if the gun—why the mallet too?) and was disturbed by Raoul Vernet and hit out at him—why return the gun to the drawer? He didn't wait to pinch anything, nothing's missing—having hit the guy he just chucked down the mallet and did a bolt. So why put the gun back in the drawer?'

'If he's found armed, his sentence is much heavier.'

'Well, but why not just bung the gun down with the mallet? After all, he'll be charged with assault anyway, not just carrying arms; and if he could show that he picked the weapon up in the house, it won't count as *carrying* arms. . . .'

'Well, well,' said Cockie, crossly, 'I don't suppose he stopped to work it all out on squared paper.' Anyway, what the hell: they all knew damn well that it was not an outside job.

He went out to the front door steps and standing there under the rather crooked glass transom rolled himself a cigarette, looking out unseeingly at the passing stream of buses and cars and lorries and vans and bicycles and carts. His mind was terribly disquieted. Thomas Evans and Matilda; Rosie, old Mrs. Evans, Melissa Weeks—these five; plus Ted Edwards, if you liked, only Tedward had been half a mile away at his surgery. But so had Rosie. And Mrs. Evans was old and dotty and had an arthritic right arm. So that left Thomas and Matilda and Melissa. Matilda had been, quite simply, alone upstairs; alone in her bedroom, she 'hadn't heard a sound' of all that violent occurrence in the hall one floor below (but then neither had old Mrs. Evans, so perhaps that cancelled that out; for the old girl was acute enough in her hearing). And Thomas had been for two hours out in the fog on a 'fake' errand, with nothing to prove that he had not slipped back into the house. And both Matilda and Thomas might have had vengeance as a motive. Melissa—Melissa had no alibi either, that had so far been proved; and Melissa had an odd air of keeping something back. But apart from the fact that she seemed to have no possible motive for murdering the man, could a young girl possibly have committed this crime? Cockrill had been a policeman too long, not to know that crimes are committed by the most unlikely people—not excluding young girls; but could any young girl have devised and carried through that business about the gun?

The gun! I must be getting old, he thought; giving way to 'intuitions'. But from the moment that gun business had entered his head, he had found himself stuck with the notion that it must be right. A hint of proof to the contrary and he knew that long training would have overcome 'feelings' and he would have abandoned the notion forthwith; but so far there had been nothing but corroboration.

You hold a gun in your right hand; a 'blunt instrument' in your left. The gun is not a gun really; the victim doesn't realize it, but the gun won't work. *You* know; you know because you are an inmate of the house. So you must use the other weapon. But the other man is not going to stand still, facing you, and let you swop it over to your right hand and hit him on the head with it. You must deflect his attention, you must make him feel safe to turn away from you, or at least to allow you to get behind him—you must persuade him into such a position as will present his head at the most vulnerable angle. . . .

But how? And how do you know which the vulnerable angle will be?

As to the first 'how'—that was easy; and it explained so much. *You got him to use the telephone.*

You have taken the gun and the mallet out of the bureau drawer; you know they are there because you are an inmate, or a familiar, of the house. You attract his attention and he comes out into the hall. You stand there with the gun in your right hand, the mastoid mallet, concealed from him, in your left. You gesture with the gun. 'Pick up the receiver. Dial the number I'll give you.' He's astonished; but he's mightily relieved. All you want him to do, apparently, is to make a 'phone call. Uneasy, no doubt, alarmed, no doubt, he is nevertheless to a great extent disarmed. He picks up the receiver and stands in the characteristic attitude of a man starting a telephone call: bent a little forward over the dialling part of the instrument, which stands on the not very high bureau; right forefinger poised, head bent, looking down. He has seen so many films in which a man forces another man to telephone by poking a gun in his ribs; he is not astonished when you slip round a little behind him. You change the mallet into your right hand—and strike. Still clutching the receiver, he pitches forward across the desk. You chuck the mallet down, you drop the gun back into the half-open drawer, pushing it closed with your knee in an automatic gesture; you walk quietly out of the house. He does not move. After you are gone, it is true, he comes-to and, finding the receiver still in his hand, summons up strength enough to dial the number which, with the word DOCTOR, all in huge letters, is written on the wall, just within his line of vision. But that doesn't matter; you wanted him to be dead, that's all, and he as as good as dead, he will certainly die. *You* know that, because . . .

You know that for the same reason that you knew which would be the most vulnerable spot.

You know because you are a doctor.

CHAPTER NINE

THE last patient, clutching the last signed form, sailed off out of the surgery as though she owned it (which, as a matter of fact, reflected Thomas, she more or less did what with State Medicine and all that), and he was free to go home to lunch. He scratched his name on the bottom of a few more forms, pushed the whole lot into a folder, scribbled a note to Tedward who would be taking the evening surgery, and hitched down his hat from its peg; there was a knock at the door and, without even troubling to be resigned about it, he hitched the hat back again, sat down at the desk again, and called: 'Come in!'

But it was not a patient; it was Detective Inspector Charlesworth, very palsy-walsy and civil-spoken but obviously not at all at ease. Would the doctor mind running round to the station with him—he had a car outside. There were just a few questions. . . .

Thomas went very white. 'I see. Yes. Can I just telephone first to my wife?'

But to Matilda he only said that he was frightfully busy and would get a snack across the road before starting out on his afternoon rounds. He knew that Charlesworth watched him alertly, even while he telephoned; watched that his hand didn't go to a drawer and slip out a nice little suicidal pellet, watched that he didn't suddenly dart round the table and make a run for it. He tore up the note for Tedward and left another for the secretary who was out at her lunch; would Tedward cope with the afternoon's rounds, somehow. 'O.K. Inspector. That's all. Let's get on with it.' It was hideous and uncanny to feel how closely at his shoulder Charlesworth walked; guarding him—guarding him, Thomas Evans, just an ordinary person, just a rather shabby, rather hard-up, rather overworked little general practitioner, who was being 'taken to the station'—to be charged with murder.

They gave him some sandwiches and a large cup of tea with masses of unwanted sugar already in it. There was a uniformed man there, a sergeant; and Sergeant Bedd—and Mr. Charlesworth in his natty grey suiting. They all sat on stiff wooden chairs round a small wooden table. 'Just a few questions, doctor. Now, about this message on the telephone pad. . . .'

At first he thought they were a bit dense; they asked the same questions over and over again, suddenly, irrelevantly; coming back to the message, leaping forward to his return to the house, shooting back again to his wanderings in the fog. 'You say you telephoned home, but you got no answer?'

'The line was dead. He'd ripped out the cord as he fell, if you remember. I suppose that was it.'

'When did you mention that you first tried to 'phone?'

'*I* don't know,' said Thomas, shrugging. 'What does it matter?'

'Funny little things turn out to matter,' said Charlesworth sententiously. 'Where did you 'phone from?'

'A call box,' said Thomas. 'I've told you.'

'You said it was—where?'

'I told you I hadn't a clue and I still haven't. I saw the light glimmering through the fog, I thought I might try and find out a bit more about the message that might help me, I mean Melissa Weeks might be back and of course I thought it was she who had taken the message. I couldn't get any reply so I gave up and came home.'

'You didn't get Operator to check or anything?'

'No, I just gave up.'

'You gave up pretty easily?'

'You think it's suspicious because I didn't give up trying to find the address; and now you think it's suspicious because I suddenly *did*. I'd been out for two hours, I was cold and weary and fed up, it was the end of a long, long day. Yes—I gave up pretty easily. You can say if you like that I was rather thankful for the excuse to pack up and come home.'

'What time did you try to ring?'

'I don't know. I started home straight away, so you can try working backwards if you like.'

'And how long did the return journey take you?'

'I've told you, I *don't know*. It seemed a long time crawling through the fog, but between half an hour and a quarter of an hour, I honestly couldn't say.'

'So we can't try working backwards, after all?'

'No, so you can't,' acknowledged Thomas with a rueful grin.

'Anyway you arrived home at ——?'

'At about ten to ten,' said Thomas patiently.

'To find this man murdered?'

'Yes. They were all still standing around the body—the whole family were there, and Dr. Edwards.'

'You were naturally frightfully shocked?'

'I was mildly surprised,' said Thomas.

'And yet you were calm enough to consult your watch— for the first time that evening, apparently—and discover that it was ten to ten?'

Thomas dropped his hand on his knee with a little *clop* of exasperation. 'My dear, good Inspector! The body was discovered at about twenty to ten, everyone says I came in about ten minutes later. You can work it out for yourself. *I* did.'

'Anticipating that you would be asked?'

'I worked it out the first time I was asked,' said Thomas. 'This is the fourth time. I've got it by heart now.'

'The minute you got in, you sent Dr. Edwards for the police?'

'Not the minute I got in; fairly soon afterwards. At least I didn't send him—he volunteered to go.'

'Well, well, which ever way it was. . . .'

'Funny little things turn out to matter,' quoted Thomas savagely.

'Perhaps you'd like to just go over that again. . . .'

'I wouldn't like it at all, but if it's necessary to your case against me, by all means let's. I got in at—whatever time it was; about ten minutes after they'd found the man dead. I asked or they told me, I can't remember which, about sending for the police; they pointed out that the telephone cord had been ripped out by the fall and they hadn't been able to ring. I said perhaps one of us had better go round by car and Dr. Edwards said *he* would. As you know, he fetched up at the police station about ten minutes later, which further confirms the madly important point about what time I got home. A police sergeant came back with him and took over. That's all I know.'

'You didn't—as the owner of the house and all that—you didn't think of coming yourself for the police?'

'What the bloody hell did it matter who fetched the police?' said Thomas, furiously.

'It didn't matter a bit, of course, as far as the police were concerned. But why *did*n't you go?'

'I haven't a clue why I didn't go. Tedward said he'd go and that's all there was to it.'

'It wasn't because you'd put your car away in the garage and didn't want to get it out again?'

Thomas was absolutely silent for a moment. He repeated at last: 'It was simply because Edwards offered to go.'

'Had you in fact put your car away?'

'I always put it into the garage when I get home.'

The garage at the Maida Vale house ran in under the kitchen on the left of the front door, at the basement level of the house. The ground rises up from Maida Vale to St. John's Wood and the houses there are built into the side of the rise, over semi-basements, with the front door up some steps, fifteen or twenty feet above the level of the wide thoroughfare of Maida Vale, which forms an extension of the Edgware Road, through to Kilburn. A straight drive led into the garage, across the pavement. Charlesworth said, slowly and steadily: 'On this occasion—did you, in fact, Dr. Evans, put your car away as soon as you arrived?' As Thomas once again hesitated, he stopped him altogether. 'Doctor, I think perhaps at this stage I ought to caution you. You seem to be finding these questions difficult and the last thing we want is to trap you in any way. You've got a right, if you want to, to refuse to answer anything more without your solicitor present; anything you do answer from now on will be taken down and may be used in evidence.' He added miserably: 'I'm sorry to have to do this,' and ground the butt of his cigarette into the ash tray. Mr. Charlesworth was really a very nice young man.

'That's all right,' said Thomas. 'I realized what it was all leading up to. You're going to charge me?'

'That depends on the answers to one or two more questions. I want to know whether you went to your car again that night; and I want to know whether anyone else went to it; and I want to know what happened to the shoes you were wearing when you came home.'

Thomas was terribly pale—terribly pale. Charlesworth said: 'Take it easy. I don't want to rattle you.'

Thomas summoned up a smile. 'Thank you very much, Inspector. You're being very decent about it. I'd better say first that of course I didn't do this thing. As for the rest, no—I didn't go out to my car again that night. I put it in the garage before I went into the house and nobody else can have gone to it because I'm the only person who has a key to the garage—I handed it over to the police later on, that evening. And I handed my shoes over too; we all did. We'd been puddling around in the blood, I suppose and they were messing about with footprints and things.' He added, lightly: 'I suppose you've still got them, because I haven't had them back. Wanted as exhibits at my trial, I wouldn't be surprised?'

'Together with the mat from the front of your car,' said Charlesworth. 'Marked with Raoul Vernet's blood. And you say that after you got home at ten to ten that night, you didn't go back to your car.'

Matilda was not a fainter. She wished very often that she was, she wished she could swoon and cling and have hysterics and be made a fuss of and get it all out of her system that way; but, worse luck, she was one of those who, from the first impact of the blow, are calm and clear and impress everybody by their fortitude (or callousness), and only afterwards pay a price in jangled nerves and exhaustion of spirit and pain and helplessness and a bleak despair, that comes too late for sympathy or help. 'I'm sorry,' said Charlesworth, looking at her white, still face. 'It just had to be, that's all.'

'What does *he* say?'

'Not very much.' He dragged forward one of the big,

square, pale-green drawing-room chairs. 'Do sit down, Mrs. Evans. I'm afraid it's a shock for you.'

She sat down on the arm of the chair. 'Do you mean to say he doesn't deny it?'

'Well, he said he hadn't done it; but he said it as a sort of formula, he made no secret but that it was just "for the record". When we charged him he just said that there wasn't any point in saying anything at this stage. Which,' admitted Charlesworth, 'was quite true.'

'But what in God's name have you got against him? Merely that he was driving about in the fog. . . .'

'Mrs. Evans—he put his car away as soon as he got back to the house. He got some of Raoul Vernet's blood on his shoes—well, that's easy enough, most of you did; but traces of blood were found on the mat in your husband's car. How did they get there, if he didn't go back to his car after you found the body?'

'Well, the next day——'

'We collected all your shoes that night; and also the mat under the driving seat of the car. That blood must have been there before he came into the house at ten to nine.'

Matilda was silent, sitting quietly on the arm of the pale-green chair, against the glow of the coral-coloured curtains. 'He *must* have gone out to the car some time, that's all.'

'He himself says he didn't. Only he has a key—is that right?'

'Yes. The garage is left unlocked all day.'

'He had locked it after garaging the car. And it's he who says he didn't go back.'

'Well, he just must have.'

'When, for example?' said Charlesworth.

'I don't know when. We were all messing about all over the place after we found poor Raoul. . . .'

'Did *you* see your husband go out to the garage? Or did anyone else?'

'No, but . . . Well, we all dispersed. Melissa put on one of her well-known acts, though what it was to do with her I don't know, she didn't even know Raoul, she'd never heard his name unless I happened to mention it to her that morning, which I can't remember whether I did; but anyway she threw a drama and I got Rosie to take her into the office and quiet her down. Yes, and it was at the same time that I took Gran upstairs, because I remember saying to Rosie, "You cope with Melissa while I take Granny back to bed." And Tedward had gone for the police; so that would leave Thomas alone, with poor Raoul's body. Perhaps that's when he went to the garage?'

'If so, why doesn't he say so? And anyway, what for?'

'He may have gone to put the car away.'

'He says he put it away when he arrived back. He always does, doesn't he?'

'He may have forgotten—he may not have put it away this particular time.'

'That would suggest that he knew that this *was* a particular time! Why depart from his usual procedure?— unless, of course, he knew what was going on in the hall.'

'*I* don't know,' said Matilda, wearily. She added: 'He's probably "shielding" somebody: they always do in books and he's just the sort of person, the silly chump.'

'They may in books,' said Charlesworth. 'But not in real life, they don't. I mean, people shield people, even murderers; but not to the extent of getting themselves hanged for it—you can take it from me! And anyway, who would he be protecting?' He added, in alarm: 'Now, don't *you* start!'

She gave him a rather wavering smile. 'Well, *I* don't know, Mr. Charlesworth; it's all the most horrible, ghastly, fantastic mistake and I suppose it'll all be all right in the end; but meanwhile . . .' She got up off her chair-arm. 'Can I see him? Where is he?'

Thomas was at the police station where he would remain for the night until he should appear before a magistrate next day and be taken off to Brixton to await his trial; in a narrow little cell, white tiled, with a tiny window of thick glass high up in the wall and a tiny peep-hole in the door. A narrow wooden bench ran down one side and was the only furniture in the room; four blankets were neatly folded at one end of it—one for a pillow—and at the other was the huh-ha, its chain dangling outside the cell so that he might not be tempted to tear it down and strangle himself with it. A suicidal drunk howled forlornly in the cell across the way and now and again slow footsteps clomped down the corridor and a voice called out to stop that bloody row; Thomas knew that as the footsteps passed his own cell, an eye was applied for a moment to the peep-hole—that there was no corner or crevice of the cell in which he could feel himself really to be alone. Now and again he wondered if the death of Raoul Vernet had really been worth all this; but he knew that it had.

Next day at the police court, he was allowed a few words with Matilda, sitting gripping her hand on a hard wooden bench with other prisoners also muttering to their friends and lovers, in little groups round the room; a bare, cold room stinking of dust and disinfectant with an ink-marked table in the centre and the wooden benches all round the walls. Afterwards he was in a small courtroom with a magistrate in plain clothes at a huge desk on the dais, under the lovely carved Royal Arms in their colour and gold; himself in a little, raised dock, fenced in with modestly ornamental wrought iron, the whole so narrow that he could hardly stand up in it, let alone sit down on the six-inch bench. It was all very informal. The court buzzed with ceaseless comings and goings and murmurings and mutterings, outside in the corridor where witnesses waited like hospital patients on benches against the walls, the chattering rose to a deafening crescendo and a very new young policeman put his curly head out through the door and shouted, 'Quiet, *please!*' and drew in his head again with a mock-bridling movement, winking at his colleagues: there!—what do you think of that for a first effort, eh? Under some misapprehension, the door from the cells was opened and a prisoner was marched in, looking scared and strung-up, and hurriedly turned round and marched out again more bewildered than ever. Mr. Charlesworth lounging against the wall behind the witness box was suddenly galvanized into action, stepped briskly into the box and embarked upon a brief recital of events at the station the day before. ' . . . the prisoner was then charged and he said, "There's no point my saying anything at this stage, is there?" ' He was silent, his hands on the edge of the square witness box, his arms rigid, looking alertly into the magistrate's face.

The magistrate shifted at his desk. 'Yes. Now, Doctor Evans—are there any questions you'd like to ask?'

Thomas looked round him vaguely. 'Well, no, I don't think so.' He caught Charlesworth's eyes, and Charlesworth almost imperceptibly shook his head. 'No, definitely not, thank you.' A funny place to be looking for guidance—but still!

'Do you apply for legal aid?'

Do I apply for legal aid? What the hell's the use, thought Thomas, of asking me questions I can't properly understand. I suppose they're so used to their jargon that they can't imagine everyone else isn't. Did legal aid mean free legal aid, or what? 'I'd just like to see my solicitor, I suppose,' he said to the magistrate. (Poor dear Mr. Burden—how was he going to like *this*?)

And it was all over and he was being whisked off through the prisoner's waiting-room, down the stairs to the cells again; there to wait for a full complement of prisoners before the van drove them all off to Brixton gaol. He caught one parting glimpse of Matilda's face, stretched with a palpable effort into a smile; her eyes gazed lovingly after him through a mist of tears. He could not know how gallant and small he looked between his two tall escorts, with his pale face and untidy, faded gold hair, his hands thrust down angrily into the pockets of his jacket. He flung her back a smile and she raised one hand with the thumb stuck up and gave it a little uh-uh jerk, as though to say: It's O.K.! It's in the bag.

But it's me that's in the bag, thought Thomas, ruefully. It was not much fun.

It was a brisk November day. Cockie hugged his old mackintosh about him, jigging from one foot to the other to keep himself warm as he waited for Charlesworth to emerge from the police court. He appeared at last, with Sergeant Bedd. 'Hal*lo*, Inspector. Just the chap I want to see.' He jerked his thumb over towards a pub. 'Come on; we'll talk when we get there.' In the saloon bar, as yet fairly empty, he sat his guest down at a little round table with a raised brass rim round it, and asked what he would have. 'Get us three bitters then, Bedd, will you, like a good chap? I want to talk to Mr. Cockrill.' To Cockie he said, in a phoney American accent, 'I expect you're plenny mad with *me*?'

'I've got no right to expect anything,' said Cockie. 'I

think you might have warned me before you actually charged him, but I suppose you had your reasons.'

'It all happened so quickly; and it was after I saw you yesterday, I wasn't expecting to charge him; but when I got back from Maida Vale, they'd established this blood on the mat in the car—same group as the body and all that. What was I to do?'

'I'm not complaining,' said Cockie. 'It's just that it would have been easier for me to talk to Mrs. Evans and all that.' He reminded Charlesworth: 'They're personal friends of mine.'

'I know, I know, and if I'd had the slightest intention of charging him, I swear I'd have let you know. To tell you the truth, I rather surprised myself. But there it was—the blood's established and he trots out that he's never been back to the car after seeing the body. I couldn't go on questioning him without the caution.'

'The feller's a doctor,' said Cockrill, grumpily. 'He's probably wading about knee-deep in gore all day.'

'Not in this gore; not with great dollops of brain floating about in it.'

'Of brain?'

'Well, not actual chunks of grey matter,' confessed Charlesworth, leaning back in his chair to fish in his pocket for a packet of cigarettes. 'But traces. Now, a G.P. doesn't get that kind of blood on him, not unless he's been dealing with an accident case or something, and he hasn't had any recently—he admits it. Then when I questioned him, he— well, he baulked a bit, you know, went white, all the usual signs.' He held out the packet. 'Cigarette?'

'No thank you,' said Cockrill, gruffly. He produced his own tobacco and papers and started rolling one. 'So you charged him?'

'How else *could* the blood have got into the car?'

Sergeant Bedd came back with the three glasses balancing each other in his big hands, and manœuvred them down on to the table. They went through automatic gestures of good health, but Cockrill did not even put his glass to his lips. 'He's shielding someone; that's the long and the short of it.'

'That's what his wife said. O.K. he's shielding someone: but who?'

'There are three women in this case—four if you count the old lady.'

'This wasn't a woman,' said Charlesworth. 'Take it from me.'

Inspector Cockrill was taking nothing from Mr. Charlesworth. 'Not a woman? Prove it!'

'The telephone message proves it. "Someone came in and hit me with a mastoid mallet".'

'Rosie's not sure; it may have been "a *man* came in and hit me with a mastoid mallet". '

'Well, if it was,' said Charlesworth, gaily, 'then it wasn't a woman, *was* it?'

'All right; settle for "someone".'

'Good. Well, here we have Raoul Vernet standing in the hall and someone comes in and hits him with the mallet. "Comes in" you observe: not "comes down". So that counts out two of them, because both the Mrs. Evans's, old and young, were upstairs, or at any rate in the house; so he wouldn't have said "came in".'

'One of them might have gone out and come back,' said Cockie. 'And anyway, Rosie may have misheard: she's quite unreliable.' Still, it was no part of his desire to throw suspicion on old Mrs. Evans, or on Matilda either.

'Well, all right, skip "came in". There he is standing in the hall; the light's on—Mrs. Evans left it on when she went upstairs. Now—Matilda Evans marches up to him and takes a crack at him. Would he ring up and say "someone"? Of course not—he'd say, "Matilda came up and dotted me one." Same goes for Rosie Evans, only of course she was out of it anyway. Then, take the old lady; surely he wouldn't say, "someone"?—surely he'd say "an old woman came in and hit me"? You must agree with that!'

'Yes,' said Cockie, slowly, 'I think I must.'

'And Melissa Weeks; if Melissa came up to you and conked you—you wouldn't call *that* "someone", would you? You'd say, "a girl came in", or you'd kind of remark on it, you'd say "some little bit of a girl came up and blipped me"—I mean, you'd be so surprised. It all sounds rather feeble,' said Charlesworth, thoughtfully, 'but I honestly do think it's incontrovertible or whatever the word is. It can't have been any of those four women, so it must have been a man. And the only other man . . .'

Cockrill had already worked round to the same conclusion, by a different route. It must have been a doctor, and the only other doctor . . . The only other man, the only other doctor, had been half a mile away on the other end of a telephone; if one thing in the whole damn show was certain, it was that. 'Someone came in and hit me with a mastoid mallet. . . .' If it had been a woman, surely he'd have said 'a woman'. But no: 'Someone', or 'A man'—'came in and hit me with a mastoid mallet. . . .'

The creamy bubbles whispered round the rim of his glass as he set it down on the table and sat staring into its amber depths: staring, staring down with eyes as bright and clear and brown as the clear, brown beer itself. Opposite him, Charlesworth too sat staring into his glass. 'I'm sorry about it, Inspector, but there it is: I hate it myself, I had a beastly time bringing him in for the job, telling Mrs. Evans and all that—I like them both. From all one can see, the chap was no great loss and if he seduced the girl, then he certainly wasn't—but the point is that whether he did or not, quite obviously Thomas Evans believed that he had. He's a doctor, he must have tumbled to what was wrong with her; then, a mysterious assignation—with this foreigner suddenly appearing from Geneva, Mrs. Evans anxious to talk to the man alone, the girl anxious to avoid him, going off out into the fog. . . . Dr. Evans is dotty about his young sister, he thinks she's the last word in lily-white innocence, he sees her as seduced and betrayed and all the rest of it. He goes out, mills round for a bit till he sees by the lights that his wife's left the feller alone in the drawing-room, goes into the hall, gets out the gun and the mallet from the drawer and calls him out into the hall. He forces him to the telephone with the dud gun, swops over hands and conks him one with the mallet. Out to the car again with a bit of blood on his shoes; drives round some more, shows up all horror when the time comes.' He glanced up from his beer, eyeing tne little Inspector anxiously. Surely it all hung together, surely it must be true? For the millionth time he wondered secretly whether he had not been over-impulsive in getting Thomas Evans charged. But damn it all—there was a case against him, and against nobody else. He insisted: 'It was a man, it was probably a doctor. And the only other man, and incidentally the only other doctor, was half a mile away when Raoul Vernet rang up.'

The shaggy ash trembled on the end of Cockrill's cigarette, broke and fell like a grey snowflake, softly on to the table. He put out his hand and absently brushed it away, leaving a dry, grey smear. He said, dreamily: 'If Raoul Vernet rang up.'

Charlesworth looked up sharply. 'If he rang up? We known damn well he rang up.' Sergeant Bedd, doubting, murmured a word and he took it up from him. 'Collusion?

You surely don't suspect collusion between those two—Dr. Edwards and that girl?'

'Not collusion,' said Cockrill; 'no. Rosie would be a very bad person to collushe with—you wouldn't dare. She'd blurt it out two minutes later, all fluttering eyelashes and ackcherlies. Somebody spoke to her on the 'phone, that's certain; but whether it was Vernet. . . . And of course, if it wasn't. . . .' His eyes shone with the joy of it, the relief of it.

'Why the hell shouldn't it have been?' said Charlesworth, angry with anxiety. 'Of course it was Vernet: why shouldn't it have been?'

'Only that Vernet was a foreigner.'

'O.K., so he was a foreigner—he could still use the 'phone, I suppose? He spoke quite good English, by all accounts, plain English, perhaps, not fancy stuff, but there was nothing fancy about that message.'

'Except perhaps for the mastoid mallet,' said Cockrill, comfortably.

CHAPTER TEN

Rosie was ackcherly utterly *mis.* about Thomas, to think that poor, darling Thomas was mewed up in some frightful gaol and really, let's face it, all because of her. If only she hadn't been so naughty in Geneva, or, since really that had been inevitable because one was the way one was and one just couldn't help it, if only that stupid old Raoul hadn't come whizzing over in his beastly aeroplane to sneak to Matilda about her goings-on. . . . It was sort of fun at home, ackcherly, at least not fun at all of course, but frightfully exciting with police tramping about everywhere and reporters ringing up and coming to the door and climbing into the garden over walls and goodness knew what, and some of them were *great* fun, and terribly humorous, they honestly were, only it was horrifying to see in the papers next morning what nonsense they made up . . . But still, one had to be honest, one couldn't deny that it was not what one might call dull. Of course Matilda was in the last stages of gloom and terribly cross most of the time, bursting out into fits of unreasonable ill-temper, Gran alternating between hilarity and deepest depression, Melissa for ever in tears and tremblings, and poor, darling Thomas . . . For the hundredth time she said plaintively to Cockie that surely it must have been a burglar all the time; because it was idiotic to think that Thomas . . .

'Do *try* and remember about that 'phone call, Rosie.'

'But I *have* remembered,' said Rosie. 'I've told you all all about it, over and over again.'

'You don't think,' said Cockie, all casual, 'that if you were on the spot you'd remember perhaps? Some littld extra thing?'

'I might,' said Rosie, doubtfully. Anyway it would be something to do; the reporters seemed to be falling off a bit to-day, and everyone at home was *hell*. She climbed thankfully into a taxi with Cockie and went round to Tedward's house.

Ted Edwards also, was sick at heart for his friend. Already late for his afternoon surgery, he still hung miserably about the house with his hands in his pockets, staring out of the window at the bleak, pewter-grey of the canal. Of course there was no real danger; one way or another they would get Thomas out of it, even if he had to confess to the thing himself. Not that the police could possibly prove anything against him; but it would create a diversion—indeed, it would be rather fun. Only quite how to set about it was the thing. . . .

Rosie appeared suddenly at the window and scrabbled on a pane with her long, curved, pink nails like a cat pleading to be let in. When he got round to the front door, Inspector Cockrill was there too. They explained their errand. 'Of course,' said Tedward. 'Go ahead. Only I'll have to go off and leave you to it, because I'm late already; and I've got all Thomas's stuff as well as my own. But Rosie can show you all right, she knows her way round.'

'What about the old trout—hasn't she come back?'

'No, indeed,' said Tedward. 'She's "sent for her things" in dudgeon; it's obviously not the thing for me to have got mixed up in a nasty murder.' He laughed. 'She's probably working on her reminiscences of me already; what I have

for breakfast and how I wear out my socks. Bad cess to her!'
He went out to his car.

'I do adore Tedward,' said Rosie, watching him as he
manœuvred his stubby form through the narrow door and
subsided into the driver's seat. 'He's so sort of solid and
comfortable. Tedward Bear I call him; it makes him so
mad!'

It was true that it made Tedward mad: mad with that
ravening hunger of his for something more tender from her,
or something less—better that she should be cold and
disregarding altogether than torment him with her innocent
coquetries, her little, offhand pet names and dabbing
caresses that proclaimed aloud that to her he was no more
and never would be more than dear old, tubby old Tedward Bear, comfortable and kind. He let in his gears with a
grinding jerk and shot forward through the gate, his eyes
blinded by the mist of his idiotic tears. I *must* get over it, he
thought; I *must* shake it off. A fat, cross-grained, hard-up
old buffer like me, slavering over a girl of half my age . . .
It was disgusting, it was absurd, he was ashamed of his
weakness in persisting in this octogenarian folly; but the
moment he set eyes on her, so fresh and spring-like in her
ebullient health and gaiety and that sort of overlying
innocence of mind—all his resolves were scattered to the
wind and his head was in the stars—and his heart in his
boots. He shot across the stream of the traffic turning out
into Maida Vale and a volley of curses brought him
abruptly to his senses. He flapped a penitent hand at bus
and taxi drivers, and continued more soberly towards St.
John's Wood: all unaware that in the house he had left, his
belovéd was unwittingly settling down to prove him a
murderer.

The house was on the simplest possible plan: the front
porch opened on to a wide corridor running straight

through to the back door, with the stairs leading up off it; to the right of the front door was the sitting-room and behind that the surgery; the window of the surgery, close to the back door, looked out on to a pleasant small London garden. But a tangle of outhouses beyond kitchen and dining-room on the far side of the house rendered the garage inaccessible except by a good deal of awkward manœuvring; even knowing it as well as its owner must, Cockrill could see that it must have been tricky on a night with a pea-soup fog. He went back to Rosie, curled up in the comfortable armchair before the Cosy stove in Tedward's surgery with the cat, like a lump of carved anthracite curled on her knee. 'What on earth have you been doing, Cockie?'

Cockie modestly h'm-h'm'd. 'Oh, I see; beg your pardon. Well, what now?'

'I want you to tell me exactly—but exactly,' said Cockie who had caught this dreadful expression from Rosie herself, 'what happened here, night before last, when Raoul Vernet died.'

'Oh, *lor*'!' said Rosie; it was so boring, going over and over the thing. 'Well, I've *told* you. I got here just about nine. Tedward went out and made me a cup of tea. . . .'

'You were in here? In the surgery?'

'No, we went into the drawing-room and he lit the gas and made me sit in a chair and nurse the cat while he got the tea. I was a bit frozen, what with the fog and all.'

Cockrill went through the dividing door into the other room. 'You took the 'phone call in here? Or in the surgery?'

'No, I just picked up the extension in the drawing-room. It was right by my hand.'

'Come through here and show me.'

Rosie heaved herself up reluctantly and came through from the surgery, the cat hanging contentedly over her shoulder like a fur; its black tail twitched in ecstasy as she ruffled her fingers through its shining short coat. 'You *are* a *nice* cat,' she said to it.

'Never mind the cat. Now you were sitting—where?'

'Oh, Cockie, what does it *matter*? I was sitting here and Tedward put the tray here on this table by the telephone. So then he said I ought to go home, because I'd been so long coming, you see, and I was a bit worn out what with the baby and all. Ackcherly that's what I'd come to talk to Tedward about; and also because I wanted to get away from Raoul.'

'But you didn't have time to discuss it?'

'Well, no, because Tedward said I looked rotten and I ought to go home to bed and he'd get the car out and leave it ticking over and warming up a bit, and I suppose I could have talked to him while I finished my cuppa, only then the business of the telephone call happened and we never got round to it.'

'Well now, yes, this telephone call; that's what we've come about.'

'I just went on with my tea and in about a minute the 'phone went and the voice said all that about come quick and someone hit me with a mastoid mallet and all the rest of it; and then Tedward came back and I told him and we whizzed off.'

'And it was a foreign voice?'

'Well, yes, of course, because it was Raoul's voice,' said Rosie. 'I mean, wasn't it?'

'That's what I'm not so sure about,' said Cockie.

'Not Raoul's voice? Then whose?'

'Supposing,' said Cockie, very carefully, 'that I suggested to you that it was—Tedward's voice?'

Rosie sat down with a plonk on the edge of the drawing-room armchair and the cat slid indignantly off her shoulder and scrambled on to the back of the chair and sat there angrily. '*Ted*ward's?'

'Can you see any way that it might have been?'

'*Ted*ward's? No, of course not. As if *Ted*ward . . .'

Cockie sat down on the chair facing her and leaned forward and took her plump, tapering hands in his. 'Rosie—I know you're fond of Tedward; but you're fond of Thomas too, aren't you; you're more fond of Thomas than Tedward? After all he's your brother—and a very good brother too.'

'Well, yes, of course. . . .'

'So, of the two—wouldn't you rather that Tedward was a murderer?'

'I don't see how he can be anyway,' said Rosie, shrugging off the issue as usual. 'How *can* he be?'

'Supposing—supposing he hadn't got the car out then at all? Supposing he'd run round to the nearest call-box and rung up this number and pretended to be Raoul. . . .'

Rosie made a little ducking, denying movement of her head. 'Well, first of all he *had* got out the car, because there it was ticking over outside the front door, and it takes simply ages to get out of Tedward's garage, even at the best of times.'

'Suppose it had been ticking over there, all the time.'

'It couldn't have,' said Rosie. 'I'd have seen it when I arrived.'

'If it had been just round the corner, outside the garage, ticking over—it wouldn't have taken him a moment to drive it round, would it?'

'Good lord,' said Rosie, 'what a thing to think of!'

'But it's true *isn't* it?'

'I suppose it could have happened; but anyway, it doesn't matter because how could he have rung me up? And anyway, why?'

'Never mind why. Now, you know this place very well: is there a telephone call-box anywhere near?'

'No, there isn't,' said Rosie promptly. 'There isn't for miles. I know because when the line conks Tedward has to get out the car and drive to the pub.' She added intelligently that it would have taken him hours to get through the fog to any pub that night.

'What about the house next door?'

'Oh, pooh,' said Rosie, contemptuously. 'As if he could! I mean the people could tell you in a minute, and then where would he be?'

This also was very much to the point. 'Is there another 'phone in the house?'

'No, there isn't. There's one in the surgery and the extension. in here and an extension by Tedward's bed upstairs, for night calls; and that's all.'

'Of course he *could* have rung through from the real 'phone to this extension.'

'I'd have heard him,' said Rosie. 'It's only in there.' She jerked her chin towards the adjoining surgery.

'He spoke very low.'

'Well, yes, I suppose so. But, anyway, how could Tedward have got the bell to ring? I mean, it's too much coincidence to think that it just conveniently rang at that moment and he cut the other person off and crashed in.'

Cockrill had always known that through the solid ivory of Rosie's head ran a streak of the shrewd common-sense of her Welsh forebears. He respected it now more than he ever had done. 'That's what I can't make out, Rosie, either. Suppose . . . Suppose he'd arranged with Operator to ring him at just that time?'

'How did he know that it would be the right time? I didn't even arrive on schedule—I was late. And, anyway, he'd have had to say something to Operator, "thank you"

130

or something, and he couldn't, because I lifted the receiver while the bell was just on its third or fourth ring and the voice chimed in immediately. Be*sides*,' said Rosie, waxing quite enthusiastic, 'what's more to the point is that you'd only have to check that with Operator.'

'If I thought of it!'

'If Tedward was the kind of thinking-out murderer that you want him to be,' said Rosie, 'he wouldn't take risks like that.' She added that anyway, Cockie *had* thought of it now so he could just ring up Op. and find out.

'Yes, I shall some time,' said Cockie. But he knew that she was right. 'You aren't such a mutton-head, Rosie, as one sometimes thinks.'

'I know,' said Rosie with modest complacency. 'People are always finding that out and being surprised.'

The cat, perceiving that things were settling down again, crept off the chair-back and established himself with contented wrigglings on Rosie's lap once more. Cockrill left them there, the fair head bent over the bright, dark coat, and went softly through the door to the surgery closing it behind him, and out of the further door into the passage and so round to the garage. A minute, perhaps less than a minute, to run the car round to the front door, if it were standing there round the corner, ready and ticking over. He went in and stood with his back to the Cosy stove, deep in thought. Tedward's big desk was up against the window, looking out on to the little garden; the telephone stood there, guarding its secrets with a closed, black mouth. He got out his papers and rolled one of his shaggy cigarettes. Ted Edwards must be a good doctor to consult; practical, comfortable, unformidable, warm-hearted—rather like this room. A big screen hid the cupboard of bottles and instruments, the examination couch, the 'business end' of it all, and there were big, easy chairs where, when all that was over, he might sit and talk to those that needed it, like a friend; opening the doors on the bright, warm glow of the anthracite stove. . . .

So why, when Rosie arrived, cold and tired on a dank, bleak night, had he taken her through from that cosy room into the drawing-room and 'lit the gas fire' for her?

The window slid up with very little sound. He put the telephone out on to the sill and closed it down again. Outside, with the telephone cord at full stretch, and the receiver in his left hand, he could just reach the back door bell with his right; and what is recognisable about a telephone bell is not so much its tone as that characteristic rhythm, that shrill ring-*ring*, ring-*ring*, ring-*ring*. . . .

'Hallo?' said Rosie's voice, piping up at him from the receiver, held absently away from him in his left hand. 'This is Dr. Edwards' house, but I'm afraid he's not here. . . .'

CHAPTER ELEVEN

MELISSA opened the door to Cockrill that evening when, triumphant but depressed, he left the house on the canal bank in the hands of Charlesworth's minions and went back to Maida Vale. Rosie had gone off upon her own occasions; it was all too silly and Tedward would just laugh, but on the other hand it certainly was most peculiar and Cockie was terrific; all the same, they'd called him in to help them, not to go and make out that poor Tedward had done it. . . . Even for Thomas. . . . 'Surely we needn't go and tell the police, Cockie? I mean let them find out for themselves if they want to.'

'I *am* the police,' said Cockie.

'Yes, but I mean not to us, you're not; and you promised. . . .'

'No, I didn't,' said Cockie. 'I made no promises at all, and I've got my duty to do.'

'Well, of course Tilda will be glad about Thomas, but she'll be jolly mad about Tedward, I can tell you.'

Fortunately Matilda was still out, doubtless upon her ceaseless activities in support of her husband's cause. Melissa took him into the kitchen and made him a cup of tea. She looked very white and scared these days and her eyes were heavy, with dark lines under them; her hair hung forward floppily over her face and Cockrill thought idly that it was true, perhaps, these young creatures did, subconsciously, seek to shelter behind these masses of forward falling hair, and idly wondered what Melissa could have to hide. He leaned back against the Aga, warming the seat of his trousers on its cream enamelled surface, 'This is nice, Melissa. A little oasis of peace.'

'The kitchen always seems sort of comforting,' said Melissa. 'It's warm and shiny and kind of everyday; you can forget for a little while—all this.'

'About the murder you mean?'

'Has there been any news about Stanislas, Inspector Cockrill?'

'No,' said Cockie. 'He certainly seems to have been a mysterious young man.' If he ever existed, he added, not out loud.

'Yes, he was mysterious, Inspector. That was the thing. It isn't me that's made him mysterious, it isn't even him not turning up like this. He was mysterious anyway; I mean, like not telling me who he really was, no address or telephone number or anything like that.' Stanislas had, in fact, had a telephone number; one dialled it and simply asked for 'Mr. Stanislas', nothing more on pain of death; a jolly, common voice replied that it would see if he was in and, probably on pain of death too, reported guardedly, In and coming in a minute or, without embellishment, Out; but Melissa had thought fit to exaggerate the cloak-and-dagger mystery of Stanislas for the benefit of the police, to whatever small extent it remained susceptible of exaggeration. 'It makes it a bit awkward for me but still I don't suppose it matters very much, does it? I mean, I didn't know Monsieur Vernet, I'd never even heard of him till the day he was coming here, so it couldn't be anything to do with me; could it, Inspector?'

'No,' said Cockie; 'I don't suppose it could.' The police had found nothing in Tedward's house by the time he left, to confirm his theory of the trick with the telephone; but it could have been done. And if it had been done. . . .

A small cushion flew past the window and landed with a soft thud in the garage drive below the kitchen. 'Oh, *blink!*' said Melissa. 'She's begun again!' She put down her half-finished cup of tea. 'I'd better go up; it doesn't so much matter at the back of the house but it's awful right out here on the main road.'

Mrs. Evans, however, was sitting on the sofa, the picture of innocence, busily pinning a lace cap on her hair which was balanced on her knee. She unhurriedly clapped it back on to her head at sight of Inspector Cockrill, where it sat rather crookedly on top of what was already there, the lace cap crowning it all. Melissa went across automatically and set it straight, skewering it into position with a couple of pins. 'Thank you, Melissa; and thank goodness you've come, dear, now you can relieve me of this horrible child.' She smiled tenderly at her great-granddaughter. 'Would you believe it, she's now started throwing things out of the window. The things these children think of!' She smiled with delighted mischief at Cockie, standing in the doorway, delicately embarrassed at the episode of the hair. 'Do come in, Inspector, and don't stand there.'

Melissa swooped upon the child and bore her out, Emma squealing like a pig, whether with rage or delight it was hard to tell. Mrs. Evans gestured to a chair with a thin old hand, weighted down with unfashionable thick, gold rings. 'Sit down, dear Inspector Cockrill, and talk to me. Really, after an hour of tick, tock, the nursery clock, you can't think how welcome a civilized chat will be.'

Cockie sat down in the chair across the fireplace from her. 'Help yourself to some sherry—well, never mind if you've just had tea, they'll mix up in the end; there's the decanter beside you. No, not for me, thank you—I'm much

135

too old and dotty to be allowed to drink: under the fumes of alcohol, God knows what I might get up to!' She eyed him brightly with her teasing glance.

'God might have His doubts—but I think you'd know all right,' said Cockie, teasing back.

She gave him an almost imperceptible wink. 'You're much too discerning.'

'I won't give you away,' he said, laughing.

'You see it—well, it gets very dull up here.' She sat silent, her hands lying quiet in her lap, her lovely, thin old face looking down, brooding, at the heavy rings with their multitude of little sparkling stones. 'Life was so gay in the old days, Inspector, and there's so little left of it now—the old, gay, well-to-do, careless, flirting days, when I was a girl, when I was a young married woman. I was a great flirt, you know, really an accomplished flirt; you might almost say a professional flirt. My husband encouraged me; he loved to see me making my conquests, he said it would be a waste to neglect such a gift.' She relapsed for a moment into a daydream. Cockrill, beginning to suspect where all this was leading, put in a gentle murmur. She came at once out of her abstraction and her voice took on a tinge of purpose. 'And it was quite a gift, Inspector, it really did amount to a touch of genius to be able to flirt as we did in those days—so gracefully and delicately, to be able to break hearts just a little and not too much; and ones own heart not at all. And all innocent and above-board and unhurtful, not like the furtive scrabblings of nowadays; or scrabblings not nearly furtive enough. It's all physical now and not intellectual at all, as far as I can see; all do and no talk. Of course with us it was *all* talk; and perhaps that was bad too in its way—perhaps we were sex-repressed, only of course we didn't have a name for it so it did seem to trouble us less.' She shrugged delicately. 'The modern people would say that it did trouble us, underneath. They'd say that that's why I throw things out of windows in my old age.'

When it came to protecting Thomas, old Mrs. Evans was obviously not going to be far behind. At this rate, however, confession would not come till midnight. He said nothing about a new theory and a new suspect, but gently prodded the wandering sheep in the direction in which it apparently wanted to go. 'Rosie, at least, won't be throwing things out of windows in *her* old age.'

'No, indeed,' said Mrs. Evans. She was silent again, her head bent over her hands. She said: 'Of course, Inspector, it's not *always* just because I'm bored that I throw things out of windows.'

'You mean you really are—some of the time at any rate—what you like to call "dotty"?'

'Don't you think it may be a bit dotty to *think* it fun to throw things out of windows?'

Cockrill shrugged. 'It depends how bored you are, I suppose.'

She gave him her twinkling smile. 'Well, I really am dreadfully bored; but it's true that—sometimes I do find that I've been out of control, I find that the thing's got a little bit beyond me and I haven't been responsible for some of the throwings. It's like—it's like letting yourself doze off and then waking up and finding you've been to sleep.'

'And that's the kind of sleep you were in on the night of the murder. That's what you want to tell me?'

She clasped her thin fingers; he could see that the heavy rings made pink marks, pressed sharply against the faded white skin. 'You're a very intelligent person, Inspector; I've always known that. But not at first; I was as wide awake as you are—and that's saying something!—when Matilda left me; having helped me to take off this top-knot of mine and undone my staylaces. She had to hurry away and leave me to get on with it because she had left her guest all alone; and she still had the baby to do.' She repeated it. *'She'd left him all alone, you see; and she still had the baby to do.'*

'Yes,' said Cockie. 'I see.'

'Innocence is a curious thing,' said old Mrs. Evans, dreamily, and yet very wide awake. 'I think of Rosie as, essentially, an innocent. I think that what she has, she gets from me—I think she's a born flirt. Perhaps if I'd lived nowadays, I wouldn't have been "sex-repressed" either; I don't know because I never had the opportunity to be other than I was. But Rosie did; Rosie had unlimited opportunity to carry the whole thing a stage further—a great many stages further—than I did. I can't take credit to myself for not being what she is; I didn't have the chance, that's all; and when things went wrong, I couldn't blame her for taking the chance that I might have taken if I'd had it. But I'll tell you who I *could* blame—I could blame the one who had taken advantage of her innocent flirtatiousness and taught her to carry it all those steps further; who has started her on a road that gets less and less innocent all the way. I could blame him.'

'I see,' said Cockie again.

'And of course being so dotty,' said Mrs. Evans, eyeing him guilelessly, 'I'd hardly be responsible if the thing preyed on my mind till I . . . I mean, they don't hang potty old women like me, *do* they? A nice, gay, criminal-looney-bin, I suppose, and after all one couldn't say that was dull!'

Cockrill sat forward, his elbows on his knees, rolling a cigarette with quick movements of his stained, brown fingers. 'You're telling me this because of Thomas, I suppose?'

'You do see that Thomas is protecting me?'

'Everyone thinks that Thomas is protecting someone.'

'Who else but me?' said Mrs. Evans. 'It could only be me or Matilda. And it isn't Matilda.'

'How can you be so sure of that?' said Cockie, quickly.

'My dear—do you think Matilda would have kept silent for one moment? Don't you think she'd have been proclaiming it from the housetops that Thomas was innocent?'

'She has the child to consider.'

'Even for Emma, Matilda wouldn't let Thomas suffer, not for one moment, for a thing she'd done. And it wouldn't do the child all that much good—either way, it would have one parent a murderer. No, no, of course it wasn't Tilda; *you* know that, Cockie, you know her too well. And Thomas would know it too. So there's only me. Melissa Weeks isn't in the thing at all, why should she be?—and anyway, Thomas wouldn't risk his neck for *her*; and Rosie was with Tedward, so it couldn't be Rosie.'

'Of course, Thomas would suffer to protect Rosie.'

'But Rosie's out of it.'

'Would he suffer, do you think, for Tedward? If he thought the murder was justified?'

'Tedward was with Rosie,' said Mrs. Evans, shrugging. 'So it doesn't arise.'

'If it did arise, Mrs. Evans—if Tedward could have killed this man, if the murder could, in your minds, have been justified—would you do this for him? Not for Thomas, but for Tedward?'

Mrs. Evans was silent for a long, long time. She said, at last: 'Do you know something against Ted Edwards?'

'It's just possible—that it may have been possible—for him to have done this thing. And in that case . . .?'

Mrs. Evans got up and stood before the fire, her frail hands hooked on to the high mantelpiece, looking down into the glowing coals. 'In that case . . . Well, this is a family affair, Inspector. Tedward, to all intents and purposes, is one of us; as far as Raoul Vernet's death is concerned. Rosie is at the centre of it all—and Tedward's in love with Rosie, poor man. If he killed Raoul Vernet on Rosie's account— yes, I'd "do this" as you call it, for Tedward too.' She looked him in the eye. 'Whatever you mean by "this".'

'I mean a confession of murder; that you believed Raoul Vernet to be Rosie's seducer and took advantage of Matilda's being cooped up in the nursery with the child, to creep downstairs, take him unawares in the hall and hit him on the head and murder him.'

'Standing on the stairs, a bit above him,' said Mrs. Evans, 'one could add a good deal of force to the blow. It was rather horrible when he didn't quite die.'

'Would that be why you rang up?'

'I couldn't just leave him lying there bleeding, could I? Of course, it seems silly trying to get a doctor for him when I'd just done my best to kill him.' She added that it was a bit like preventing murderers from committing suicide so that they wouldn't die before you hanged them, only the other way about if Cockie saw what she meant. 'If he'd died outright, that would have been another matter.'

'So you rang up pretending to be him?'

'Well, I couldn't say it was me, could I? I thought I improvised rather brilliantly.'

Inspector Cockrill thought that Mrs. Evans was improvising pretty brilliantly now. 'If his life had been saved. . . .?'

'Well, it would have taught him a lesson anyway,' said Mrs. Evans, shrugging.

'But I meant where your safety was concerned.'

'Oh, well, as to that—I didn't think actually he could have seen who it was. And if he had and he'd died and whilst he was dying he'd said something to Tedward—I knew I'd be safe with Tedward. If he'd survived. . . .'

'Yes; if he'd survived and had seen you. . . .?'

She shrugged again. 'I don't think I thought about it then; if I did, I suppose I thought it would have been worth it. I've only got a few more years to live and they couldn't hang me, could they?'

'They could put you in prison,' said Cockie.

She turned back to the fire again, not looking at him. 'What—a dotty old thing like me?'

'The legal definition of dottiness is that you're unable to judge whether an action's right or wrong. But you say you knew.'

She lifted her head and he saw that she was very tired, that the thing was becoming an effort to her, almost more than she could carry through. She drove herself forward, however, into the final spurt. 'I knew? Knew what?'

'Knew what you were doing when you killed this man.'

Mrs. Evans glanced at the window, glanced at the cushions on the sofa, looked back at the window again and picked up a cushion. She said vaguely: 'Did *I* kill someone?'

'Isn't that what you're confessing to the police?'

'Me—confessing?' said Mrs. Evans. 'I don't know what you're talking about.' She put down the cushion slowly on the sofa. 'My dear Inspector—do use some of your wonderful intelligence. If I'd been going to confess, do you think I wouldn't have sent for that young Charlesworth days ago, and saved my poor boy all this? Of course I can't confess. "How do you know?" they'd say; because you see, if I did know that would be prison for me, the rest of my days; the most frightful frustration because it would be so dull that I'd long to throw cushions every minute, and yet no windows low enough to throw them out of! No, no, of course I knew nothing about it, of course I had to wait and—just put the idea into your head and start you all on the road to finding out. From this moment forward, I shall

141

deny every word of it; if I prove to have killed him, then I had no idea what I was doing, poor mad old thing.' She smiled at him but her hands were shaking and her eyes were bright with tears. 'I don't remember anything about that night till Matilda came up and told me what had happened; and I don't remember a word of this conversation with you.' She sat down on the sofa with a bump. 'So there! From now on—it's up to you. Only do be quick and find me out.'

He went over and sat down beside her and took her trembling hand. 'Don't worry too much,' he said. 'Thomas will be safe, without this sacrifice. And as for proving anything against you—I wouldn't know where to begin.'

'You could begin with my wig,' said Mrs. Evans. 'Matilda took it off for me before she went to do the child. You just ask her if, when she came up to tell me the man was dead, she didn't notice that it was on again?'

Matilda, as it happened, had meanwhile come in and was sitting downstairs in the office; Melissa had made yet another pot of tea. 'I was just coming up, Cockie, to rescue you from Gran.'

'She's been quite sane all afternoon,' said Melissa who persisted in regarding Mrs. Evans as a candidate for immediate certification with only occasional lucid periods. 'Really quite all there—hasn't she, Inspector?'

'*Quite* all there,' said Inspector Cockrill. When Melissa had gone off to the dining-room for the sherry decanter he said: 'What's this about her hair?'

'Her hair?'

'The old lady's false hair. She now says she had it on when you went up to her room—after first seeing the body.'

Matilda reflected. 'Well, yes; she did have it on. I noticed it with about a quarter of my mind. I'd taken it off for her when I first went upstairs.'

He sat in a characteristic attitude, his narrow behind perched on the edge of a chair, knees parted, elbows on knees, hands dangling between them, tobacco-stained fingers playing with a cigarette. 'I don't suppose it means anything. She heard the commotion in the hall over the body and reached out and clapped her toupée on, so as to be respectable in case of emergencies.'

'She'd have to have arms ten feet long; it was on her dressing-table. She must have got out of bed to get it; and if so, why go back?'

Melissa returned with the sherry and went through a routine genteel fuss about accepting a glass. Tedward came in with Rosie. They both looked white and weary and Rosie had been crying. She pulled off her silly little hat and fluffed out her fair hair and fished a lipstick out of her handbag and plastered a further layer on her scarlet mouth; but she did it all absolutely automatically. Tedward went to the fireplace and turned and faced Cockie. 'I hear that you made some discoveries at my house this morning.'

Rosie was certainly, as Cockrill had said earlier, a very bad person to collushe with. He stopped rolling the cigarette for a moment and was still, looking back into Tedward's eyes. 'Yes. And you know what we discovered?'

'You worked out how some trick could have been played with the telephone. That doesn't mean that it *was* played, however? I mean, there's no proof?'

'I expect Charlesworth's men have looked into all that by now,' said Cockie. 'Scratches on the sill and so forth.'

'I see. The dear friend of the family, of course, has duly Told All?'

'I am a policeman first and a friend of the family next,'

143

said Cockie. 'You all knew that.' He glanced at the clock. 'I daresay Charlesworth will be coming round.'

'I daresay,' said Tedward, sourly. He went over and sat down beside Rosie on the sofa, taking her hand in his. She left it there, hooking an arm through his arm, leaning against him confidingly; he looked down at her with a little, loving, comforting smile and it came to Cockie, watching them, that, despite the discrepancies in age and temperament, here perhaps would have been the answer to all Rosie's troubles—though he doubted, wryly, whether with marriage to Rosie, poor Tedward's heartaches would have been at an end. Tedward pulled himself together a little. He gave a brief, apologetic smile. 'I'm sorry, Inspector. Of course you have a plain and simple duty to do. Matter of fact, you actually got in ahead of me. I was going to Charlesworth myself.'

'You too have joined the Protection of Thomas Society?'

'I was going to confess to the murder of Raoul Vernet; if that's what you mean.'

'It's an epidemic,' said Cockie.

'The others are trying to be heroic. It's easy enough when you didn't do it—not such fun when you really did!'

'You haven't been in the first rush,' agreed Cockie.

Matilda lay back, withdrawn from them, staring into the fire. Thomas in a police station cell, Thomas in that terrible little narrow dock with his pale hair all on end, Thomas herded together with criminals in a—would they actually take her Thomas in a Black Maria, a sort of hideous, horrible, music hall joke? And Thomas in the hospital ward of a prison, moving in a sort of resentful dream through a whole crowd of other men 'on remand', real criminals, real murderers; there had been a case in the paper the other day of a man who had raped and strangled a girl he never had seen before, and another of a man who had injured a woman in a pub fight, stabbing her horribly with broken glass—would *they* be there with Thomas?—men like that, all living together in a prison ward, bed next to bed, eating with them, companion to them—all watched, every movement studied, every word, to see whether they would, when the time for trial came, be 'fit to plead'. What did Rosie's grubby little sins matter, compared with this? She was a tart, just a natural born tart, poor child, and here was Thomas, with all his quiet goodness and integrity, living like a murderer among murderers, closed in with low understanding and cruelty and vileness. . . . I hate her, she thought; I hate her for this and I always shall. .

But Tedward sat close to Rosie, his hand over hers. 'I wasn't going to let Thomas suffer—not in the end. I had only to say one word to save him; I knew he was willing to put up with a few weeks in prison, even a trial, knowing that I could always save him in the end. He thinks it's for someone else of course—at least I suppose so; but the facts are the same. He sympathized with the killing of Raoul Vernet and he's willing to suffer if the killer can go free. And by the time the trial was over, by the time they started looking for someone else—well, I'd have had a much better chance of escaping altogether. I knew Thomas wouldn't mind putting up with a bit, if he knew. And I didn't see why I should hang unless I had to, for having settled accounts with that brute.' He shrugged and gave a bitter, small smile. 'And now my beautiful gesture comes too late.'

There was a rattle of cup against saucer, a crash as cup and saucer fell to the parquet floor. Melissa stooped automatically and grabbed at the empty air to save them, but, not touching them, straightened herself, unaware that she had moved. Her eyes did not leave Tedward's face. She cried: 'You? *You?*'

They all turned their heads, astonished, to stare at her with wide, startled, uncomprehending eyes. She moved her head from side to side, her mouth foolishly open; she could not speak. Cockie said, sharply: 'Why should you be so surprised?'

She ignored him. She tried again to speak, and her teeth chattered together uncontrollably. She blurted out at last: 'You say *you* killed him?'

Oh, God, thought Matilda; *now* what? She said, impatiently: 'Of course he didn't Melissa! They're all running round protecting each other and there isn't a word of truth in any of it, not one word.' To Tedward, she said: 'Don't go on and on, darling, do for God's sake leave it—what's the point of all this, why go accusing yourself? Thomas didn't kill the man, they can't do anything to him in the end. Leave them to find that out for themselves, don't go complicating matters, making everything horrible for everybody, irritating the police and putting them even more against us all.' And she burst out cheaply and bitterly that everyone was glorying in it, making martyrs of themselves, having a wonderful time in the limelight while poor Thomas was doing the real suffering, caged away all alone in that dreadful place. . . .

Melissa disregarded her. She said to Tedward, still staring, 'How *can* you have killed him?'

Cockrill cast his cigarette into the fire with a flick of his wrist. He got up and took a pace forward, facing her. He said again: 'Why should you be so astonished, Melissa? What's behind this?' And he broke off and glanced across to where, in the shadows, the door had slowly opened; and glanced sharply away again. The door remained half open; nothing moved.

In the bright light about the fireside, attention was focussed entirely on Melissa. She stood, as she had leapt up from her chair, the broken china at her feet, a thread of spilt tea winding its wormy way from out of the little deposit of sugar and tea leaves in the bottom of the cup. Tedward sat upright on the sofa, still holding Rosie's hand, but looking up into Melissa's face with bewildered concentration, Rosie curled up beside him, her mouth a little round O of slowly dawning comprehension and alarm; old Mrs. Evans looked lost in her deep chair, clutching at the wide arms with thin, nervous hands; Matilda had relaxed back against her cushions, exhausted and distressed by her outburst of weary protest. Melissa fought down the chattering of her jaw. She said, again, 'But why should you kill him?'

Tedward looked down at Rosie's hand. He shrugged. He said: 'I killed him for very excellent reasons, Melissa, which are nothing to do with you. I killed him because he deserved to die; I killed him because it would prevent any more unhappiness, to ourselves or to other people; and I killed him because it gave me great personal satisfaction to do so.' He leaned back, smiling. 'On the day I'm hanged, don't all get into a huddle and go into mourning; it will have been worth it, and that's what I shall be thinking.' Without turning his head, he added: 'All right, Inspector Charlesworth, standing there in the doorway; now you've heard it all and you can declare yourself. You're creating a hell of a draught.'

Charlesworth came into the room, followed by Sergeant Bedd. Cockrill gave him a questioning glance and he almost imperceptibly shook his head. Tedward intercepted the exchange. 'What—no proofs? No chips out of the window-sill, no finger-prints on the back door bell? You'd better get busy with the neighbours, Inspector. Perhaps they heard my car ticking over all that time, round the corner of the house.'

'Thank you,' said Charlesworth. 'That's a good idea. I will.'

'What *is* this idiotic trick, anyway?' said Matilda. 'Everybody knows Tedward was with Rosie in his surgery at the time that Raoul was hit.'

'No, darling,' said Tedward. 'That was a doings, very brilliant but not brilliant enough for the Yard.' He was cool, quick, mocking, but he drew his hand across his face in a gesture that gave away his intolerable inward weariness. 'I'll tell you. You see—the moment I heard that this man was coming, I got the idea that I would kill him: somehow or other—I didn't know how. My first idea was to wait outside, of course, and just hit him on the head as he left the house; but you'd probably ring up for a taxi and see him into it, so that wouldn't be any good; and I didn't think the doorstep of the Ritz was a very suitable spot for slaughter either. Then I thought that you would have to leave him for a bit when you went up and did the baby and I began to work out whether I couldn't engineer it that he would be left alone. Oh, it was all frightfully vague in my mind; but it sort of built itself up, I began to take steps that would help it along, just in case. . . . I mean, Gran would be upstairs in bed by then, and it was Melissa's day out because you'd told me so. I knew I could get Rosie over to my place if I said I'd discuss getting rid of the baby; so there was really only Thomas. That was the first step I took—writing down a call, and leaving it on his pad; if nothing came of it, it wouldn't do any harm. And if I was going to kill the man in the house, then I'd better use weapons from the house, that anyone might have picked up, a burglar or someone; so I took the mallet and the gun on the way out: I thought the mallet would do fine, and I haven't got one of my own, of course—besides that would have been fatal. And then it looked as though there were going to be a hell of a fog, and I thought that that would probably help if I could take advantage of it—and it did. The only thing was that I'd have Rosie on my hands.' He smiled down at her.

Charlesworth stood listening with all his ears. He wondered if he ought to be giving the feller the official caution; but he hadn't made up his mind to charge him yet—it was true that there was no evidence whatsoever at the house on the canal bank, and moreover he already had one prisoner in custody over this crime! I'll leave it, he thought; I haven't invited him to make any statement, and if we want it again, it looks as if he's ready enough. . . . He prompted: 'So you made a virtue out of necessity?'

'Yes,' said Tedward. 'I decided that Rosie should be my alibi—and a very good alibi you were too, my pet,' he added, smiling down at her again, 'until the telephone let me down! Well, never mind. I faked the 'phone call, Tilda; I'd planned it for earlier, as soon as you'd have gone upstairs, but this little wretch kept me waiting. Still, all was not lost. I rushed her into the car; if by the time I got to the house the nursery light had been out, it would all just have been a mysterious hoax; like the phoney message calling Thomas out. But the light was on. I left Rosie sitting in the car and I went in and killed him. Didn't I, Rosie?'

Rosie said nothing; but she looked down dully at her hands and at least made no dissent.

Matilda sat staring at him, staring at him. . . . It all sounded so true, coming from Tedward in this quiet, level voice, coming from Rosie, speechlessly acquiescent. And if it were true . . . She said: 'You did tell me he couldn't have been killed outright at the time of the call. I suppose—I suppose you knew the next doctor to see him would have known he hadn't been dead for long? So—you told me he'd just died.'

'Yes,' said Tedward. 'He *had* just died; I'd just killed him.'

Melissa still stood, with the broken cup and saucer at her feet, the trickle of tea. 'I don't understand. You say it was you who killed him? How *can* you have? And, anyway— why?'

Tedward was silent; not for him to bandy Rosie's name with Melissa Weeks. Charlesworth said, curiously: 'Why should you be so astonished? He's explained it. Rosie doesn't really constitute an alibi at all. He made some excuse to leave her sitting in the car while he came in ahead of her—"to see what had happened", I suppose, save her a shock and all that.' Rosie looked up swiftly, but he went on: 'He whistled the feller out into the hall, banged him on the head, and rushed out and brought her in, pretending he'd found him dead. And as for why—well, Rosie was having a baby. He killed her seducer, that's all—he killed the father of her child.'

Melissa took one step forward. The thin china crunched beneath her heel, her mouth was a hole in her white face, her eyes were witless, her hands curled up into fish-white stiffened claws. She cried: 'The father! The father of her child! Good God!—she didn't even know who the father was.' Her eyeballs rolled upwards under the lids, she went off suddenly into scream upon scream of hysterical laughter; and Rosie slid out of the safety of Tedward's arm and, slowly toppling, slumped like a pink and white jelly to the floor.

CHAPTER TWELVE

I SUPPOSE, thought Matilda, I shall live through all this and somehow come out sane at the other side. She looked at Melissa, lying back shuddering and sobbing in a chair, at Tedward's sick white face as he bent over Rosie, heaving unbeautifully on the floor. She said: 'The whole thing's nonsense. Rosie's been showing off to Melissa, that's all. She was in love with a student in Geneva, she practically lived in his atelier or whatever they call it, and this is his baby. She told me the whole thing.'

Old Mrs. Evans looked up sharply; and sharply closed her mouth and looked down again. Tedward saw it. He gave them a smile that was almost terrible. He said: 'Go ahead, Mrs. Evans—what did she tell *you?* She told me he was an elderly roué who got her drunk.'

'Fisherman,' said Mrs. Evans, briefly. 'Young. Moonlight on the lake.'

Rosie moaned and lifted her head. 'We'd better get her up to bed,' said Tedward, 'and give her a sedative.' And he smiled again, a different smile altogether, and said to Matilda: 'Don't take on for my sake, love; my illusions never really ran very deep—at the back of my idiotic heart, I think I knew all the time. What she was, I mean.' He shrugged a little. 'They can't help themselves,' he said.

They got her, moaning and flopping about, up to her little room; Matilda shrewdly suspected that she preferred unconsciousness to the necessity of speech but, in the end, flopped on her bed, she clung to Tedward, holding his hand against her cheek and weeping bitterly. Matilda left them to it. 'She's probably thought up a new one by now,' she said to Cockie, who waited with Charlesworth in the office downstairs. To Charlesworth, mightily anxious for a word with Rosie which would corroborate or explode the theory of Tedward's guilt, she said untruthfully that he had already administered a sedative and that Rosie was more than half asleep. 'Surely you can ask her in the morning? It'll keep.'

But in the morning, Rosie refused to utter. She crept down to the office and sat hunched over the fire, reiterating merely that she wouldn't talk to anyone but Tedward. 'You can't,' said Charlesworth. 'He's at the police station, under interrogation; and the longer you keep me here, the longer they'll keep him there. . . . One word from you . . .'

'I've thought it all out, and I won't say a thing until I've talked to Tedward.'

'Very well, talk to him on the telephone.'

'What, with all Scotland Yard listening-in?' said Rosie. 'No thank you.' When Charlesworth had gone, promising dire things to witnesses who refused to co-operate with the police she said to Matilda: 'I shall write to him, that's all,' and gathering up a large stack of notepaper from Thomas's desk, retired to her room upstairs. Matilda could hardly bear to answer her: a grubby, promiscuous little trollop, that was all—and for her Thomas was shut up in that dreadful place (What is he doing now, now this minute? Is it hateful, is he wretched and bewildered and impatient, is he wondering what we're all doing here, at home and free . . .?), and Tedward was—or was not, God only knew—a murderer. She felt relieved when nearly two hours later Rosie came down with an envelope in her hand, and announced that as everyone was so stuffy and beastly she would just go out, that was all, and not stick around to be disapproved of, and Melissa was a jolly untrustworthy person and not deserving of a person's confidence, and rather than stay home to be treated like a criminal or something, one would simply be out of the house all day and not bother to have any lunch. . . .

'Good,' said Matilda. 'That'll save me a lot of trouble.'

'And you needn't think I'll worry *you* for any more help, Matilda,' said Rosie, tossing her head.

'Good,' said Matilda again. 'That'll save me even more trouble.' It's mean and unworthy, she thought, jibing at the poor little beast like this, and she does look white and rotten; but I just can't be nice to her this morning, I just can't. She snatched her child out of the way of an over-tipped pot of boiling water and smacked it soundly for having its life saved. Emma took no notice either of the spanking or of her mother's remorseful embraces, but trotted off gaily, singing Cuppa Tea an'a Piece of Wood, a lyric of her own composing. Rosie flounced off down the front steps and, true to her promise, was seen no more till the evening. Matilda turned her attention to her disordered house.

She was putting the baby to bed that night when Cockrill arrived back, after an exhausting day. 'Forgive me, pet, if I go on with this ghastly chore. Look, sit down there, out of the way, and for God's sake tell me what's happening.' Emma stood, slender and firm with her aureole of fiery hair, in a foam of white towel, as she dried her vigorously by the nursery fire. Cockie subsided into the rocking chair. 'I suppose I can't smoke?'

'Yes, yes, of course, smoke away. We'll fling open windows and things afterwards. Only do *tell* me.'

'All I can hear about Thomas is that he hasn't said anything more. He's seeing Whosit to-morrow.'

'Mr. Granger. I saw him yesterday; I've been dashing about like a lunatic, trying to get things fixed up. Our

Mr. Burden said we ought to get a solicitor "more used to dealing with this kind of thing". He's a nice man, this Granger. He's going to "try and get James Dragon", whoever James Dragon may be: what a name!'

'He's what's called an eminent K.C.'

'He can't be too eminent for me.'

'I hope he won't be too *expen*sive for you.'

'We can always sell the house,' said Matilda, dismissing it.

The nursery chair was damned uncomfortable. Cockie rocked backwards and forwards, his short legs almost leaving the ground each time. 'Re. Tedward—they've had him at the station all day.'

'What does that imply?'

'Questions, questions, questions,' said Cockie. 'A rest on one excuse or another, and then the same questions; different people putting the questions: different ways of putting the questions. . . .'

'They haven't arrested him or anything?'

'They already have a slight embarrassment of arrested persons,' said Cockie, dryly. 'And I don't quite see what they can arrest him *on*. The trick with the telephone could have been played, but there's nothing at all to show that it was; no signs, apparently. Of course *he* says that it was—but we also have an embarrassment of confessions. You don't charge people on their own, unsupported admissions.'

'Rosie's the only person who could confirm it; whether she came in with him, I mean, or waited outside in the car. It all hangs on that.'

'She hasn't said anything?'

'Not a sausage. She finally declared that she'd write to Tedward, and spent hours in her room, in the throes of composition, I suppose, because she's not exactly fluent with pen and ink. Now she's gone off in a huff at being caught with the lilies of purity down.' She enveloped the

154

baby's pink body in a cloud of white powder. 'All *I* can say is that when I got to the turn of the stair Rosie was certainly with Tedward—they were standing looking down at Raoul's body and she was close beside him. But of course that's not to say that she hadn't followed him in afterwards, or that he hadn't gone out to fetch her as he says.'

'As Charlesworth says,' said Cockie.

'Well, whichever way it was.' She knelt on the rug, staring into the fire. The baby, quiet for a moment, stood in the golden glow, in the curve of her arm. 'Do you know, Cockie—the bare thought of him lying there used to turn me sick; I never could endure the sight of blood and accidents and things. I can't bear to see mice in traps and flies on sticky paper and cats catching birds. . . . But now—I seem to have got over that, it doesn't shake me any more. I can't even think of Raoul any more, alive or dead; only Thomas, Thomas, Thomas all the time, and this hideous muddle of Tedward and Melissa and Granny; and Rosie, damn her for a trouble-making little bitch!' She tied off the rope of Emma's white, spotted dressing-gown and gave her a pat on her tiny behind. 'Well—poor little devil; she's got her troubles too—in all this hell and high water one's forgotten that; I mean the baby and everything.'

'What on earth's to become of her?' said Cockie.

'Oh, God only knows.'

'I was thinking last night that Ted Edwards might have made an honest woman of her; but that was while he still thought she was a dove deceived by an elderly eagle with the aid of strong drink.'

'He had no illusions by the time dear Melissa had finished,' said Tilda.

'Green-eyed envy,' said Cockie, drawing on his cigarette.

'Thank God Thomas wasn't there—it would have broken his heart.'

'He'll have to know some time,' said Cockie.

'Well, yes, it must all come out in the questions and things. Poor darling—one more horrible shock for him. But different from—last night; I mean, that was vile, that screaming little neurotic of a Melissa and Rosie rolling about in mock faints and things, and Tedward looking like death. . . .'

'The little minx!' said Cockie.

'Little nymphomaniac, more like.'

'I meant all these stories: all true, Matilda, you see—but each one selected to suit the confidante of the moment; and most brilliantly. *You* might be expected to sympathize with an affair of first love, two young things in the grip of their emotions; Tedward got the betrayal by the experienced roué, the old lady got the story of the strong silent man, sweeping her lit. and fig. off her feet.' He shook his head, the smoke of his cigarette curling up thin and blue between his brown fingers. 'She's a lot more shrewd than one gives her credit for. One's always noticing that.'

The baby had eaten its apple and had its teeth cleaned and now lay back in her arms and began its ritual good-night crooning. 'Sorry, Cockie, about this frightful row, and the awful part is that I have to join in too.' She sang rather tunelessly the first lines of a song called Three-mice-unable-to-see . . . 'Now you sing, darling, so that mama can talk.'

'More pleess,' said the baby.

'No, no, you sing, baby sing.'

'Potty, potty, pot-ty,' sang the baby

'Well, all right, though not quite the theme one might have chosen.' She shushed it for a moment at the sound of soft footsteps on the stairs outside and called out, 'Rosie?'

'I'm going to my room,' said Rosie's voice. 'I don't want any supper.'

'You needn't think I'm going to bring you any,' called Matilda, through the door, 'because I'm not.'

Rosie was understood to reply that she didn't *want* any, thank you, she had just said so; and they needn't think they could treat her like Lady Godiva one minute and start bringing her supper and things the next! 'She means send her to Coventry, I suppose,' said Matilda, shrugging. 'Let her get on with it!'

'Porty, porty, por-ty,' sang the baby, showing off; it looked at Cockrill shyly from the corners of its eyes but he disregarded it ruthlessly. 'What on earth can Rosie have been writing to Tedward about?'

'I suppose she wants to know whether or not to support him in this "confession" of his. It looked, last night, as if she'd agreed to, though she didn't actually say anything; still, she didn't deny it.'

'She didn't show any great astonishment,' said Cockie. 'They'd obviously discussed what he was going to say.'

'It *must* be all a nonsense,' said Matilda uneasily. 'I mean, sometimes I think I'd welcome anything that would set Thomas free, but to think that Tedward really was a murderer. . . .' She got up and the baby's singing increased in volume and silliness lest by any chance she should be imagining that it was ready for its bed. 'You don't think, Cockie, that it could have been done that way? Or do you? It was *your* theory in the first place.'

Cockrill got up too and the chair rocked backwards and kicked him violently in the backs of his legs. 'Damn this infernal thing! Oh, beg the child's pardon!' He jabbed out his cigarette on the nursery mantelpiece and hurriedly flapped away the ash with his cuff. He said: 'I don't know what I believe, Matilda. There's no question of my having a theory—I saw that the thing with the telephone might have been cooked and I proved that it *could* have been cooked—that's all. As you say, it all rests with Rosie.'

'And then who's to know whether Rosie's speaking the truth?' She plonked the baby down in its cot where it sang porty-porty-porty in a sillier voice than ever and went off into peals of self-conscious laughter; and said, wearily, tucking down its waving legs: 'I wonder what my poor darling's doing now!'

Her poor darling was at that moment sitting very unhappily on the edge of the bed while the gentleman of the broken glass bottle, who had taken a fancy to him, sat very close beside him and poured out his confidences. 'Schizophrenia, you see, Doc.—that's what's the trouble with me. You being a doctor, you'll understand better than what these louts of coppers seem to do. Schizophrenia—invalided out of the army with a touch of it, I was, and I daresay it's got a bit worse since then.' He seemed quite delighted about it. 'Carve up the lot of you, I wouldn't be surprised, if I got into one of me moods.'

'Good,' said Thomas. 'That would save the hangman a lot of trouble.'

But they would never hang Thomas. They'll never hang *me*, thought Thomas. They could keep him here as long as they liked and meanwhile the truth was slipping away, slipping away with every hour that went by—little facts forgotten, little truths overlooked, conclusions confused, deductions made more uncertain: all silted over, hidden away, finally obliterated by the sands of all-concealing time. They can keep me here as long as they like and when it suits me to march out, I have only to say a word; and even then they can't do anything to me—*I* haven't confessed to the murder, *I* didn't tell any lies, or none that they can prove. Only about the car. And about the car, I can simply say that I'd forgotten; Tedward will bear me out, Tedward can prove that, though I never set eyes on Raoul Vernet till I came in and found them all standing over his dead body in the hall, I may still have got blood on my shoes and so into the car. . . . They would never hang Thomas; Tedward knew the truth about him, Tedward, in their own good time, would see to that. . . .

And they would never hang Tedward. They'll never hang *me*, thought Tedward, standing at the window of his lonely room, looking out at the leaden grey of the canal. They wouldn't charge him while they still held Thomas, and they wouldn't release Thomas until they were very certain that the case against him had collapsed or until the case against himself was proved beyond all possibility of doubt. They'd never hang Thomas and they'd never hang Tedward. When Thomas was good and ready, when he gave the sign that his willing self-sacrifice might now come to an end, then he, Tedward, had only to speak a word, to say that he'd forgotten about Thomas's car—and Thomas was free. That he himself had forgotten all about the car, had built up a case against himself to confuse the issue, to help Thomas, to delay things and muddle things up. . . . That now it was unnecessary because he had suddenly remembered—fool that he was!—about the car. As for himself—Rosie had no more waited in the car than he had. She had been close at his shoulder when they went together into the hall of the Maida Vale house and saw Raoul Vernet lying there dead on the floor. Whether they would have taken Rosie's word for it or not, that was the truth—

and they could never prove otherwise; their case against
him was just a nonsense; a desirable nonsense from all but
the police point of view, since it confused the issue against
Thomas, against the person that Thomas was trying to
protect. . . .

But they would never hang old Mrs. Evans, anyway.

At home, in the house in Maida Vale, Mrs. Evans had
decided to help out, during the utter demoralization of
Melissa, by making a little something towards the evening
meal: just some nice, simple Crèpes Suzettes. She had
started very early in the afternoon so as to give the batter
time to stand, but somehow it was all going rather slowly
and the place seemed an absolute mass of flour. Flour was
not what it had been in her day, thought Mrs. Evans,
distractedly flapping clouds of it off the table with the skirt
of her overall; it seemed to fly about most dreadfully. And
there wasn't an orange in the place and not a drop of
liqueur; and really Matilda had been unreasonable about
her taking just a drop, just the merest half bottle of the
baby's government orange juice. Muttering fretfully to herself, she trotted about the kitchen, plunging everything into
ever worse confusion. The crèpes were little and round and
wafer thin, but they did seem to be mainly composed of
large holes which must surely be wrong? Struck by an idea,
she went over to the kitchen looking-glass and, with a
certain amount of manœuvring, removed the lace cap from
her toupée and tried the effect of a pancake there instead.
It was terrific: one would patent it at once, the advantages
were indubitable—her mind played gaily with a whole
series of brilliant advertisements: no outlay on costly Rose
Point or Honiton, no washing, no ironing, easily disposed of

(by inward consumption), invaluable if overcome by hunger on a long train journey or stranded in a desert, just the thing in time of famine. . . . One would make a whole stack of them on a Monday and work one's way through. 'A pancake a day Keeps the laundress at bay!' thought Mrs. Evans and, enchanted by these flights of fancy, forgot all about her disablement and put up her right hand to take the pancake down from her head. But the hand fell back; and, as she jacked it up with the other and slowly scrabbled the lace cap back into position, the laughter died out of her bright old eyes. The police wouldn't be such fools as not to cotton on, sooner or later, to the fact that never for one moment, from the stairs or anywhere else, could she have lifted those feeble arms and felled a man to the ground. They would never hang old Mrs. Evans for this crime or put her in prison or even a loonie bin. I'll have to think up a better one than that, she thought, if I'm going to keep him safe. . . .

And they would never hang Melissa. Melissa crouching on her divan bed in her basement room, wept and gloomed and was sick with dismay and despair—but only because of the hideous things she had blurted out last night, only at the thought of her own betrayal of what, after all, had been sacred confidences, only because of the horrified, the incredulous, the sorrowful looks she had brought to the faces of those who had never been anything but kind to her. Not for any fear of herself, not for terror lest one day she must hang by the neck till she was dead. For, after all, she had only to say one word; had only to speak one name to clear herself—had only to blurt it out as last night she had blurted out the chronicle of Rosie's sins—had only to tell them the dreadful truth as the murderer had, in so many words, confessed it to her. Melissa could give the murderer away, confession and all: they would never hang *her*.

Or Damien Jones: they would never hang Damien Jones. For the police knew nothing of Damien Jones, knew nothing of Damien's sudden tendency to limp, knew nothing of how wearily Mrs. Jones' pet lodger, Mr. Hervey, dragged himself up the stairs after his long day's work, collecting subscriptions for his insurance firm; knew nothing of any meeting in the house in Maida Vale, that night of the fog. The police would never associate Damien with this crime at all, for only one person could tell them that he had been there, and that person would never breathe a word of it. They would never hang Damien.

And they would never hang Matilda, for Matilda had no sort or kind of motive to murder Raoul; and if she had killed him, would never for one moment have permitted her husband to suffer in her place. It was as simple as that. They would never hang Matilda for this crime; and they would never hang Damien and they would never hang Thomas and they would never hang Tedward; and they would never hang old Mrs. Evans and they would never hang Melissa. And they would never hang Rosie. . . .

Inspector Cockrill went upstairs to Rosie's little room. Rosie lay back against the pillow, with only the street lamp shining in from outside to illuminate the room, and said in a dying-away voice that she felt very ill and would he please go away.

'I will when you've answered me one single question,' said Cockie, standing over her bed in the darkened room. 'Only *you* can help us, Rosie; only you can say whether Tedward could have killed Raoul Vernet or whether he could not. I don't say "whether he did kill him", I say "whether he could have". Now, tell me the truth.'

'I feel very, very ill,' said Rosie. 'I can't answer any questions. Please go away and leave me to sleep.'

'This is me, Rosie, not the police; not officially the police. You called me in, yourself, to help you all. I can't do a thing for you unless I know the truth. I don't for one moment believe that Tedward could have killed Vernet, all in a half-minute like that; but unless you tell me in one word whether or not he went into the house alone—I'm stuck, I can't go on. Now, tell me the truth.'

Rosie flopped back against the pillows and closed her eyes. He put out his hand and caught at her shoulder and jerked her to a sitting position. 'Don't play games with me, Rosie; don't play for time. I'm not going to leave this room till you give me an answer.'

'I don't know what you're talking about,' said Rosie, querulously. 'Please go away.'

'Did Tedward, or did he not, go into the house alone?'

She turned her head from side to side on the pillows and gave a sort of hollow moan. 'I feel terrible. Please go away and let me sleep.'

'I'll let you sleep the moment you've said this one word—yes or no.'

'I've taken something,' said Rosie. 'I'm too dopey. I can't talk.'

He hammered with his clenched brown fist on the table by her bed. 'Stop play-acting! Yes or no?'

'Yes or no—what?' mumbled Rosie, passing a lax hand with a gesture of exaggerated weariness across her face.

He pulled down her hand. 'Yes or no—did Tedward come into this house alone?'

The hand dragged limply out of his; she said at last, 'Of course he did,' and moved the hand again and laid it with a childish gesture which, in the dim light he could only just discern, upon her heart. 'Go away, please, Cockie, and let me sleep. Now I've told you. Yes—he came in alone.' Her eyes closed, her hand slid softly down and rested against the turned-back edge of the bedclothes. 'Good girl,' he said, and went away, satisfied.

They would never hang Rosie; for Rosie had cried wolf once too often and one who might, even then, have saved her life, had come away all unsuspectingly and left her to die.

CHAPTER THIRTEEN

INSPECTOR COCKRILL, shocked temporarily into old age, tottered to the telephone and asked for Charlesworth. To him he said, briefly: 'You'd better come over. Rosie Evans is dead.'

'Dead? Rosie Evans? How *can* she be dead?'

'She's stopped breathing,' said Cockie in a blind rage and slammed down the receiver.

Matilda, sick and sobbing after a night of horror, walked through a round of necessary duties in a stupor of sorrow and remorse: of sorrow for the young life suddenly ended, for the beautiful body lying so still, out of mischief at last, and in peace, of sorrow for Thomas who must break his heart all over again; of remorse for hasty anger, for too little understanding, too little patience, too little love. In the office, Tedward sat with his head in his hands, as colourless and motionless as stone. Downstairs, Melissa wept noisily and cooked up a drama about it's all being her fault, upstairs old Mrs. Evans sat by the dead girl's bed and gave herself over to the quiet grief of those who have seen the passing of so many friends. The doctor whom Tedward had called in during the night, paced up and down the long drawing-room with its unlit fire and said again and again that he was most frightfully distressed, Mrs. Evans, that he had done all he could, that by the time he saw her, it was already too late . . . Matilda brought him coffee. 'I'm sorry it's only this; there's no one to cope except me.'

'My dear Mrs. Evans, for goodness sake don't think of me.'

'I'll try and scramble some breakfast together later.'

'Please don't worry about *me*,' he said again.

'You'll tell Inspector Charlesworth. . . .?'

'I shall have to tell him I think it was some kind of overdose; some kind of abortifacient. I can't not tell him.'

'No, of course not,' said Tilda, hopelessly. 'You'd have thought we had enough to bear, wouldn't you?—without . . .' She stopped. 'Without Rosie going and landing us in for this,' she had been going to say.

Charlesworth arrived, anxious and nervy, concealing it in a flurry of jerky activity, of questions, notes, orders, cancellations, reprimands. The doctor introduced himself. 'Under the circumstances, Dr. Edwards didn't feel that he ought to handle the case himself, certainly not on his own. He seems to be a close friend of the family; and then all this murder business. . . .' It was self-explanatory. 'I think he was right.'

'What time did you get here?'

'Two o'clock this morning. Mrs. Evans heard her moving about some time after midnight and went up to her; but I gather she was pretty far gone even then. Frightful retching and vomiting and all that. They'd done a lot already when I got here, but it was hopeless.'

'Did she say anything, do you know?'

'Not to me; she was past it by the time I saw her, and I think by the time Mrs. Evans found her. They don't seem to know what happened, anyway.'

'She was supposed to be having this illegit. How could she have got hold of an abortifacient?'

For answer the doctor produced a large white handkerchief, tied into a bundle, and slowly untied the knot. I noticed these in the waste-paper basket in her room. I had a closer look at them, and then I thought I ought to keep them for someone in authority. I fished them out and wrapped them up; it was easy enough, they were all occupied with the patient.' He was rather miserable about it. 'It seems a bit mean—but what else could I do?'

What else indeed? A dozen little white envelopes, tiny white envelopes such as pharmacists use; each with the legend, 'To be taken as prescribed', each labelled POISON, each with the name and address of a different chemist. 'Quite small doses, probably,' said the doctor. 'Harmless by themselves. But twelve!'

'She must have gone round collecting them,' said Charlesworth. He spelt out the addresses, Paddington, Bayswater, Westbourne Grove, Marble Arch . . . 'Juggle them about a bit and you can practically trace her route; she must have just walked along, popping into each of the shops she passed.'

'But where did she get all these prescriptions from?'

Rosie had got the prescriptions from Thomas. They were written on his headed writing paper, signed with his name; twelve prescriptions each for a small dose of a proprietary drug. A young lady had come in, the day before, said the various pharmacists, and presented a prescription which seemed to be quite in order; and here, if the police doubted them, were the originals. . . . Twelve prescriptions which, all added together, amounted to certain death.

Pushed into Rosie's handbag was a thirteenth prescription, dated two days ago. Written across the bottom were the words, 'Repeat once'. It had been stamped by a Maida Vale chemist, but the second dose had not been applied for. Charlesworth himself visited the chemist, and later confronted Tedward with the prescription. '*You* gave Rosie Evans this?'

Tedward was still sitting, dumb and unmoving, in the office, where Matilda was coaxing a reluctant fire. He

lifted an unshaven face and looked back at Charlesworth
with bleary eyes. 'What about it?'

'It's an abortifacient.'

'I know,' said Tedward. 'She was having an unwanted
baby.'

'You mean you were helping her to get rid of it?'

'Oh, go to hell,' said Tedward and relapsed back into
his coma.

Charlesworth took him by the shoulder and shook him
roughly. 'Give your mind to this. She died of the stuff.'

'It wouldn't hurt a fly,' said Tedward.

'Enough of it would.'

'Well, she didn't have enough of it. This was for a small
dose, two small doses that wouldn't have done her any
harm—or any good either, for that matter—if she'd taken
them together. But I told her to take them three days
apart.' He looked more closely at the paper and added,
indifferently: 'She's never even cashed the second one.'

'Why give them to her at all, if they'd do no good?'

Tedward put his head back in his hands. 'Oh, dear *God!*
I gave them to her because she begged and badgered and I
thought it would keep her quiet and prevent her from
running off to some phoney who *would* "help" her. There
was nothing wrong with them, they might just as well have
been aspirin.'

'Then why not have palmed her off with aspirin?'

'Because Rosie was not a damn fool,' said Tedward
shortly.

Matilda sat back on her heels, brushing away a strand
of hair with the back of a sooty hand. 'Anyway, how could
this small dose of Tedward's have made any difference?'

Charlesworth spread out the twelve prescriptions.
Matilda, craning forward to look at them from her position
on the hearth, said, sharply: 'But those are Thomas's!'

168

Charlesworth turned the papers so that she could more easily read them. 'Yes—they are, aren't they?'

'But Thomas—well, Thomas wouldn't give her all those, he wouldn't sign a dozen prescriptions at a time, he wouldn't dream of it. And anyway, he didn't know about the baby.' She stared at them, terror-stricken. 'Yes, they're his. . . It's . . .'But suddenly she said: 'But they're dated yesterday.'

'Yes,' said Charlesworth. 'All of them.'

'But yesterday. . . . But yesterday, Thomas was in prison. And the day before. *And* the day before.' And she raised her head and said urgently: 'Rosie took a lot of his headed notepaper upstairs. She said she was going to write to Tedward. She was up there for hours.' She swung round on Tedward. '*Did* she write to you?'

'No,' said Tedward. 'What would she write to me about?'

'And then she came down with something in her hand. I thought it was an envelope for posting; and she went out and she was out all day. And then she came in and went straight up to her room, and later on when Cockie went up she was already in bed and she said she felt ill.' She said, triumphantly: 'She had Tedward's prescription. She copied it out on Thomas's paper, all these times, and signed his name.' She looked more closely at the forged signatures. 'They're frightfully bad, really; but of course, on this official paper, how would the chemists know? They had nothing to compare with. It wasn't as if it were a large dose or anything frightening like that. . . .' And she buried her face in her hands, dizzy with relief, and said: 'It's nothing to do with Thomas—nothing at all.'

'So that's all right, isn't it?' said Tedward, savagely sarcastic. 'What does anything matter if Thomas is in the clear?' He got up and blundered out of the room, out into the cold November garden and up to the stone bench beyond the leafless mulberry tree, and there sat down and buried his head in his hands once more. They saw the baby trot up to him, full of excited confidences, gazing up into his face with her head on one side. He lifted his hand and pushed her so roughly away that she fell down and, picking herself up, ran bawling into the house. He did not even lift his eyes to look after her.

If only, thought Cockrill, they would not all be so sorry for him because he had been the one to get up and go away leaving Rosie to die! He supposed that somewhere, fathoms deep down in him, he was sorry himself, but he had for so long gradually overlaid with the matrix of self-protection, the small pearl of pity in his arid old heart, that he no longer felt capable of this kind of distress. Far more than their sympathy he would have valued a simple recognition that he had done what each of them, knowing Rosie, would have done, that it had been the natural thing. But no! Sitting round the drawing-room on the day of her funeral, sick with the scent of inappropriate lilies, uneasily conscious of the casket of ashes which was already so pathetically becoming no more than a faint, faintly ludicrous, embarrassment, they forced on him still their generous, kindly pity. 'For God's sake,' he said to Charlesworth, 'let's go out to a pub and drink in some nice fresh air.' But at the pub, with beer glasses in their hands, it resolved itself into the same old round, whether she had been as ill already as she had claimed to be, when she must have taken the stuff to have arrived at that stage, the how, the why, the who. . . .

'We sound like a couple of ruddy owls,' said Charlesworth.

'Owls are remarkable for seeing in the dark; but it was too dark for *me*, in her room that night.'

The inquest had been adjourned 'to allow the police to make further enquiries'. 'Though what on earth we're supposed to discover, I don't know.'

'I knew Rosie Evans pretty well,' said Cockrill. 'I must say I don't see her working out all that.'

'The alternatives. . . .'

'The alternative is that someone put it into her head—either to help her or the other thing.'

'Who on earth would want to kill Rosie Evans?'

'I don't know,' said Cockie. 'Who on earth wanted to kill that poor, inoffensive Frog?'

The curve of the great Edwardian bar glowed ruddily in the dreadful pink neon lighting; in the intricate carved wooden shelving behind the bar, bottles were reflected back and back again in their mirrored recesses. They repaired to an alcove, horribly upholstered in red, and sat down uneasily on the rexeline-covered seat. 'Let's begin, anyway, by taking the charitable view. Dr. Edwards, in all innocence, gave her the original prescription; with or without advice she thought up this bright idea of getting a larger dose, and she went and overdid it by accident.'

'Or by design,' said Cockrill, sombrely.

'What, suicide? But why?'

'She was having an unwanted baby. Everybody had lost interest in her, nobody was helping her, they were all taken up with the business of the murder. Old Faithful, who might still have been counted on, had suddenly learned that she was nothing but a nymphomaniac; for that matter, they'd all learned that, and her stock was at zero.' Cockrill drained his glass and set it down with a bump. 'Not that I believe it; she was not the type.'

'One so often hears that said,' said Charlesworth, sud-

denly looking much older than his years. 'But these kids—
they do, you know, don't they? They're all froth and
bubble—they haven't much stamina. One does find them
giving way to sudden fits of despair.'

'This wasn't a fit of despair,' said Cockie. 'It was a
carefully thought out, elaborately carried out plan.' He
collected the glasses and went to the bar with them;
Charlesworth watched him carrying them back towards
him, shouldering his way crabwise through the crowd, not
spilling a drop. He said, as he sat down: 'No—suicide's out.'

'Then, still in sweet charity. . . .'

'There's no charity in this thing,' said Cockie. He stared
down into his glass with troubled eyes. 'Don't let's fool
ourselves. This wasn't a mistake. Suppose someone wants
to help her, damn it all—they know that Dr. Edwards'
dose won't amount to much, they suggest this way in which
she may make it more—surely to God they might tell her
twice as much, or three times as much, or if you like four
times as much! But twelve times! Twelve times! Nobody in
their senses would take such a risk.'

'They might have suggested less and she thought she'd go
one better.'

'But she went nine or ten better,' said Cockie. 'She
wouldn't go one better to the extent of twelve times the
dose; not even Rosie.'

'On the other hand, Rosie did take that much.'

'On the advice of somebody she trusted,' insisted Cockie.

Charlesworth thought it all over. He said, slowly: 'We're
now talking of laymen?'

'We're talking of Matilda Evans and old Mrs. Evans and
Melissa Weeks.'

'Of course it *may* have been a non-layman; a doctor?'

Cockie shrugged.

'I mean, Thomas Evans could have put her up to it

before he was taken into custody. We've nothing to prove that he didn't really know about the baby business, all along.'

'He may have,' agreed Cockie. 'He may have put her up to it and Dr. Edwards may have put her up to it. Neither of them could legitimately have given her such a dose as would terminate the pregnancy; they might see it as a way to help her without incriminating themselves. But if no layman would make such a hideous mistake—how much less a doctor.' The pastille tin in which he kept his tobacco shot off the slippery surface of the seat and clattered on to the floor. 'Blast the bloody thing,' he said, and stooped and groped about for it. 'I'm old,' he said, straightening himself with a hand to his back. 'I get feelings in my bones. I've got a feeling in my bones that this thing's murder. . . .'

But murder by whom? By the murderer of Raoul Vernet —or were they to believe that *two* killers lurked in that little group of plain, everyday people centring upon the house in Maida Vale? By Matilda Evans, then? But Matilda had never for a moment believed Raoul Vernet to be Rosie's seducer; she had believed her lover to be a young man, a student. And what reason had Matilda to murder Rosie, to murder her by a cold, reasoned, premeditated plan? Only that, by 'getting herself into trouble' Rosie had made trouble for them all.

Or old Mrs. Evans? But old Mrs. Evans could not have lifted her crippled hand to strike the blow; nor would she have had any reason, for she too had been told a story of a young man, a big, strong, young fisherman from the East, sweeping poor, fascinated Rosie off her feet. Mrs. Evans had had no reason to kill Raoul Vernet; and no reason to kill Rosie, whom she held so little responsible for her sins.

Well, Melissa Weeks then? Melissa seemed hardly likely to have avenged Rosie's seduction so drastically, even if she had not known that she would have to take on an army to do the thing properly. As for Rosie—what had Melissa against Rosie Evans, except for an occasional boy friend pinched, an occasional hope destroyed? And Thomas—Thomas who had been in prison while the plot against Rosie had been in action, who loved Rosie with all his heart; who purported to have known nothing of Rosie's love affairs? Or Tedward? 'Whether or not he could have killed the man,' said Cockie, 'or whether or not he would have—can you conceive that he would have killed this girl? He was in love with her, he's been in love with her since she was an adolescent. He'd discovered that she'd been deceiving them all, he'd discovered, if you like, that if he'd killed Vernet, he'd killed the poor chap on an absolute misconception of the whole affair. But even so . . . You see, if he started this thing he must have started it that night; he must have suggested it to her when he took her upstairs, under the guise of "administering a sedative", What?—just because he was disillusioned in her? It doesn't ring true; it simply doesn't ring true.' He shook his head and the tin box shot off the shiny seat again and on to the floor. 'But I get feelings in my bones these days,' he said, retrieving it again. 'And I've got a feeling in my bones that this thing's murder —murder by suggestion, by a person or persons unknown.'

Three days later, at the renewed inquest, the jury, bewildered by a plethora of possibilities and alternatives, chose the most exciting and brought in a verdict to precisely the same effect.

CHAPTER FOURTEEN

So, labelled now as person or persons unknown, the Maida Vale household stumbled through the necessities of routine, with Tedward, a ghost in the familiar, shabby old overcoat that, in a night, seemed to have grown so much too big for him, stumbling in their wake. Interviews, questions, answers, instructions; the police, the curious public, the ever-present press. Not a day but their names appeared in the papers, with inaccurate details of their private lives, with grey, smudgy photographs, misleading headlines, misrepresentations of the 'recollections' of their friends. 'Mrs. Evans', 'Rosie Evans', 'Dr Edwards' were household words. If it were true that eating created appetite, thought Matilda, the public had been fed to starvation point. They awaited with avid eagerness the reappearance of Thomas in the magistrate's court.

Thomas had almost looked forward to this day; a break, anyway, in the deadly sameness of life in his prison ward, with the constant companionship of his friend with the touch of schizophrenia. It was not very pleasant when one got here, however; perched up in the damn little narrow dock with no room for one's legs, and one's self-conscious back turned to the people in the long narrow benches so close behind one. There was quite an array here to-day, a smooth gentleman representing the Director of Public Prosecutions hurriedly mugging up his notes, his own solicitor, Mr. Granger, and a youngish barrister, patently anxious, representing Mr. James Dragon in the prisoner's interests. The public squashed and squeezed into the gallery behind him, which was not a gallery at all really, but a sort of loose-box, very long and nearly as narrow as his beastly dock, and raised not more than a step or so above ground level. He thought he caught a glimpse of Damien Jones there, among the crowd; it was very decent of the kid to have come. . . .

The gentleman from Public Prosecutions had probably just been doing a crossword after all for he had obviously no hesitations about his piece. He stood up and rattled it off, very clear, very brief, very fair. 'That is the case against the prisoner, Your Worship.' The case against the prisoner was that the victim had seduced the prisoner's sister, or at any rate the prisoner had believed he had; that the prisoner had put forward a false alibi, a previously planned false alibi, claiming to have been called out on a visit to a sick child in a house which, in fact, proved to be untenanted; that the weapons used in the killing had belonged to the prisoner and the prisoner, as a doctor, would have known how and where to strike; and finally, and surely conclusively, that there had been found in the prisoner's car, traces of the victim's blood which could not have got there unless he were the murderer. Or let the gentleman from Public Prosecutions put it in this way—the prisoner had arrived back after the discovery of the body *and by his own admission had put his car away before entering the house*; by his own admission, he had not returned to the car. How then, could those traces of the dead man's blood, have got into the prisoner's car? 'That is the case for the prosecution.' The gentleman from the D.P.P. sat down. And a damn thin case it is too, he said to himself.

Witnesses, witnesses, witnesses. . . . Detective Inspector Charlesworth, Detective Inspector Cockrill, Matilda, nervous and anxious, hardly taking her eyes off Thomas, expert witnesses, out of turn because they had urgent business elsewhere and were anxious to be released as soon as possible, if His Worship could make it convenient to the Court. . . . So am I anxious to be released as soon as possible, thought Thomas, ruefully; and he wondered how soon *that* would be convenient to the court and whether it would be ever, whether he had not tied this noose a bit too effectively about his own neck. Melissa Weeks, nervous and gabbling, Gran, nervous and charming, Tedward. . . .

He walked slowly and heavily, like an old man; and Thomas remembered Rosie and made no more jokes to himself. 'I swear by Almighty God that the evidence I shall give to this court shall be the truth, the whole truth and nothing but the truth. . . . Yes, I arrived at the house with Rosie, with Miss Evans, at about twenty-five to ten . . . Yes, I left my car in the road outside. Yes, I removed the ignition key; it would be an automatic action, I always do. . . .' A clerk took it all down in long-hand, filling up pages and pages of foolscap with large, flowing writing, enormously widely spaced. Counsel waited to put each new question till the clerk had finished with the last. Now and again he said, 'Just a minute', and the magistrate asked witness to go a little more slowly, please, because this gentleman had to take down what was being said. At the end of the witnesses' evidence he would read it all back to him in a rapid, monotonous gabble and witness, stepping down from the box, would be invited to sign it and would do so, with much fumbling for glasses and preliminary scratchings, trying out the police court pen. . . .

Counsel for Thomas Evans was on his feet. 'Dr. Edwards —did you see the defendant's car outside the house when you arrived?'

'No,' said Tedward.

'You have told us that you left your car and went up into the house?'

'Yes,' said Tedward.

'Followed by Miss Rose Evans,' said Counsel, skating delicately over any question as to how closely Miss Rose Evans had followed.

'Yes.'

'And later saw the defendant enter the hall through the front door?'

'Yes; about ten minutes after I got there.'

'Did you observe anything about his attitude to the presence of the dead body in the hall?'

'He seemed very shocked and surprised,' said Tedward.

'He seemed very shocked and surprised; as though he were seeing this body for the first time?'

'Yes, certainly.'

'And then, Dr. Edwards, what did you do?'

'Well, one or other of us suggested that as the telephone wire had been torn out by the fall, I should go for the police; so I went back to my car.'

'I see. And on this occasion, did you see any car outside the house?'

Leaning against the wall behind the witness-box, Charlesworth shifted from foot to foot in an agony of suspense. On the answer to this one question, so much hung; if Thomas Evans were committed for trial, what was one to do about Dr. Edwards, about his confession, about Rosie's confirmation of his confession, about the faked telephone call? They had let the thing drift too far, that was the truth of it; in face of the verdict on Rosie, ought they not to have withdrawn the charge against Thomas and started all over again? But they had not; and whichever way it went, he, Charlesworth, would get the brickbats, that was certain.

And rightly so; he had been too damn hasty in charging Thomas Evans. Ted Edwards had thrown out hints that he could clear Thomas Evans; if he didn't do so now . . . Charlesworth prayed fervently to heaven to intervene.

And heaven intervened. The dead hand of Rosie, which in life had tumbled the little pawns about so violently, stretched forth from her casket of ashes and picked up one little pawn and tossed it out into the sunshine of freedom; and thrust another on to the vacant square. And Tedward put his hand into the dead hand of his love, and let it move him where it would. 'Yes. This time there was a car outside the house: Thomas Evans' car.'

'Whereas there had not been a car there ten or fifteen minutes before, now his car was there?'

'Yes.'

'Which you know very well?'

'Oh, yes,' said Tedward. 'I've known it for years.'

'I see. You're aware, of course, that the defendant stated to the police that he put his car away, as usual, when he arrived at the house?'

'Yes,' said Tedward. 'I think in the shock and fuss he must have forgotten.' In reply to the Magistrate's reminder that they must not have his thoughts, please, he amended: 'Well, let's put it this way: in the shock and fuss I forgot all about it myself.'

'You forgot you had seen the defendant's car outside the house when you went out to fetch the police?'

'Yes. As soon as I remembered, I told the police,' said Tedward, who had told the police just as soon as it suited them all for him to do so and not a moment before.

'And when you returned a little later with the police——?'

'The car was not there,' said Tedward.

'In the interval, he had gone out and put it away?'

'I suppose so, yes.'

'You know that the defendant positively states that he did not go out again?'

'Yes,' said Tedward.

'That he put his car away and locked up the garage before he came into the house?'

Behind him, the police witnesses stiffened to immobility against the wall, all about the court there were little knots and little whisperings. He knew that Mr. Charlesworth's seconds were preparing to throw in the towel. And he looked across at Thomas and the dead hand of Rosie lifted the noose over Thomas's head, and came and slipped it gently about his own. And he lifted his head, with the noose about his neck and said, loudly and clearly: 'He couldn't have put it away. He's forgotten, he's made a mistake.' He said more quietly, 'When I drew up in front of the house, I overshot my mark a little, in the fog. And there's no question of my car being moved, I'd left it locked. He did go back to his car after he came into the house, he went back to put his car away, and by then he had blood on his shoes.' And he smiled and said, directly to Thomas, in contravention to all court etiquette: 'My car was right across the entrance to your garage, old boy.'

The dead hand of Rosie reached up and jerked the noose tight.

CHAPTER FIFTEEN

And so it was Tedward who was brought to trial at last for the murder of Raoul Vernet—in Court No. 1, of the Central Criminal Courts, familiarly known as the Old Bailey; with Mr. Justice Rivett on the bench, Sir William Baines for the Crown, Mr. James Dragon defending. . . .

He stood at the foot of the narrow steps leading up to the dock; a thin, stooping, elderly man, now, in a suit much too large for him—no trace left at all of the comfortable solidity, the broad, friendly smilingness, the air of youth, the easy-going pride and integrity, the reliability and strength; only that ghostly, ghastly, heart-breaking, eternal pretence at cheerfulness. A decent bloke, the two prison officers said, who brought him to and from the court and throughout the trial would sit in the dock with him; already they had started an elaborate 'book' on his chances of condemnation or acquittal and, supposing the former, of his being reprieved or finally topped. Odds would fluctuate enormously during the course of the trial, especially before and after speeches by counsel and the summing-up; reaching fever point while the jury were out and again at the time of the inevitable appeal. By the day set for the actual topping, everyone in the prison world would have a little something, if only a couple of cigarettes, on the fate of Edwin Robert Edwards, charged on indictment that he did on November 23rd, of last year, etcetera, etcetera, etcetera.

Meanwhile, said the two prison officers, he seemed a very decent bloke.

They stood at the narrow stairway that leads up into the dock, one with his hand on Tedward's arm, one at the angle of the stairway where he could see the signal from the dock. There were three loud knocks and a sudden shuffle of many feet over their heads; the man on the stairs jerked his head and the man at his shoulder said, 'Here it comes, cock,' and gave Tedward a friendly shove. Their broad shoulders almost brushed the tiles as they went forward up the narrow stairway, from the tiled landing with its row of cells, the iron stairs twisting down to more tiled landings, more rows and rows and rows of cells, all with the pervading smell of dust and disinfectant. He came up into the great dock; from the vast dome above his head, light flooded down upon white walls, oak-panelled, upon carved wood and tooled leather, upon a sea of pink faces, white wigs, black gowns, here and there a touch of bright colour, and straight ahead of him, a splash of scarlet. It was like coming up from a public lavatory into a London park; and it was six long weeks since he had looked upon the faces of free men.

The court was resettling itself after the entry of the Judge. Mr. Justice Rivett was well over seventy and he had never got used to murder cases, never. Criminals were another matter he would say (*ad nauseam*) to his colleagues on the Bench, but a murderer was really a creature of accident; and every time he picked up that infernal square of black, and, carrying it folded in his hand as a woman carries her gloves, walked through that door heralded by the three knocks, in his bunched red dressing-gown of a robe, with the little tie wig perched over his own white hair, it turned his stomach over, it honestly did. So much abdominal churning necessitated a battered little tin of assorted pills known as 'my Neurotic Box' whose absence from his clerk's desk, close to his own, would have rendered his lordship a murderer in his own right. He glanced up and met the anxious eyes of the man in the dock; and thought, Another decent one—damn and bloody hell!

Tedward stood quietly at the front of the dock, a man on each side of him, raised a couple of feet above the rest of the court, level with the dais opposite him, with its seven great carved wooden, leather-backed chairs for the Judge and any Lord Mayors or Sheriffs or Aldermen who happened, by duty or inclination, to be there. Since it was not the opening day of the session, no Lord Mayor was present to see poor Tedward turned off; but a Sheriff in an ancient dark blue robe with a piece of rather tatty-looking black fur round the edge, sat ungracefully in the end chair, toying with his chain of glittering plaques. He looked at the rather shabby, rather untidy figure in the dock who, nevertheless, bore a hall-mark that he envied; and thought, Fancy!—a gent. For he himself was not a gent.

Between the two gents on dais and in dock, the long table with its brown-paper parcels of 'exhibits', its bulging envelopes and files; sitting at the table, the police officers concerned and the experts, Tedward's own solicitor, Mr. Granger, just below him, and further up the gentleman who stage manages the trial for the Public Prosecutor. Along the wall to his right, rising rows of benches; in the first counsel for the defence and the Crown, with their juniors; behind them barristers, robed and wigged, listening to the case from interest or curiosity or for the education of their minds; behind them again the 'fashionably dressed women' who would be in the papers to-morrow, having managed to wangle the coveted places there. Above them, eager faces peering down from the public gallery. To the judge's right, the witness-box, with the shorthand writer crouched in his little stall at its feet, fountain pen scribbling rapidly; and beyond, the two rows of benches where the jury of twelve sat solemnly regarding the man (a nice-looking chap too, just an ordinary person like theirselves) whom they were probably going to have to condemn to die. Some of them were pleased about it, exulting in their importance; some of them resentful. You had to come. You suddenly got a letter demanding your attendance on pain of lord knows what; and then there was a lot of hanging about and delay, two or three days sitting here in this very court, in the benches behind the dock, waiting till, as each new trial began, the names were shaken up in a box and at last your own turn came. Still, a murder trial was something; a bit more exciting than most of the stuff they had listened to while they waited, forgery and fraud and such—though some had been fruity enough, goodness knew, not to say downright naaaaarsty. . . . Below them were little loose-boxes housing the police and officials of the court; below them again, on the level of the table, a bench crammed to suffocation with the gentlemen of the press. There was a tremendous amount of hushing and shushing and everybody tried to be wonderfully quiet; the court was so furnished and designed as to make this as difficult as it could possibly be.

Outside the court, on the flagged, first floor landing, on narrow benches against the chilly wall, for hour after hour sat old Mrs. Evans and Matilda and Thomas and Melissa, waiting to be called as reluctant witnesses for the prosecution; trying to convince themselves that this was not all a hideous, horrible dream; that Raoul Vernet was dead and Rosie was dead, and they were here at the trial for murder of their dearest friend. The wide stone staircase curved on up above their heads and a ceaseless stream of people cast careless glances at them and idly wondered who they were.

In Court No. 1 the Clerk of the Court got to his feet and

mumbled out something which, if anybody could have heard it, would have signified that Edwin Robert Edwards was charged on indictment that on the 23rd of November in last year he had murdered Raoul Vincent Georges Marie Vernet at an address in Maida Vale, London. He raised his voice to add, chattily: 'Well, Edwin Robert Edwards, are you guilty or not guilty?'

One had gone through most of it once already at the Magistrate's court; but of course that only committed you to come here and stand trial for your life. This was more, sort of—conclusive. Tedward said in a voice not his own, 'Not guilty.' His attendants took him by the upper arms and shoved him gently backwards on to a wooden chair. Sitting down, with his head and shoulders only just appearing over the wooden side of the dock, he felt less assured than ever, he felt he lost every last vestige of dignity. Still, one couldn't stand up for three days, or however long it lasted. . . . Through the hot swimminess in his head, thoughts darted like little fishes. Two or three days; and at the end of that time he would know, perhaps, his exact 'expectation of life'. How many times he, himself, had been called upon to deliver the death sentence. . . . Had the victim cared two hoots, then, about the cosy glow of the stove in his comfortable old surgery? Had the careful preparation really made very much difference, had the promises of help and friendship to the end meant anything at all? Yet surely it was better, thought Tedward, than to stand here under this bright white light and be told abruptly that within so many weeks now, one was to hang by the neck till one was dead. . . . And he tore his mind from that glimpse of home because it brought with it a vision of Rosie, curled up in the big chair by the stove, running her hands through the shining, short black hair of the Anthracite Cat. Rosie's white hands were grey now, part of a heap of grey ashes in a carved wooden box that nobody quite knew how to dispose of.

The Crown was represented by the Attorney-General, Sir William Baines, commonly known as S'Will; and a jolly good name for him too, thought many an optimist who had previously hoped he might just get away with it. It was his task now to run through the outline of the case for the benefit of the Judge—who knew all about it anyway—and the jury who must be asked to pretend to themselves that they hadn't read every detail of it in the papers: to outline the case for the prosecution, to make a sort of blank map, as it were, upon which the jury might place the facts and figures as they emerged through the evidence of witnesses. Hardly waiting for the court to settle, he got to his feet, hitched one heel up against the edge of the bench behind him, and, slightly swaying as he spoke, addressed himself in conversational tones to my lord and members of the jury. He reminded my lord, who seemed to have heard it somewhere before, and the members of the jury who would need to be reminded of it over and over again through the progress of the case, that it was for himself as representing the prosecution, with the aid of witnesses, to establish a case against the accused; it was *not* for accused to establish his innocence. And the case for the prosecution was this: that this man, Edwards, had struck and killed a man whom he believed to have seduced the girl he loved. Not that it was for the Crown, members of the jury, to prove a motive; it need not matter to the jury why the thing had been done, only that it be proved *to have been done by this man*. But in this case—in the submission of the prosecution—the motive was perfectly clear and it was important because without it, the jury might think that there was nothing whatsoever to connect the accused with the murdered man. He had not known the man; until the day of the crime, it might be that he had never so much as heard the name of the man: and yet, if one accepted the motive put forward by the Crown, then it would seem that these very facts operated in favour of his having killed the man. For Raoul Vernet was not, in fact, the betrayer who had seduced the girl; and Counsel would try to prove to them later that the accused, Edwards, was the only person concerned who might have supposed that he was.

'Now, I think I had better start,' said Sir William, changing feet, 'by taking you back to the third week in November last year, when Rosie Evans arrived back from six months in Switzerland.' He took them back to the third week in November and through the history of Rosie's revelations and the family reactions to them; easily, comfortably, conversationally, he sketched in the scene, the lovely, shabby old house in Maida Vale, the old lady in her room upstairs, the young lady in her flat in the basement, the devoted brother and the not quite so blindly indulgent sister-in-law; the casual routine which in one respect only was not casual at all—that the baby must be brought up with absolute regularity and that this regularity extended to nine-thirty in the evening when its mother, without fail, went up to the nursery to attend to its infant needs. . . . (The jury, and indeed the whole court, indulged in a sentimental vision of the, as yet unseen, Matilda sitting quietly in the firelight suckling her Littel One, and were later rather shaken at discovering that the child was well over two years old.)

And this habit, this unfailing habit, members of the jury was well known to everyone, was a sort of family joke—certainly was well known to the accused; and it was the contention of the prosecution. . . .

Forty minutes later he concluded abruptly that he would now call witnesses to support what he had been saying (which as far as the jury were concerned was entirely un-necessary for Tedward was as good as in the condemned cell already), and wriggled his cramped leg free from its un-comfortable angle and sat down with a bump, raising his seat slightly from the bench to add: 'I call Matilda Evans,' and sit down again.

Matilda, who always dressed in black because it made her look thinner, had gone out and bought an entire outfit of navy blue, because to wear black at Tedward's trial did sort of seem . . . Well, anyway, she had bought a blue frock and a blue coat and a blue hat with two white wings to it, tremendously gay. She felt frightfully fat in the blue and her new shoes seemed to echo like thunder through the hushed court as she followed the officer across the polished, linoleumed floor, round behind the dock and along the narrow pathway between the central table and the jury box. Up some polished steps, clatter, clatter, clatter, and into a little wooden box like a pulpit with a canopy. Her head felt full of Thermogene, everything swam in a blur before her; but as she lifted her eyes, trying to focus, trying to shake her mind free of its stupor in preparation for the ordeal to come, she felt the mists clear a little and there in the clearness, was a face she knew—so thin and drawn and unhappy, and yet still the strong, the reassuring one, looking across at her with a little, affectionate smile that said, 'Go to it, love, everything'll be all right, you'll see!' Tears pricked her eyelids; she looked down again. The usher, in a black gown, thrust a prayer book into her hands and she swore by Almighty God in a very croaky voice and gave the book back to the man.

She had been through most of this once already in the magistrate's court and was familiar with the curious means to which counsel must resort in obtaining the required information from his witnesses, without asking questions that would put the answers into their mouths. ' . . . And the next day—did you see someone . . .?' ' . . . That morning— did you do something . . .?' She obediently volunteered, therefore, that Raoul Vernet had been her friend (she departed somewhat from the oath she had sworn a few minutes earlier, in describing the exact nature of her friendship with Raoul, but consoled her conscience with the reflection that the oath applied only to relevant facts and that this had really nothing to do with the case), and that he had rung her up on the morning of his death and said that he 'wanted to have a talk with her'. No, they had never got around to their talk. . . . Well, all right, Counsel might think that was curious, but she supposed a Frenchman would have too much respect for his digestion to spoil his dinner with an unpleasant discussion. 'You know what French people are,' said Matilda, falling into her own easy stride as the mists of unfamiliarity gradually cleared and she began to see Sir William as just a rather attractive man trying to get her to admit something she didn't want to— just like so many attractive men, all one's life!—'they're always worrying about their ventres and things, aren't they?' As to why she should have expected it to be an unpleasant discussion, well, it usually was when people said in that sort of dark way that they 'wanted to talk' to you. She glanced up at the judge, sitting austere and remote behind his great desk, just a little to the right of the black and gold sword that hangs, point up, beneath the Royal Arms, and for an instant thought that she recognised an answering gleam; excitement rose in her as she felt the old magic begin to work, knew that she had won him over, knew that so the jury would be won over, knew that for all Sir William's cleverness, while she was in the witness-box the court was 'on her side'. Sir William saw the lift of her head and the light in her eye, and thought: I shall have to keep on the right side of this one! She was his witness but she was frankly reluctant. The man in the dock was her friend.

So they came at last to the hour of the murder. 'Did you then—go somewhere?' 'Yes, I went upstairs.' 'What did you do there?' 'Well, first I went to my—well, actually she's my grandmother-in-law, to help her to get ready for bed. . . .'

A couple of minutes with Gran, five minutes alone in her room, 'doing her face', back to Gran for another five minutes or so, and then to the nursery as the clock struck half-past nine. As she went she had called down that she wouldn't be long, but there had been no reply. No, you couldn't see down to the hall from there.

'You were upstairs in all—about how long?'

'Between twenty and twenty-five minutes.'

'During this time—did you hear any disturbance in the hall?'

'No, I didn't,' said Matilda. 'But you see . . .'

'Just answer the questions, Mrs. Evans; don't elaborate.'

Matilda went slightly pink and folded her lips. Sir William thought, Now I've done it!—but I had to stop that one. Having gained the admission he wanted, however, he was a great deal too clever to press the point or even to ask a further question to make the significance clear. The defence would do that for him, they couldn't help themselves, when they came to cross-examine. 'Later on, however, did you hear something in the hall?'

'No,' said Matilda with an air of bland surprise; *not* elaborating.

'You heard nothing?'

'No,' said Matilda.

'Well, come, you haven't lived in a world of silence from that hour to this. When did you next hear something?'

'When I opened the door and went downstairs to the hall,' said Matilda, with a most regrettable air of sucks to you.

With nobs on, thought James Dragon, lolling back against the polished wooden bench, watching his colleague with an air of pitying surprise not lost, and not intended to be lost, upon the jury. When at last he rose to cross-examine, he came straight back to this point. 'While you were upstairs—you heard no sounds at all from the ground floor?'

'No, nothing, till I came out and went downstairs and found Dr. Edwards and Rosie in the hall.'

'Did you hear them arrive?'

'No, I didn't,' said Matilda.

'You didn't hear the car? Or the front door opening?'

'No, I didn't. But the window was closed while the baby was out of her cot.'

'Earlier, you were in old Mrs. Evans room?'

'Yes, but I didn't hear anything from there either,' said Matilda obligingly.

'It would have been possible, then, for this man to have been killed in the hall, *at any time during the twenty-five minutes when you were upstairs* without your hearing a disturbance?'

'Well, he was, *was*n't he?' said Matilda. She had seen something of Mr. Dragon during the nightmare of preparation for Thomas's trial, and knew just where she was with *him*.

'Now, you looked down to the hall and—well, just describe in your own words the scene you saw there.'

It would be there for ever, petrified in her memory like a fly in amber—herself, with her hand on the banister at the turn of the stairs, the front door standing open with the grey fog curling in and, wreathed about with the fog, like a scene from the witches' heath in Macbeth, Tedward standing with Rosie close at his shoulder, her hand clutching his sleeve, both lifting their heads sharply to stare up speechlessly at her; and at their feet, the long, thin body in the too bright suit, the pointed brown shoes, toe down to the floor, the ringed blue socks; the terrible head. 'They were standing close together. . . . Well, I took it for granted that they'd come in together. . . . No, nothing at all to suggest that she came in after him. . . . They both just looked horrified. . . .'

'At what stage did Dr. Edwards say that the man was dead?'

'I think it was almost the first thing. I said, "Is he dead?" and he said "I'm afraid so," or something like that.'

'Did he say how long he'd been dead?'

'Well, at one stage he said that he didn't think he'd been dead very long.'

'Dr. Edwards—the defendant—he said that? He said that the man had not been dead very long?'

'Yes. He said, "He wasn't killed outright,"—at the time of the telephone call, I suppose he meant—"he's only been dead a minute or two." '

' "He's only been dead a minute or two"?'

'Yes.'

'In view of the case against the accused—that he had himself just killed the man, a minute before, that would seem a dangerous admission on his part?'

Counsel for the Crown turned back a page or two of his notes and scribbled in the margin; plans for his closing speech ran like a Mr. Jingle conversation, through his mind. 'Clever move—other doctor back any minute—police surgeon too—confirm time of death—going to be known anyway—suggest it himself—get it in first. . . .'

'Was any reference made to the telephone call?'

'Yes, he said—well, I can't exactly say how it came about

or what order it was all said in, but he did say that it must be nearly half an hour since Raoul Vernet had rung up and said he'd been hit, and that he must have passed out and been lying there unconscious. . . .'

The shorthand writer in his little box just below the witness-box was perhaps the only person in court who was not quite sorry when Matilda, with a tentative little bow to the judge, was led away to a seat tucked down on the left-hand side of the dock; heaven send him a brief, snappy one next, thought the shorthand writer, upon whose aching hand Matilda's otherwise rather charming verbosity had made excessive demands. His prayer was granted, for Thomas Evans came next and anything less chatty it would have been hard to imagine. He wore the resentful look he always assumed when he was ill at ease, and spoke in a low, grumbling voice. He was very pale and his hair, which had been brushed down ruthlessly into a sort of ordered thatch, now stood on end again with the weary passing through and through of his fingers as they waited wretchedly on the bench in the corridor outside the court. Yes, he had known the accused for a long time; they were in partnership together. Yes, he had had a sister named Rose Evans. Yes, his sister was now dead. Yes, the accused had known her for many years, since she was a child. Yes, the accused was much older than she was, twenty years older than she was. . . .

'Was he fond of your sister, do you know?'

'Yes,' said Thomas.

'Very fond of her?'

'Yes,' said Thomas.

'Had you, in fact, reason to believe that he was in love with her?'

'Yes,' said Thomas. He lifted his head and looked across the intervening space to where Tedward sat heavy and sad, staring back at him; and his look said, What can I do, old boy?—they've subpœna'ed me and got me here and I've sworn an oath to tell the truth: and that *was* the truth, wasn't it? No easy compromises for Thomas Evans; the truth was the truth.

They came to the message, the message that had been written on his pad. It had been there when he came in that evening. He hardly remembered the thing—he had copied the name and address into his book and chucked the little paper into the fire. Well, the fire had been there and he had thrown the paper *in*, that was all. No, that was not his usual procedure, but messages were usually written down on a pad, and he naturally didn't throw the *pad* into the fire each time. No, this message had not been actually on the pad, but on a small piece of paper lying on the pad. No, not very unusual: if someone took the message on the upstairs extension, they'd write it down on any handy scrap of paper and leave it by the pad. Well, all right, Counsel could think it as casual as he liked; we did not all live our lives in hourly expectation of having to produce exhibits for a murder trial. . . . He mumbled an apology at his lordship's intervention, but his expression said, Then tell this damn fool not to comment, and I won't either.

The court had heard from Matilda that Tedward had called at the house that morning. Could the writing on the slip of paper have been Dr. Edwards writing? 'It could have been anybody's writing,' said Thomas. 'It was in printed letters, the address and a couple of words of diagnosis.'

'Is it usual to have such messages taken down in printed letters?'

'You haven't seen my secretary's handwriting,' said Thomas.

'Might Dr. Edwards have known of your secretary's habit of taking down these messages in printed writing?'

'He might have.'

'He was a constant visitor to your home?'

'Yes.'

'So he almost certainly did know?'

'Yes,' said Thomas, bleakly, once again; and Sir William's Mr. Jingle ran through his head again, 'Called at house—heard man was coming—resolution formed—note left in surgery—mallet—gun . . .' But they had not yet come to the mallet and the gun; he stopped jingling and applied himself to the task of extracting in monosyllables from Thomas that Tedward would have known where the mallet was kept, and in looking for the mallet might well have come across the gun. As to the fog. . . . Counsel had never quite made up his own mind whether or not the fog had been necessary to Tedward's plan. Matilda had admitted, grudgingly because she did not see where the question might be leading, that already that morning there had been signs that by nightfall the fog would be thick. He might as well get them all to agree to that; if he found later on that he didn't want it, he need not use it. Thomas duly admitted that he had actually remarked that morning that it 'looked like fog'.

Really, the jury quite pitied that poor Counsellor for the Prosecution, the way the Counsellor for the Defence kept looking at him as if to say, You poor thing, can't you think of nothing better than *that?* They sat in two patient rows of six, dutifully trying to remember every single answer to every single question, and utterly fogged as to what it was all leading up to, except that of course he *done* it, but they mustn't make up their minds to that till the end. One thing, that Mr. Dragon did look so contemptuous about all this stuff about the fog. And then going for the doctor like one o'clock. Dr. Evans, you don't set up to be a weather prophet. . . .? When you say you thought there would be fog. . . .? So that you couldn't have *counted* on there being a fog, if you had happened to want a fog that night. . . .? In fact, all you could say was that you thought there might possibly be a fog. . . .?

('Fog useful after all—lead old James up garden about fog—plan not affected either way by fog—leave girl in car—close door of hall—couldn't see anyway— . . .' The fog would keep Thomas Evans out of the way for a longer period, but then the crime had been planned for much earlier, no doubt; for a quarter past nine, perhaps, as soon as Matilda Evans went upstairs; it was Rosie's late arrival that had kept them back till almost the last moment. 'Even so—all not lost—arrive at house—no light in nursery—plan abandoned—telephone call an unexplained hoax. . . .')

At five to one, his lordship looked up at the clock beneath the public gallery and said civilly to S'Will that if it suited *him*, perhaps this would be a convenient moment to adjourn? Sir William, who knew all about the Judge's digestive troubles during the course of a murder trial said yes, certainly, m'lord, of course, of course. Tedward awoke from a sort of dream of pain and stupor and, at a touch on his arm, rose to his feet. His lordship gathered up the black cap; it lay, a narrow, folded square, through the ring of his thumb and forefinger, falling equally across his palm and the back of his hand. He bowed to the court and the court, including a great many people who had no call to do so, since he was not addressing his courtesies to them, bowed back. The Sheriff hitched up his fur-edged gown and stood aside at the door and his lordship bustled through. He thought, I hope to goodness they've laid on something reasonable for my lunch. The prison officers touched Tedward on the arm again and he turned with them and plunged below; they had laid on something very reasonable for *him* at any rate, and he ate it, all alone in his narrow, tiled cell, at the tiny table, perched on the single, small wooden chair. The smell of dust and disinfectant pervaded all.

In the end, they had all gone wretchedly and self-consciously down to the Garden of Remembrance and deposited Rosie's ashes in an arbitrarily chosen spot. For a moment she came to the door of his cell and said that she was too utterly *mis.* to see him cooped up there, and to think that it was ackcherly, let's face it, her who had put him there; and she put out her hand to him and he clutched at it, and saw that it was a hand of ashes, really, of pale, pink and white, feathery ash, like cigarette ash, that broke and fell the moment he touched it. Oh, well, he thought, scrubbing away the vision from his aching eyes, what the hell!—in a few weeks time I shall be dead and out of it. But he thought again, with bitter pain, that Rosie had been like this vision of the ashen hand; you thought that she was real and you put out your hand in faith, to her reality and her loveliness; and she fell away to dirt and ashes at your touch.

It was extraordinary, it was fantastic, even after all they had been through during the various appearances, both of Thomas and of Tedward, at the Magistrate's court, to be having lunch during the adjournment interval of Tedward's trial—to be sitting in a restaurant, eating their lunch as though they were ordinary people, jostled against by ordinary people, whose eyes would have popped out of their heads had they known that these were important witnesses at the trial of Dr. Edwards—*you* know, that chap that done that Frenchman in, hit him on the head with a mastoid mallet, just like what they must've used on our Ernie in hospital, and I'm sure if I'd've know what they did there, hammering away at the pore child with a great sort of a hammer like that, I'd've never have let him go. . . . Cockie sat with them; he was being called, in his private capacity, as a witness to the scene on the night of Rosie's death. 'Yes, I know you've already given evidence about it, Tilda, and probably they'll ask Thomas too, when they resume this afternoon; but they have to get what everyone says—not just a selected few of the people who were there. There might be discrepancies.' He broke off as the waitress came round with their plates of chicken casserole. 'It looks like boiled handkerchiefs,' said Matilda. 'Well, never mind. . . .' When the girl had gone, she said: 'You're sure they won't ask you about—later on?'

'I shall testify to being the last person to see Rosie alive,' said Cockie briefly; and once again wished to God they would not all feel sorry for him because he had been the one to get up and go away and leave Rosie to die. He said, coldly: 'Her name must come up a good deal, and there has to be formal evidence as to why she's not here to testify. That's all.'

'If they ask you what she said about Tedward . . .?' said Thomas hesitantly.

'I've told you, they won't ask me; they can't.'

Matilda sat staring down at her untouched plate. 'Just if they did, Cockie—you wouldn't say . . .? I mean, it would be the end of Tedward, if that was said, flat out in court.'

'I daresay Cockie would get round it,' said old Mrs. Evans; she flashed him a smile that had stood her in good stead throughout her life—a smile that said that men were so clever and strong and kind that all one had to do was just rely on them, and everything would be all right. 'Cockie doesn't want poor Tedward to suffer, any more than any of us.'

'You are all very pig-headed,' said Cockie, crossly. 'What the soldier said is not evidence, and what Rosie said to me is not evidence because she did not say it in the presence of the accused; they can't ask me, and that's flat.'

'You told Inspector Charlesworth,' said Melissa in a resentful voice; honestly, thought Cockie, seldom could an apparent murderer have been so loyally defended by the witnesses for the Crown. 'My dear child, the police hear, and act upon, a great many things that can't be produced in court. The rules of evidence are peculiar to themselves.'

Thomas wound strings of stewed chicken round his fork and put the resultant bundle back on his plate, in disgust. 'What about a "dying deposition", Cockie. That doesn't apply?'

'The whole point about a dying deposition is that it must have been made in the knowledge that one was going to die; the law assumes that at such a time, a man will speak the truth.'

Thomas put his knife and fork together and thrust the plate away from him. He said: 'Yes, I see. And of course we don't know whether or not Rosie knew she was going to die.'

'The fact that at the last moment she did tell the truth,' said Cockie, 'does seem to suggest that she did.'

The choice of puddings was narrow and all of them were horrible. 'Could we have some biscuits and cheese, please, and the coffee at the same time; and we're in rather a hurry.' To Cockie, Matilda said, keeping her voice low so that the closely crowded tables about them might not hear what they were saying, 'How does one know, Cockie, that that was the truth?'

'Why in God's name should she have told a lie?'

'Charlesworth's brilliant idea,' said Thomas, 'was that Tedward killed Rosie—or let her kill herself with the stuff— to prevent her saying just what, in the end, she did say.'

'Poor Tedward,' said Matilda; 'who would have given Rosie the sun and the moon and the stars!'

'It was because I told him about all her lovers,' said Melissa in a low voice. Her nervous fingers fiddled ceaselessly with the corner of her napkin where the hem was coming undone.

Matilda was sorry for the girl; she looked so white and worn-out, nowadays, with dark shadows under her eyes and a look of cowed despair that was dreadful in one so young. Thomas made matters no better; he was not unkind, but he could not get out of his mind that she was the instrument through which had been shattered for ever such last little shreds of his happy illusions as had been left to him; and he could not be kind. Matilda said: 'If Tedward could have killed Rosie, Melissa, it wouldn't have been because of that: or it wouldn't have been like that—thought out and planned and put into deliberate operation. If he had hated her because of what you said, he might have raised his hand against her then, in the moment of the first shock. But he didn't hate her; he may have ceased to love her, I think in a sort of way he did—but he didn't begin to hate her. You were there—you could see that.'

'Charlesworth could say,' suggested Cockie, shrugging, 'that it was a combination of the two. He wouldn't have killed her, even to save his own neck, because he loved her. But, having ceased to love her—he might have killed her.'

'Except that it wasn't a case of saving his own neck,' said Thomas. He reached for the bill and glanced at it and folded it over again on itself, but he still had no idea what the figures were. 'All Rosie could say was that he *had* come into the house before she did; in other words, that it was possible for him to have killed the man. That wasn't going to convict him; the police still had to build up a case, which they'd probably have built up anyway, because nobody was going to just take Rosie's word for it, if she'd said that he didn't go into the house ahead of her. And rightly so.' He unfolded the bill again and this time fished in a pocket for the small roll of crumpled notes which was his fashion of carrying money about. 'Rosie would have lied like a trooper for Tedward, if she'd wanted to; and the thing is that she would never have let him go through this, she'd have contradicted herself right and left to save him. And she could have; nobody knew anything about that last hour or so, except Rosie. She could have "remembered" that Tedward was only in the house a split second before she was, or she could have made up something about the telephone call which would have made that trick impossible.' The waitress brought his change, and he dropped a couple of coins back on to the plate and got to his feet. 'Whatever it was that made Rosie say that about Tedward at the last minute, she would have told lies to save him in the end. Of all people in the world, Tedward was the very last to have wanted her to die.' His arms flailed as he heaved himself into his coat. He said, irritably, 'Come on—we'll be late.' Everyone else had been ready for five minutes at least.

Mr. Justice Rivett looked at the clock in his room across the corridor from the court, and sighed and had recourse to his Neurotic Box; in the corridor, counsel and their colleagues settled their wigs so as to be comfortable for the next two hours, having recently been notified that the habit of lifting them off in court and wriggling them on again, really did not look well; up in the gallery *hoi polloi* pushed and craned, below them the fashionably dressed ladies squeezed themselves not much more decorously into their inadequate seating space. The jury, who had broken up into groups during their lunch in the jury-room and so made friends, filed back into their places; it was odd how familiar the court seemed when they thus returned to it. Cockrill and Melissa and old Mrs. Evans returned to their weary wait in the corridor, and Matilda to her place in the body of the court. An usher stood at the ready with Thomas at his side, waiting to go back to the witness-box; in the dock, a prison officer was alert to give the signal for Tedward to start up the narrow stairs, as though his slow ascent were some nightmare sporting event. Three loud raps at the judge's entrance, the court scrambled to its feet, stood, bowed, sat down again; and, unleashed, Tedward began mechanically to stump up the stairs, and Thomas to clatter across the floor to the witness-box. Sir William gathered a handful of papers in one hand, tucked up one heel against the bench behind him, and asked another question as though the last had been answered just a moment ago. Outside, the January darkness slowly descended upon the great dome, and along the oak panelling round the recesses of the walls, strip lighting burst into its fluorescent glow. Outside, the newsvendors chalked up in red on their board-papers, 'MAIDA VALE MURDER CASE: MRS. EVANS IN THE BOX,' and round the arched doorway a little crowd of early home-goers assembled in the hopes of distinguishing her by her picture in the papers, as she walked down the steps; or of seeing the great black gates open and a dark closed-in van drive away with the murderer and seven other inferior criminals caged up in eight tiny boxy compartments inside. In fact, so distinguished a malefactor would have a car all to himself: a discreet dark car with drawn blinds, slipping in silent anonymity through the byways to Brixton; but they were not to know that and they confidently reported at home having 'seen the murderer'—Mum and Dad and little Ruby were thrilled; and it did make something to talk about after the uneventful office day.

CHAPTER SIXTEEN

WE are like the ten little nigger boys, Melissa,' said old Mrs. Evans, sitting chilled and weary on the bench outside the court. 'Only you and me left now.' She quoted: 'One got frizzled up and then there was one,' and added thoughtfully that in America they did call it being 'grilled' she believed.

'Call what being grilled?' said Melissa absently, too much appalled by the thought of the ordeal to come, to pay much attention to anything dotty old Mrs. Evans could have to say.

'Being cross-examined,' said Mrs. Evans.

'It's all right if you just tell the truth,' said Melissa stoutly.

'*And* the-whole-truth; *and* nothing-but-the-truth.'

'You're all right if you've got nothing to hide,' said Melissa again.

'Nothing to hide: but then, who in this world has nothing to hide?'

'Well, you for one, Mrs. Evans, I should think,' said Melissa, humouring the old thing.

Mrs. Evans looked down at the little chips of diamond and sapphire, sparkling in her rings. She shifted her tack. 'Who do *you* think, Melissa, really killed that man?'

Melissa shrugged sullenly. 'The police say it was Dr. Edwards; isn't that enough?'

'Not for me,' said Mrs. Evans. 'They said it was my son, Thomas, a little while ago; but it wasn't, after all.'

'Well, who is there left?' said Melissa. She had brought a magazine with her, hoping to be allowed to read it in peace and—now that she had decided on her plan of campaign— put the coming ordeal out of her mind till the moment arrived. Now, however, on this cold, hard bench, almost within reach of the glass swing doors behind which an innocent man stood in peril of his life, it seemed sort of— indecent—to be reading a lot of tripe about girls marrying their bosses and countesses improving their complexions, and the new tulip neck. She said: 'Anyway, they'll never convict Dr. Edwards, so what does it matter?'

'Why not?' said Mrs. Evans, sharply. 'Why shouldn't they convict him?'

'Well, I thought you just said that you didn't believe he did it?'

'My dear child, who on earth cares what *I* believe? I'm not on the jury, am I? And, after all, as you yourself say— who else?'

'As far as the jury's concerned,' said Melissa, 'anyone else. The jury don't know anything about the rest of us.'

'They've all been reading the papers all this time. I know they're told to "put it out of their minds", but after all, of course they can't really do that; I mean, they can't just forget that the police from the first were convinced that it wasn't an "outside job", they can't just forget how few people that leaves in! And they must have read about Thomas being charged and released, and about me having arthritis and not being able to hit people over the head, worse luck; so that only leaves you and Matilda. And they know all about your alibi with that Belgian prince or whatever he was; no, he was a Pole, wasn't he?—or wasn't he? He never did turn up, did he?'

Melissa swung round on her, violently. 'What do you mean by that?'

Mrs. Evans looked blank. 'My dear child, what is the matter? I only said . . .'

'If the police accept my alibi . . .'

Mrs. Evans sat for a long, long minute in silence staring down at the little, sparkly stones. She said at last, slowly: 'I've been trying to think, Melissa, why I should have thought for a moment that that man was a Belge. I've remembered now: it was Raoul Vernet, *wasn't* it, who was a Belge? Everyone always goes on as if he'd been French, but he wasn't, he was a Belgian. He came from Brussels, he was on his way there when he died.' And she put out her hard old hand and caught Melissa by the wrist and said, '*When* was it you were at your finishing school in Brussels, my child?'

A uniformed arm pushed open the glass swing-door of the courtroom; a voice cried: 'Next witness: Miss Melissa Weeks. . . .'

The light in the wooden canopy over her head turned Melissa's smooth hair to a casque of shining bronze. Devoid of other armour, she took refuge behind it, drooping her head so that the burnished sweep of it covered half her face; her voice was an almost unintelligible whisper, she clutched at the wooden ledge of the witness-box with shaking hands. Self-consciousness run riot, thought Sir William irritably; he had only a few routine questions to put to her, she had been through it all before at least twice in the Magistrate's court. The judge, sorting through his box with a forefinger in search of a certain kind of pill, glanced up and said impatiently that the witness had nothing to be afraid of and she really must speak up. It was very important that they should all hear what she had to say. (Not that it is, he thought; the jury know the verdict already—and nothing she or anyone can say will change their minds.) Now—would she please turn and face that gentleman over there, and he would put his question to her once again and this time they *all* wanted to hear her reply. Sir William, infected by the prevailing desire for more noise, bawled out his question once more; and Melissa, thus harried, croaked out harshly that yes, she had heard voices in the hall and gone up from her basement flat and seen them all standing there, Dr. Edwards and Mrs. Evans and Rosie, all standing there looking down. And she had seen the body lying there on the floor, croaked Melissa, concentrating fiercely on making herself audible, only this time the feet were sticking up in the air and she realized that they must have turned him over on his back. . . .

The hush fell by degrees; as though touched by the wand of the wicked godmother, first counsel, then judge, then jury, witnesses, spectators, officials, the prisoner and his wardens in the dock were stricken silent and immovable, till at last, for a long moment, all was absolutely still. It was like the lull before an earthquake when all nature holds her breath in terrified anticipation of the violence to come: heavy, oppressive, menacing, interminable. And yet it ended; there was a sharp crack as the judge snapped-to the lid of his cheap tin box, and he leaned forward, over the arm of his chair and said in a voice almost as sharp as the crack of the box: '*What do you mean by "this time"? Had you seen it before?*'

Melissa stood shuddering in the little box, her white hands gripping the ledge, her face like a dead face, white and blank with wide-open, sightless eyes. Her mouth opened and shut but no sound came. She tried again, and her jaw chattered like the jaw of a cat, watching flies on a window pane; but she managed at last to splutter out a single word.

Yes.

Edwin Robert Edwards—*not guilty* of the murder of Raoul Vincent Georges etcetera, etcetera; for if Melissa had seen the body lying there before Tedward's car ever arrived at the house, then that was the end of the case against the accused. . . .

Both counsel were on their feet, looking for guidance to his lordship. He sat for a long moment looking down at the little box in his hand, and then opened it and replaced the digestive tablet. 'Let the witness sit down and rest for a moment.' He motioned to the woman police officer, standing uncertainly on the steps leading up to the witness-box. 'I daresay she would like some water—or perhaps you have something a little more stimulating . . .?' He swung round and hooked himself over the other arm of the chair. 'Well, Sir William—this was *not* in the depositions?'

'No, indeed, m'lord,' said Sir William ruefully.

'No. The question now arises . . .' He leaned his chin on his hand and gave himself over to earnest consideration; but already his breakfast sat more lightly on that uneasy stomach of his, for the thought that he would not be called on to pronounce the death sentence on this sad-eyed man, who through the long hours had sat with bowed head and sagging shoulders in the dock before him.

Tedward's head was bowed no longer. He sat straight in his chair, his hands gripping the edge of the box, his eyes blazing in his haggard face. All about him the court seethed with the slightly hysterical excitement of those who rejoice in holy places. Tilda sat gripping Thomas's hand, trying to see over the edge of the dock, to signal her triumphant happiness to the prisoner there. The fashionable ladies could or could not see what on earth the girl had said that had made all this difference, and explained it to each other with greater or less sense, usually in opposite ratio to their greater or less sense of dress. Up in the gallery, a young man shoved his way through the protesting crowd and, his own face very white, stared down at the white face in the witness-box.

The consultation ended, Sir William shrugged and smiled a little ruefully again, and sat down. James Dragon rose to cross-examine. The Judge said: 'If the witness would like to remain seated . . .? Would you like to stay sitting down?' In stalls and upper circle and gallery and pit, the audience settled back in their places in eager anticipation, for though the first act might have dragged a bit, the curtain had been terrific and now things looked like speeding up. Melissa shook her head mutely in response to the judge's invitation and got to her feet and, with the back of her hand, brushed aside her hair. It immediately fell forward, heavily, over her cheek again.

Mr. James Dragon. 'Um—Miss Weeks: you say that when you came up and found them all standing over Raoul Vernet's body in the hall—that was not the first time you had seen it there? Is that what you say?

'Yes,' whispered Melissa

'You had seen it there earlier?'

'Yes,' whispered Melissa.

'How much earlier? How long before?'

'About two or three minutes.'

'Can you tell us more exactly? Two minutes? Or three minutes?'

'Three minutes,' whispered Melissa.

'Perhaps you had better, just in your own words, tell us

under what circumstances you saw this body in the hall?'
He glanced at the judge and opposing counsel; you see, I
can't extract it by questioning, his glance said—I don't even
know myself what we're talking about. 'Now—just in your
own words.'

'And I'm sure you will do your best to let us all *hear* your
words,' said his lordship, benignly.

Melissa pushed back her hair again and lifted her head.
'I—I came up into the hall. . . . No, first I went out to pool
the dog. I went out by the basement door, by the garage
in the front of the house. And then I went up to the hall
by the basement stairs and I saw him lying there.' She
stopped.

'I see. He was lying there.'

'Yes. He was lying on his face with his head towards the
bureau, and one arm sort of still half-way up the bureau;
it looked as though his feet had sort of skidded away from
under him and he'd slithered down the bureau. He had the
telephone receiver in his other hand. It was sort of lying
outwards, on the floor.'

Counsel shifted about among his papers. 'Perhaps,
m'lord, the jury might see, er, Exhibit six; that's the police
photograph of the body arranged as it was alleged to have
been found. When the police saw it, of course, m'lord, it
had been turned over.'

The jury were by now fairly well inured to photographs
of Raoul Vernet's dead body and they passed it along the
rows, earnestly studying it, two at a time, like people in
church sharing hymn books. Allowing for a good many
'sort of 's', Melissa had described the position of the body
accurately enough.

'Very well; now, you'd come up from the basement
(where as we've heard, your room is) into the hall? Why?'

'Why?'

'Yes; why did you go up just then?'

'Well, I—just went up,' said Melissa. 'I . . . Well, you see, I'd been pooling the dog and the dog wanted to go up. I expect he wanted to go to the kitchen; for a drink, he always wants a drink when he's been for a walk.'

'Had you been for a long walk with him?'

'Oh, no,' said Melissa, 'only two trees down the road, the fog was too bad.'

'I see. And he wanted a drink, so you were taking him upstairs to the kitchen?'

'Yes; and when I got up to the hall—I saw—the dead body.'

'Did you know it was a dead body?'

'Well—yes,' said Melissa, shrugging doubtfully.

'How did you know?'

'Well, I suppose I couldn't know he was *dead*. I just—thought he was. He was quite still and his head was all—horrible.'

'What did you do?'

'I . . . Well, I went back downstairs,' said Melissa, whispering again.

'You went back downstairs. All right, don't be frightened: we only want to know what happened. What did you do then?'

'I was upset, seeing him there. And I couldn't have done him any good by staying,' said Melissa, beginning to bluster. 'There it was, he was dead, and I couldn't do anything for him. At least, anyway, I thought he was dead. And in fact he was, because then Dr. Edwards came in and he said at once, "He's dead," so he *was* dead.' She looked at Mr. Dragon quite triumphantly.

'*You-heard-Dr.-Edwards-come-in?*' said James Dragon. He repeated it after her, slowly, in a voice that was almost terrible. '*You heard Dr. Edwards come in, and he said at once,*

"*He's dead.*" ' He paused. He said: 'Well, now—who did he say that to?'

'He said it to Rosie Evans,' said Melissa.

A long silence. James Dragon stood with his thumbs hitched into the sleeves of his gown and frantically searched his mind for discrepancies and snags that ought to be dealt with now. The Attorney-General leaned back with his hands in his pockets and Jingled through a last-ditch speech for the Crown. Melissa had been his own witness, he could not now turn round and cross-examine her; all that was left to him was to pour scorn on her story, when the time came for him to address the jury. 'Friend of the accused—impressionable girl—case going against him—chance to assist—no one to contradict her—unsupported evidence—unlikely story. . . .' chattered the Attorney-General's Mr. Jingle; he added in a whisper to his junior that as a matter of fact there *were* bits of her story that didn't ring true. That drink for the dog. . . .

Mr. Dragon again. 'Did you *see* Dr. Edwards and Rosie Evans?'

'No, I was on the basement stairs; I was on my way down when I heard the front door, and I heard them come in and then he said that; and then I—well, I crept down, because I was too—too upset to face them then.'

'And later you came up and pretended that this was the first time you had seen the body?'

'Yes.'

('Case of Cox and Box?—man killed while she's out with dog—Edwards back to car to fetch Rosie—this girl pops up—*he* 'back with Rosie—*she* pops down. . . .?')

'Now, Miss Weeks, just let's go back a little way. When

you went out with the dog—was there a car outside the house?'

'No,' said Melissa.

'Can you be certain—considering the fog?'

'Well, Dr. Edwards' car wasn't there if that's what you mean,' said Melissa. 'It's supposed to have been across the entrance to the garage and that's the way I went, so I'd've bumped into it.'

'And did you go straight upstairs?'

'Oh, yes,' said Melissa. 'I absolutely ran.' She added quickly that Gabriel, well, that was the poodle, had run up and she had run after him.

So not Cox and Box after all; for in that brief space, the accused could not possibly have committed the crime and gone back for the girl. If Melissa's story was true, the case for the prosecution had gone up in smoke.

If it was true.

'Now, Miss Weeks, I want you to understand quite clearly that you need not answer any question which might incriminate yourself; you see, you've put us all in a very difficult position here, we don't know what we can ask you and what we can't; but if an answer will put you in the wrong, criminally in the wrong I mean, just don't say anything and I shan't press the question. On that understanding —can you explain to us *why* you have never told this story before?'

'I was afraid to,' whispered Melissa.

'Why should you have been afraid?'

'Well, I . . . Well, you see, I had an alibi, but they couldn't find him, so I thought they would think I was alone in the house when the man was killed.'

'Is it true there were two other people in the house?'

'They didn't make any difference as far as the murder was concerned. They were both upstairs.'

'You saw the body and you thought you might be accused?'

'Yes,' said Melissa wearily.

'But—you said, didn't you? at the Magistrate's court, that you'd never met this man, that you'd never set eyes on him. Why should you think anyone would suspect you of murdering him?'

(A thin, small hand like a bird's claw, covering her own hand with its bony grasp. . . . '*When* was it you were in Brussels, Melissa, eh?') Melissa improvised desperately. 'I was—I was protecting someone else.'

'All right, well, we won't have any names mentioned in court,' said Counsel, hastily. 'Afterwards you'll be able to inform the police and they can take what steps they like. You said nothing, because you were protecting someone else. At the expense of the accused here—Dr. Edwards?'

'Dr. Edwards wouldn't have minded. He's always doing things for people. And I knew he'd sympathize with anyone killing Raoul Vernet because he thought that Raoul Vernet had seduced Rosie. And besides, of course, I never thought it would come to this. . . .' She looked round the court, at the man in the dock, at the judge in his scarlet robe, at the magpies in their black gowns and curled white wigs. 'You don't sort of think in the beginning that people will *really* be accused and *really* go to prison; you never think for a moment that there's *really* any danger of them being found guilty when they haven't done the thing at all. . . .'

The judge leaned forward. 'Now, er—(what is the witness's name? Miss Weeks?)—Miss Weeks, you know, we mustn't have what we call "comment" in court. We have been patient with you, but you must try to confine yourself to answering the questions, and just keep calm. Nobody is accusing you of anything, nobody here will accuse you of anything. You say you told these—untruths—to protect a third person. That is enough, for the present, about that third person; the police can deal with that later, if need be. You have given us your reason for concealing the truth; now all we want is for you to convince us that your second story *is* the truth.' He waved a hand towards Mr. Dragon. 'Just answer the questions, and as briefly as you can.'

But Melissa heard not a word of it. She stood with her hands pressing down on the ledge of the witness-box, her shoulders hunched, her head hanging forward, her bright hair sweeping across her eyes, and gave herself up to an hysteria of terror. They don't believe me. . . . They'll say I did it. . . . I can never prove anything. . . . All these lies. . . . She was protecting someone. . . . She was protecting someone. . . . Someone that Tedward would have offered his life to protect. . . . Counsel put a question and she lifted her head and stared across at him with terrible, burning eyes. Her mouth would not work, her lips would not obey her, her tongue was pressed against her teeth, her jaw had begun to chatter again in a rigor of helplessness, and she stared and stared and, ignoring interruptions from judge and counsel and woman attendant alike, gibbered out that they could just ask Matilda Evans, that was all. . . . Just ask her if she had not been Raoul Vernet's mistress, just ask her if she had not said on the telephone that very day, that very day that he was murdered, something about making love to her, something about not being able to make love to her; ask her if she had not said that she was disappointed, ask her if he had not said that perhaps they could do that too but now he had to talk business or something like that. . . . 'I was listening,' said Melissa, sobbing and gibbering, brushing aside interruption and protest, 'I was listening on the extension, I didn't put back the receiver, I heard it all. . . .' Ask her, *ask* her if he had not told her that night that he had been Rosie's lover, ask her if it was not she who

214

had murdered him out of jealousy. . . . 'She was alone with him. . . . She got rid of everyone else. . . . *She* put that note there to get her husband out of the way, anyone could see that. . . . And the telephone call, she could have done the telephone call; perhaps she didn't really mean to kill him, perhaps she just hit him. . . . And she never could bear the sight of blood, she couldn't bear people in pain, she wouldn't just leave him there. . . .' She swayed and gibbered and suddenly pitched forward in a dead faint, and hung like a rag doll, with dangling arms, over the wall of the box; and into the moment of quiet that followed the sudden cessation of the shrill, gabbling voice, another voice cried out, from high above their heads: 'It's not true! It's all lies! She killed him herself—she told me so!'

Mr. Justice Rivett thought that perhaps, if it suited counsel, this might be an opportune moment to adjourn for lunch?

Inspector Cockrill said a word here and a word there and minions moved unobtrusively away—the habit of authority is strong and the habit of obedience to recognized authority: it was not till later that it occurred to any of them that he had no right to be giving orders there. He said a word to Charlesworth. 'You'll be a miracle worker if you can,' said Charlesworth. 'I'm for the high jump anyway, I should think.' Up in the gallery the crowd milled and chattered about an excited boy with a white face and rumpled, curly hair; in the body of the court, Melissa forgotten, everyone stood to stare. In the dock, the prison officers recollected themselves and hurriedly took Tedward's arms and bundled him below; through the glass screen that runs round the sides and back of the dock, he caught Matilda's eye as she eagerly strove to attract his attention, and smiled at her and shrugged a 'lord knows what it all means!' and, still smiling, disappeared from sight. Cockie came up to her and took her arm. 'Cockie! That *bitch* of a girl! Did you *hear* what she said?'

'*I* heard,' said Cockie. His bright eyes smiled at her with a mischievous delight. 'That'll teach you to flirt with nasty foreigners, my girl.'

'She did take that call . . . Thomas, darling, you do realize how the conversation went?'

'I know your little ways,' said Thomas. 'Let it be a lesson to you, as Cockie says.'

They shoved their way towards the door through the crowd whom the ushers were vainly trying to shoosh out of court. 'And that man in the gallery, Cockie, what on earth did he mean, "she told me herself"? Was it Stanislas? I couldn't see properly. But could it have been?'

'Never mind all that now,' said Cockie. 'You go and get your lunch. Thomas, take her along. I'll have to stay here, but I'll tell you what I'll do, I'll take the old lady off your hands; I can fix something for her here. You'll only get her over-excited and upset, and I don't suppose his lordship will put up with any more hysterics.'

Matilda stopped dead in her tracks? 'She surely won't have to give evidence now?'

'She's next. Go *on*.'

Matilda resumed her slow progress. 'But Cockie, they won't go on with all this? I mean, they *must* let Tedward go *now*?'

'My dear Matilda, this is a murder trial. You swear in a jury, the jury's got to give a verdict, and they can't do that without hearing the evidence, at least. What do you think happens? the judge just pops up and says, "Well, what do you know, boys?—let's call it a day." '

'They do sometimes stop trials in the middle,' said Thomas, fighting along in their wake.

'Not where everything's in a muddle like this. He'll round off the evidence and get a formal verdict; he'll have to. And if you two don't get a move on, you won't be here to see it, because you won't be back from lunch.'

They squeezed out of the door with the crowd and fanned out on to the broad landing. Gran had disappeared from her bench in the corner. 'I've borrowed a room,' said Cockie. 'I'll look after her. There'll be too much gossip and fuss in the restaurants.' He left them and started up the broad stairway; leaning over to call out, 'They'll take care of Melissa here; don't worry about *her*.'

'I won't,' said Matilda grimly, calling back.

Detective Inspector Cockrill might be able to 'borrow a room' in the Central Criminal Courts, but Chief Inspector Charlesworth had no such luck. He pinned his victim into a corner of a corridor and conducted his interview there. Mr. Granger, the solicitor who had been handed on to Tedward with much of the rest of the backwash from Thomas Evans' abortive trial, had been invited to stand by in the interests of his client. Sergeant Bedd was also present. 'Well, now, my lad,' said Charlesworth, 'what's all this?'

Damien spreadeagled himself in his corner in a vivid impersonation of a (Minority) Stag at Bay. 'I'd better warn you first that I'm a Communist.'

'O.K. so you're a Communist,' said Charlesworth. 'What's your name?'

'And as a Communist I do *not* think much of the British Police.'

'As a Communist, I don't suppose you think very much of the British. Now—your name and address.'

Sergeant Bedd licked the end of his ball-pointed pen; old

Charles had given it to him last Christmas and he had to use it, but he never could get used to the damn thing not being a pencil. He wrote down the name in his notebook—Damien Jones; and a Kilburn address.

'All right,' said Charlesworth. 'What have you got to tell me?'

'I've got something to give you,' said Damien. He fished in the bulging pocket of his mackintosh and lugged out a large brown shoe which he stuffed under one arm, heaving up his shoulder to get at the other pocket and extract its fellow. Charlesworth took them gingerly and turned them over and looked at them carefully. 'What's this?'

'It's a pair of shoes,' said Damien savagely.

'Who do they belong to?'

'They belong to a Mr. Hervey,' said Damien. 'He lives in my mother's boarding house; or, as *she* would say, he's a paying guest.' He put on a fancy voice for this contemptible confession of snobbery.

'I see,' said Charlesworth. 'And what have Mr. Hervey's shoes got to do with Raoul Vernet's murder?'

'They've got his blood all over them,' said Damien.

Charlesworth turned them over again and looked at their soles. They were new shoes, but they had been worn and fairly recently; indeed, one would have thought them still rather damp after yesterday's light rain. '*I* don't see any blood on them.'

'There's none to see,' said Damien. 'I've wiped it all off. But you'll find it's there. There are always traces left, aren't there? In the seams and things.'

Charlesworth handed the shoes to Bedd. 'Do something or other with them. Now, look here, Jones, let me get this thing straight. These shoes belong to a Mr. Hervey who lodges in your mother's house. They were, at one time at any rate, stained with the blood of this murdered man, Raoul Vernet. And it was you who wiped away the blood?'

'Yes,' said Damien. 'You see it was me who got it on.'

Back in the witness-box, restored to a sort of nightmare calm, Melissa recanted right, left and centre and, lifting her white face to the gallery, said that now that—now that other people that all this time she had been so loyally protecting, had tried to shelter behind her skirts, now she would tell the truth and the whole truth and nothing but the truth, so help her God indeed! Unaware that Damien was still pinned in his corner and far out of hearing, she poured out the story of that dreadful night. Nobody stopped her, nobody checked her; she was a witness in the course of giving evidence, she had a right to be heard, and judge and counsel exchanged glances and shrugged their shoulders and gave it up. The whole thing was like Bedlam already and it might as well run its course; the police officers concerned, would doubtless be hearing all about it in due time, it was possible that the Director of Public Prosecutions might address a few remarks to his staff; but meanwhile, you couldn't stop a trial on the grounds that it had been inadequately prepared, and the only thing to do was to concentrate on trying to keep its lunacies within the limits of procedure laid down by the law. So Melissa, her white face lifted to the gallery, lived once again through the night of Raoul Vernet's death, and forgot to whisper, forgot to stumble, forgot to hide behind her curtain of curly hair; forgot the black cap and the scarlet robe, forgot the white wigs and black gowns, forgot the jury, forgot the spectators, forgot the shorthand writer below her, scribbling away, scribbling away, scribbling away. . . .

It had all been Rosie's fault, the whole thing was her fault, everything beastly was always Rosie's fault. She went through her world so gay, so lighthearted, dancing through fields of flowers on delicious bare feet, and everyone stopped to watch her and felt the better for seeing her, and thought, how enchanting, how heart-warming, how sweet! And nobody stopped to see how under the fat, white feet the flowers were broken and bruised; and nobody paused to consider whose flowers they were. So many of them had been Melissa's flowers: silly little wild flowers of hopes or illusions, crushed out of existence by the capering, careless feet. And then had come Stanislas, and Rosie had been away in Switzerland and everything had been so safe and wonderful. Rosie, it was true, had capped the story of Stanislas, mysterious background and all, with her doings in Geneva; but Melissa would rather have had a date with Stanislas, thanks, than with a Maternity Hospital, and Melissa had had a date with Stanislas for that Tuesday night. There had turned out to be a bit of a fog, it was true, but Stanislas wasn't going to be put off by mere fog. In perfect confidence that he would call for her as arranged, she had dressed herself up ('Do wear that green thing of yours, my dear; I like my women to wear green . . .'), and decided on the *other* green thing, and changed, and been ready again, and changed back again, and at half-past seven was feverishly putting a different feather in her hat and waiting for his knock at the basement door. She heard Rosie fumble her way down the steps from the front door and, cursing, wrestle with the latch of the gate. She thought, well, if Rosie can go out in it, he'll get here all right. Rosie's faltering footsteps died away, muffled in fog. There was no other sound.

An hour later, chilled and depressed, the bright eagerness faded, anxiety and irresolution setting in, and yet still with a conviction in her heart that what one so ardently desired could not, surely, be denied, she went out to the gate for the tenth time and listened, peering up the shrouded road, for the footsteps that would bring him looming up through the fog, to her. Not a sound, not a footfall, not a human voice; even the ceaseless rumble of London traffic was muffled and still. She crept along the pavement a little, feeling her way with a hand against the walls of the little front gardens of the Maida Vale houses. I'll go to the cross-roads, she thought. I can't miss him that way. It would do not the slightest good, but anything was better than waiting at home; and, after all, she might easily meet him and have just that moment more of time with him.

A little way up the hill at the cross-roads, there was a telephone booth. The thought came into her mind that she might ring him up and see if by any chance he had had to turn back and go home. She hadn't liked to go upstairs and ring, because Mrs. E. was there with her boy friend; and anyway, she hadn't dared to leave the basement door, in case he knocked and, receiving no answer, went away. She fumbled her way up the hill to the call-box, feeling in her handbag for pennies. There was somebody in the box. She went on up the hill a little way and waited. In a minute or two I'll go down and cough outside the door, she thought. It's probably only a Tender Couple gone in there out of the fog, to neck. On a bad night, you could never get *into* a Maida Vale telephone booth, they were all full of necking couples. . . .

And sure enough, there were two people in the booth. She h'mm'ed at the door, and a man's voice said, 'Oh, lor', someone wants to use the 'phone,' and added in a would-be American accent that they would have to break it up, Sugar, and go out into the cold, cold night. And a girl's voice said, 'Well, it's been nice knowing you,' also in a pseudo-American accent, and they came out and, arms entwined, started off, without a glance at intruding Melissa, down the little hill. And the man's voice said, What now? and the girl's voice said that ackcherly she simply *must* go now, because she was hours late for her appointment already and it was all his fault. And he said well then, where should he ring her up to-morrow? and she said that by to-morrow she would be overcome with shame at her shocking behaviour, and certainly would never be able to look him in the face; and they must just be passing ships or whatever that thing was, and not try and find out who each other was, because honestly, she was *not* a person who picked up people in fogs and—and had petting parties in telephone booths. And he said where *did* she have her petting parties, then, because he'd like to be there some time; and added that come on, he'd see her to wherever she was going, because he'd crashed his date anyway and might as well be hanged for a sheep as a lamb. . . . The pseudo-American accents faded as they wandered off down the hill and disappeared into the fog; and the last of Melissa's poor little field-flowers crumpled and died beneath the clop, clop, clop of Rosie's high-heeled shoes.

She went into the call-box and dialled a different number. No use ringing up Stanislas now; she knew for certain that he was not at home.

Damien Jones, however, was at home. He was having a meeting, said Damien's mother, who never could remember that a Branch Leader, even a Twig Leader, did not care to have his activities noised haphazardly abroad. 'Well, never mind the meeting,' said Melissa. 'I want to talk to him.'

But Mrs. Jones at least knew better than to disturb a meeting. 'You must,' said Melissa. 'Tell him it's a Comrade. In most terrible trouble.'

Damien, who to do him justice, could love his fellow men and wish to force them to share everything equally between them, without having to call them by fancy names, came out at once to see who this self-styled comrade-in-distress might be. To him, Melissa, weeping bitterly, choked out a garbled story of deception and betrayal, no names mentioned; only dark hints of nobility from overseas. 'I'll come as soon as I can,' said Damien, and went back, rather awed, to his Meeting. The Austrian refugees were of opinion that he should rush off at once to the rescue of the seduced lady; a warm gush of tears filled their soft brown eyes at the thought of beauty deserted and in distress. The Welsh intellectual, having satisfied himself that the parties in the case were of differing sexes, lost interest in the matter and said coldly that the Party Came First; the disgruntled adolescents, having equally assured themselves that only one man was involved and he an effete foreign aristo at that, were clamorous in offers to come along and, *en masse*, support their Leader, if there was a fight. It was twenty-past nine when Damien finally got rid of them all and arrived, through the fog, at Maida Vale.

'Twenty-past nine?' said Charlesworth. 'You're sure of the time?' The 'phone call to Tedward had finally been established as having been made at eighteen minutes past.

'Actually it was twenty-two minutes past,' said Damien. 'I looked at my watch while I was waiting for her to open the door, because it had taken me such a hell of a time to get there.' He added very seriously that he had been 'afraid of suicide'; she sounded in a frightful state.

Sergeant Bedd noted down 9.22 p.m. in his notebook. Mr. Granger thought to himself that it was all very well for these police fellows, they were used to standing on their two feet all day; but couldn't they, for God's sake, find somewhere to sit down. Where all this was getting his client, he could not see; and meanwhile, the court had long ago reassembled after the luncheon adjournment and heaven knew what evidence that girl was giving in there. As long as she did not go back on her story of Tedward and Rosie coming in together, and finding the body in the hall. . . .

'Are you telling me,' said Charlesworth, 'that you were in the house that night?'

'Only about ten minutes,' said Damien. He added kindly that the police couldn't possibly ever have found that out: nobody except Melissa knew that he had been there; the Meeting had not heard her name, his mother did not even know who it was who had rung him up; in the thick fog, no one could have seen him come and go; even if there had been fingerprints or anything like that—well, he had been in the house that morning, anyway. 'It wasn't your fault; you couldn't possibly have known.'

'Thank you,' said Charlesworth. 'You set my mind at rest. I hope my superiors will take the same view.'

'What happened when you got to the girl's flat?' said Mr. Granger who wanted to get back to court and at the moment preferred expedition to an exchange of jolly ironies.

'Well, she was most frightfully hysterical—you've seen how she can get—and I couldn't make head or tail out of what she was saying. But you see, Rosie had told me about her, so I realized what was up. What you've never realized,' said Damien with simple scorn, 'is that it wasn't Rosie at all, that Raoul Vernet came about. It was Melissa.'

'*Melissa?*' said Charlesworth, absolutely thunderstruck.

'Well, yes. I suppose she must have known him Abroad; she'd been Abroad a good bit,' said Damien, who had not been Abroad at all, 'and I suppose he's been coming over here and seeing her, because it was too long ago that she was Abroad, for her to be having a baby now, if you see what I mean. So anyway, Rosie told me about her, and I said to send her along to Us, and we'd soon fix her up with a job in the Party or something, because we're very keen on children being born outside the shackles of the old conventions and all that, only I haven't got time to go into it now. . . .'

'Thank God,' said Mr. Granger, looking at his watch.

' . . . and so, of course, when she found herself deserted and betrayed, she turned to me.'

'I see.' Mr. Charlesworth stood, hands in pockets, teetering back and forth from toe to heel. He said at last: 'And of course, at the same time, Rosie was having a baby too?'

'I suppose that would be what made Melissa confide in her,' said Damien; and he folded his firm young lips over the disillusion, the shock and the heartbreak, of Rosie's defection and Rosie's death, which only the personal terror and dread of the past hideous weeks could have done anything to allay.

'Did Rosie—when she told you about Melissa—actually mention Melissa's name to you?'

Damien considered. 'I don't think she actually did; she just said "a friend", you know how women do. But she said that I knew the friend very well and she said she'd been Abroad and various things like that. So of course I realized at once that it was Melissa.'

'Rosie had been abroad too,' suggested Charlesworth, 'and much more recently. And you knew her very well too, *did*n't you? Has it never occurred to you, perhaps thinking about it since, that Rosie was telling you about herself? That she wasn't talking about Raoul Vernet and Melissa at all?'

'Oh, no,' said Damien simply. 'Of course not. I mean, if it wasn't Melissa—why should she have killed the guy?'

And so, point, counterpoint, the duel went on; Melissa in the witness-box, gabble, gabble, gabble, her white face turned up to the gallery; Damien in his huddle in the chilly corner outside the court. . . . The poor little, pitiful impromptu plan of revenge upon Rosie, by taking away Rosie's 'steady'; the appeal to his chivalry—dark hints of passion and pain and despair, the mysterious background, the incognito, the air of cloaks and moustachios, the final betrayal. . . . All unaware that Damien believed himself in the secrets of her 'past', Melissa wept and clung and confided, and vowed that all men were brutes, were devils, were fiends, all except Damien. Damien was the only decent man she ever had met, and to no other man would she ever speak again. . . .

There was a sound at the basement door and she lifted her head sharply, listening. Stanislas! It was Stanislas, come back, perhaps with lies on his lips, but at least come back to his own true love. . . .! She left Damien abruptly and rushed out into the corridor, slamming the door of her room behind her. Stanislas! Stanislas!

But it was only Gabriel, the poodle, pawing at the door because he wanted to go out. She stood for a moment, sick and dizzy with the shock of it, the bitter disappointment, the self-abasement, the shame. 'All right,' she said at last, to the poodle. 'I'll take you.' She did not trouble about a coat, let her perish, let her die, of bronchitis or pneumonia and put an end to the bitterness of life. No one would care, and certainly she would not. She shuffled her way along the short drive-in to the garage, and turned out into the street.

Damien, so suddenly released from hysterical clingings, blew out his breath and rubbed his chin and paused to wonder what he had let himself in for. Women often had these *volte-faces* or whatever they were called, and if he was not jolly careful, he would find that reaction had set in and, on the rebound, she was transferring her affections to *him*. And of course with all that hysteria and things she was probably most frightfully passionate; for a moment he wondered whether, while preserving his pure love for Rosie, he might not indulge in something a little more reciprocal with Melissa. Chaps were always doing that kind of thing and they seemed to get away with it; the Austrian comrades made an absolute thing of it, they picked girls up on buses and in tubes and at parties with the greatest of ease, and seduced them, and deserted them too, for that matter, and the girls seemed all for it and gaily came back for more. . . . Still, if this was an example of Melissa seduced and deserted, perhaps he had better keep off! What the hell had she rushed out to do now, yelping 'Stanislas' like that, at the top of her voice? Dashed off to shoot the feller, Damien thought, grinning, and opened the door and put his head out into the passage to see what went on.

There was nobody there. He called, 'Hey—Melissa?' but she did not reply. There was a light, on the ground floor above and he went gingerly up the basement stairs and peeked into the hall.

Melissa, half-way down the little garage drive, saw the blurred square of light as the front door was flung open and the fog-dimmed figure came tumbling down the front steps and along the little path and down the few more steps to the gate. The sound of his footsteps grew fainter and fainter; running, stumbling, faltering down the road away from the house.

And the meeting next evening on the bench up in Hamilton Terrace, outside the church. 'Haven't the police been to your house, Damien?' 'No, why should they, unless you went and said . . .?' 'I haven't breathed to a soul that you were there last night. . . .' 'What did they say to *you*, Melissa, about yourself?' 'They didn't say much, they just asked me where I'd spent the evening. . . .' And *she* had told them lies about where she had spent the evening, and *he* had told her to say nothing about his having been at the house; and so they had parted, he thrusting his hands into his pockets so that he might not have to touch the hand of a murderess; she running back to catch him humbly by the sleeve and say 'thank you'—not thank you because of his compassion in not 'splitting' on her to the police, but thank you because, in his chivalry and manhood, he had killed the man he believed to have done her wrong.

'What about your coat and hat?' said Charlesworth. 'You didn't leave them at the house.'

'I didn't have a hat, I never do; and she hadn't given me time to take my coat off—I still had it on.'

'I see. And Mr. Hervey's shoes? Where does Mr. Hervey come into all this? Or is he a white rabbit?'

'A white rabbit?' said Damien. 'No, he's one of our lodgers.'

'And these are his shoes?'

'They are now.'

'But at the time of the murder, they were yours—is that what you mean?'

'Yes,' said Damien. 'You see, after the murder, I swopped.'

'After you'd got the blood on them, you mean?'

'Yes. I—well, I sort of jumped over the—the body—when I rushed out of the hall. . . . I was a bit shaken, I expect,' said Damien, apologetically.

'And you got blood on them, then?'

'Yes. And you see, if you've got blood on your shoes, it's no use trying to wash it off or anything,' said Damien, explaining kindly to the poor bloody British police; 'and if you get rid of them, that's no use either because people know about it and afterwards, when things happen, they begin wondering—I mean, your mother asks you where your shoes are and things like that, especially if they're new ones and these were fairly new ones. So the only way to hide them is somewhere where people will see them but won't look at them, if you see what I mean. Well, Mr. Hervey wears the same kind of shoes as I do, because it was him who recommended them to us, and when he got new ones, he took me along to his shop and I got some too; and of course there was nothing on earth to connect Mr. Hervey with the Frenchman being killed, so I thought if the police ever—ever connected *me* with it, they might come and look at my shoes, but they'd never look at Mr. Hervey's. So I just swopped with him, and I wrote my initials in his with huge ink letters. I think he must take half a size smaller than me, though; they've been hellishly tight all this time, and they've given me an awful blister. And he does seem to have been rather slopping about in mine, poor old boy.' He looked up guilelessly into Mr. Charlesworth's face.

'Is that all?' said Mr. Granger. ('I'll leave this to you,' he said to Charlesworth, 'and get back to the court.')

Charlesworth nodded absently. Damien, having exhausted his spate of words, had time to look about him and take stock of their effect. 'What about Melissa now, Inspector? What'll happen to her?'

'That remains to be seen,' said Charlesworth, shrugging. '*And* what happens to you.'

'Well, I can't help what happens to me; I don't see how I could have given her away for killing that brute of a man, and in France they wouldn't have taken any notice, they'd just call it a crime passionelle. Even Dr. Edwards and Thomas Evans, I thought would put up with it. But when she starting accusing Matilda, who runs around taking birds away from cats and mice out of mouse traps, or rather making other people do it, because she can't bear it herself, well, I couldn't let that go. What happens now?'

'Well, first we test your story at every point. . . .'

'You test it?'

'You have a serene confidence in its being accepted,' said Charlesworth.

'Well, damn it, it's the truth.'

'It's an explanation, anyway.'

'An explanation—what of?'

'Of the fact that you have Raoul Vernet's blood on your shoes.'

'But I tell you, it was Melissa who killed him.'

Mr. Charlesworth smiled and shrugged: 'At this moment, no doubt, she's in there in the witness-box—saying the same thing about you.'

Damien was silent for a long time, his face like a child's face, frightened and troubled. But at last he lifted his head and squared his shoulders, and set his young mouth into an ugly sneer. 'I see. So that's your little game.' And he gave a light laugh and held out his hands for imaginary handcuffs. 'One more dangerous Red out of the way,' he said.

Charlesworth thought that perhaps he flattered himself a little.

An expert witness who had been waiting two days to give evidence and saw his chance of finishing to-day getting more and more remote, slipped out of court and rang up his wife and told her to send him a telegram. At the end of Melissa's protracted appearance in the box, therefore, Counsel for the Crown stood up and said that, m'lord, Dr. Brightly had received an urgent call, and if it was convenient to opposing counsel, he, for his part, would be willing to hear Dr. Brightly's evidence now and let him get away, unless his lordship had any objection; his lordship stifled the reflection that, at the rate things were going, they might as well all get into the box together and chant their evidence in unison, and replied graciously that if it suited Counsel . . .? Mr. Dragon raised his seat from his seat for a moment and said, perfectly, perfectly, m'lord, and sat down again. Dr. Brightly therefore droned his way into the box and Charlesworth wagged his head at Inspector Cockrill and met him outside the court and produced a cigarette. 'If I don't have a fag, I shall go off my ruddy rocker. Look here, what did you mean by saying not to worry, you'd fix it?'

'Well, I meant, don't worry, I'll fix it,' said Cockie.

'Do you mean you *know?*'

'No, I don't know,' said Cockie. 'I only guess.'

'Oh, well,' said Charlesworth, disappointed. A fine time

to be playing guessing games! The truth was, the old boy was past his prime.

Cockie looked up from under his eyebrows with a gleam of mischievous bright brown eyes. It wouldn't be the first time he had 'fixed it' for Mr. Charlesworth, but these young sparks would never learn. 'You don't think I can do it?'

'How can you, if you don't even know the person who murdered the man?'

'I propose that the person who murdered the man shall stand up in court and tell us so himself.'

Thomas, Tedward, Damien Jones; Matilda, Melissa, old Mrs. Evans. 'That's so likely, isn't it?'

'Properly handled, I think it is.'

'Thomas Evans has been discharged from the case, Dr. Edwards is about to be found Not Guilty; Melissa and the Jones boy cancel each other out, the old lady could not possibly have hit the man on the head and that's flat. And Matilda Evans . . .' He paused. He said, slowly: 'I suppose there *wasn't* anything in that girl's revelations?'

Cockie shrugged and smiled. 'My dear friend Matilda is in a considerable flap about the revelations; in fact she doth protest too much, I think. But of course the more truth there was in the revelations, the less likely that she was the murderer.'

Mr. Charlesworth did not see that at all. 'If the affaire was such,' said Cockie, 'that she was capable of murdering him through jealousy, do you for a moment suppose that he would have confessed to her that he'd been having fun with Rosie? He was a foreigner, he was far away, he need never see her again: why should he tell her? What a fool the man would be!'

'Well, but Rosie might tell her.'

'She hadn't, had she?' said Cockie. 'She'd told her the father of the child was someone else—someone, incidentally,

whom Tilda could not possibly have mistaken for Raoul.
And Rosie herself laughed like a drain at the bare idea that
that scruffy old Raoul Vernet might have been her lover.
And even if she *had* told Matilda—Raoul Vernet could have
simply denied the whole thing. Rosie had had lovers enough
in Geneva; he could have denied the whole thing and that's
what he would have done—and what's more, he'd have
denied it from afar.'

'You don't seem to think very highly of the gentleman's
sense of honour,' said Charlesworth.

'I think very highly indeed of his sense of preservation:
and therefore I say that the truer it was that he was Matilda
Evans' lover, the less likely that he would have come over
here and invited her to murder him.'

'Of course she *could* have done it.'

'It's all a question of coulds and woulds,' said Cockie.
'Matilda could have, but she wouldn't have. Ted Edwards
would have, but he couldn't have; because he quite positively did not come in ahead of Rosie, and for the rest of
the time he was with her at his house or driving the car;
the old lady wouldn't have *and* she couldn't have, because,
first of all Rosie had described a totally different seducer to
her, and secondly she literally would not be able to lift her
arms to deal such a blow; Melissa Weeks could have, but
she wouldn't have, because contrary to Master Jones's
beliefs, she had not been seduced and betrayed by Raoul
Vernet; and Damien Jones could have but he wouldn't
have because why should he? He thought it was Melissa who
had been seduced, not Rosie, and he didn't know Melissa
nearly well enough to run round slaying her seducers.'

'He *says* he thought it was Melissa. How do we know
that's true? It may all be a cover-up. He was in the house
that morning, he could have fixed the telephone message
and got the mastoid mallet and the gun. . . .'

'And then waited for Melissa to ring him up and summon him round—finally getting in his bash with about half a minute to spare.'

'But we've got nobody left,' said Charlesworth.

'Only Thomas Evans; and you've had him and let him go.'

'There's no evidence against him,' said Charlesworth. 'We couldn't get him.'

'You'll find there's no evidence against the murderer,' said Cockie. 'But you'll get *him!*'

'Him?'

'Him or her; I don't mean necessarily a male.'

'But male or female—you know? At least you can guess?'

'I can—work it out,' said Cockie, slowly. 'And so can you.' He would have said more, but Dr. Brightly came hurrying out through the glass swing doors, and he caught Charlesworth by the arm instead. 'We must get back into court.'

'There's no hurry,' said Charlesworth, puffing at his cigarette.

'On the contrary there's a great hurry: all the hurry in the world.'

'Yes, but tell me . . .'

'I've told you,' said Cockie, crossly: honestly, these young men!

'You've told me? You haven't said a word.'

'I've told you that there's a hurry; this case must be decided in the next half hour, or else . . . Doesn't that mean anything to you?' He added impatiently: 'My dear fellow—can't you see it? Rosie Evans told me on her deathbed that Ted Edwards could have killed Raoul Vernet. . . .'

'But he couldn't,' said Charlesworth. 'It's been proved up

to the hilt that of all people concerned with this case, the one person who could not possibly have killed the chap was Edwards.'

'Well, damn it, that's what I say,' said Cockie. 'Then why the hell should she have told me that he could?' He shoved his companion towards the door, and at the same moment a voice murmured a name, a second voice took it up and cried it forth, a third voice echoed it louder still, voice taking up the syllables from voice like the baton in a relay race, Call Mrs. Evans, *Call Mrs. Evans*, CALL MRS. EVANS . . . Clad in her rusty black with her crumpled flat black hat set squarely on her head, and her old eyes bright with a desperate, and yet a sort of mischievous resolve, old Mrs. Evans trotted into court and along the narrow pathway between the benches and under the shadow of the high dock and up the steps and into the witness-box. She settled herself without haste, placing her handbag on the ledge beside her, rolling her gloves into a ball beside it, giving the neat result an approving pat; and lifted her head and flashed across at the prisoner in the dock a smile whose brilliance and tenderness lit for a moment with a special radiance, the already bright-lit court. The little chippy diamonds and sapphires sparkled on the thin old hands clasped, trembling, on the ledge of the box. Greater love hath no man, thought Mrs. Evans to herself, withdrawing the smile and turning to face the onslaught from the benches opposite, than that he lay down his life for his friend; and so stood there, waiting—the only person in the entire court who did not know that her friend was in no need of her sacrifice, that the suspect was no longer suspected, the accused no longer accused, the prisoner, in all but the formal verdict, free.

'Raise the book in your right hand. "I swear by Almighty God . . ." '

CHAPTER SEVENTEEN

U P in the crowded gallery they made way for the
young man who had made such a sensation by
calling out that the evidence of the curly-haired
young lady had been all lies; in the benches to the left of
the dock, Matilda sat with Thomas two or three places
away from Melissa and exchanged with her no smallest
glance of recognition; on the narrow seat beneath the jury
box, Inspector Cockrill lounged with his shoulders up to his
ears and his chin on his chest, in an agony of alternating
hope and doubt. The usher stood patiently waiting, with
one hand on the ledge of the witness-box. Mrs. Evans said
regretfully that she *was* so sorry, she did hope it wouldn't
muddle things up for them, but she was afraid she couldn't.
Mr. Justice Rivett relieved his feelings with a somewhat
over-dramatic sigh, hooked himself over the right arm of
the great chair and said, 'Can't what?'

'Can't raise the book in my right hand, my lord,' said
Gran, flashing the smile again. 'I *am* so sorry, but you see
I have this idiotic arthritis in my shoulder and I can't raise
my arm at all.' She demonstrated the restricted movement
of her arm. She *was* so sorry to be a nuisance.

'If you just hold the book so that it can be seen that you
are holding it, that is all that is required,' said the judge,
patiently. He settled back into the chair and folded his
hands across the black sash that held the untidy scarlet robe
in place, and exchanged with counsel in their benches a tiny

glance, half amused, half desperate; what on earth is *this* one going to get up to, said the glance.

Sir William rose to his feet, tucked up a heel against the bench behind him, gripped the edges of his black gown, one in each hand, dragging it down heavily from the shoulders, and launched upon the regulation questions that must be briefly put and, pray God, as briefly answered before they could decently wind up the case and all go home. His mind toyed pleasantly with the prospect of a free afternoon to-morrow; with the collapse of the case against the accused (no possible shadow of blame attaching to its conduct by the Attorney-General), it could not possibly linger on after midday to-morrow. Your name is Louisa Jane Evans . . .? (One might go out to the R.A.C. and get a game of golf . . .) You are the grandmother of the previous witness, Thomas Evans?. (Or run down and see the children at school. . . .) And you live with him at his home? You remember the evening of November 23rd? Perhaps you would tell us briefly in your own words. . . .?

Mrs. Evans obliged with a spirited account of her recollections of the evening in question, beginning with the arrival of her supper tray. 'Matilda, that's my grand-daughter-in-law, had a guest, this Frenchman. So I just sat quietly by my fire, reading.' A book by Robert Hichens, it had been. . . .

'Just stick to the relevant facts, Mrs. Evans, please.'

Mrs. Evans indulged in a small, rather pitying shrug; let Counsel remember when the time came that it was he, not she, who had dismissed Robert Hichens as irrelevant. Very well, then, at a quarter past nine, Matilda had come to help her take off her dress and her hair. . . .

'I beg your pardon, Mrs. Evans, I don't think we heard that quite correctly.'

'To help me take off my hair,' said Gran. She elaborated

gaily: 'A sort of little pancake of hair on top of my own hair, or rather on top of my absence of own hair, if you see what I mean.' She laid her left hand on top of the flat, black hat, ignoring all interruptions, swivelling round to demonstrate to the jury. 'You can't see it now because of my hat, but if you count the hat as one pancake, then there's another pancake of a bit of white lace, and then under that there's the pancake of hair: quite a little heap of pancakes, really, Crêpes Something the French would call it, only of course they'd smother it with melted butter and liqueurs and things, which would be delicious, no doubt, but would make me look most strange, *would*n't it?' A shadow passed over the eager, gay old face. 'I'm so sorry; have I been talking nonsense? I'm getting muddled up.'

'Let us just stick to events, Mrs. Evans; we want you to tell us quite shortly, *quite shortly*, what you saw and heard that evening.'

'Rather like a pancake itself when you come to think of it,' said Mrs. Evans, thoughtfully. She nodded to herself, inwardly communing. 'A little round white pancake, floating, floating, floating about in the gloom.'

Judge and Counsel exchanged glances of mounting despair. 'Mrs. Evans, *please:* I asked you to tell me what you saw that night.'

'But I *am* telling you,' said Mrs. Evans, pained. 'A small, round white pancake, floating about down there in the gloom, floating about in the dimness of the hall.' She added inconsequently that night came swiftly in the desert; if they'd paid more attention to Robert Hichens, they would know that.

Sir William shrugged hopelessly. 'I think, perhaps, m'lord . . .?'

The judge had one more try. 'Let us keep calm, Mrs.

Evans, try not to get muddled. You are telling us that you looked down into the hall that night, which we have heard was not very brightly lit; and saw——?'

'A little white pancake floating about down there,' said Mrs. Evans. She smiled up at him confidingly. 'Only of course it wasn't a pancake really,' she said.

You could see that Mr. Justice Rivett was glad of that. 'It wasn't a pancake? Then what *was* it you saw?'

'The bald top of that Frenchman's head, of course,' said old Mrs. Evans, all smiles.

Inspector Charlesworth tilted his chair back on its hind legs and, leaning perilously backwards, said over his shoulder to Inspector Cockrill: 'So this is it?'

'Yes,' said Cockie. 'This is it: at least it's the beginning.' And he added: 'Thank God it's come!' but there was no triumph in his voice and no gladness. '*You*'ll be all right now; you've saved your bacon,' he said.

But it was Inspector Cockrill who had saved Charlesworth's bacon, and not for the first time. 'You're a marvel, Cockie, honestly you are. What did you say to her: to the old girl?'

'Me? I didn't say a word,' said Cockie, surprised.

'But at lunch?'

'She had her lunch by herself; I got some sent in to her, here. I haven't seen her, not to speak to, all day.'

The muttered discussion between Judge and Counsel and the gentleman from the Director of Public Prosecution's office, having reached a conclusion and Sir William being again upon his foot, heel tucked up, fists closed on gown, an usher shushed urgently and Charlesworth, still unsatisfied, perforce righted his chair. The Judge, most unfairly, since he himself was seething with excitement and curiosity, said irritably that this was a very serious case and if there were any further outbreaks of chattering and whispering, he would clear the court of all who had no special business there, and yes, Sir William, please continue. Sir William put it to Mrs. Evans, very civilly that she was now departing somewhat from her evidence in another court? Mrs. Evans said blankly what other court was that?—she was afraid her memory was dreadfully cloudy these days. *So* sorry if she was being a nuisance, muddling things up, . . .

'You haven't told anyone before that you saw the deceased that night?'

'Of course this would be before he became the deceased,' said Mrs. Evans earnestly. 'Because I did see him afterwards, everyone knows that, when I went down into the hall with the rest of them.' His bald patch, however, had not been looking like a round, white pancake by that time, not a bit!

'No, no,' said Counsel, hurriedly. 'But you are telling us now that you did see him earlier—before he died?'

'Just the top of his head, you know, when I looked down into the hall.'

'And that would be—at what time?'

As the church clock struck half-past nine, Matilda had gone off to pot the baby; it had been immediately after that.

Mr. Justice Rivett intervened. He said that it might be helpful to the jury to just recall that the time of the tele-phone call—the call purporting to come from Raoul Vernet, saying that he had been attacked—had been, er, um, 9.18 p.m., yes, he had a note of it here, approximately 9.18. He sat up very straight with his finger still in the page, and looked alertly at old Mrs. Evans. Sir William looked desperately from his Lordship to defending counsel and back again to the witness. 'Perhaps you had just better go on telling us in your own words, Mrs. Evans. . . . (Your Lordship will appreciate that I am completely in the dark. . . .?).'

The thin old voice tinkled out clearly through the hushed court. 'From where I left off? It was about Matilda taking off my hair; and that's what led us to the pancakes, *was*n't it?' She might have been reciting Cinderella to a circle of children sitting round the nursery fire. 'Well, now, that was at about a quarter past nine, just *before* that famous telephone call, you see. And then Tilda went off to her own room, and I think she tidied up her face a bit and so on, and after about five minutes she came back and I'd got into my nightgown by then, and she helped me into bed and gave me my Horlicks, and then she went off to do the baby. It was just half-past nine, because we heard the clock. So I sat there in bed, reading my Robert—my book,' corrected Mrs. Evans, glancing with mock apology at Sir William, 'and suddenly I heard a noise. It seemed to be coming from the hall. I listened for Matilda but I didn't hear her come out of the nursery so I hopped out of bed myself, to have a look. But first I popped my hair on, of course, and my teeth in.' She went off into a fit of little giggles and, recovering herself, explained that she had nearly said that she'd popped her hair *in* and her teeth *on!* 'So silly!' said Mrs. Evans, biting on a knuckle looking up naughtily into the disapproving face of the Attorney-General. She added: 'Because what *would* I have looked like?' and went off into giggles again. But her eyes were swimming with unshed tears of terror and loneliness: all by herself there in that little box under the pitiless glare of the bright, hard lights and the hundreds of bright, hard eyes, smilingly talking herself into a place of everlasting lights, of ever-watching eyes, where the windows would be too high to throw things out of and cheer life up. . . .

'Why should you have been so careful of your appearance, Mrs. Evans? Who did you expect to see?'

Mrs. Evans pulled herself together. 'Who? Well, that Frenchman, of course.'

'You expected to see Raoul Vernet?'

'There was nobody else in the house, *was* there? At least I didn't think there was.'

'You thought you heard Raoul Vernet moving about in the hall? What did you think he could be doing there?'

'I thought he was probably trying to find the downstairs huh-ha,' said Mrs. Evans, simply. She shrugged. Hospitality was hospitality, the shrug said, and in the absence of his hostess it was obviously up to anyone else in the house to see that no guest was permitted to wander wretchedly about in search of physical relief. 'For all I knew, the poor man might be in agony.'

'So you looked over the banisters . . .?'

'One has to go just a little way down the stairs.'

'And you saw . . .?'

The prisoner in the dock got heavily to his feet and said in a loud, clear voice: 'And she saw—me.'

Reproof from Bench to dock, reviving sips of water for shocked witness, mutter, mutter, mutter between Judge and counsel and stage manager and accused's solicitors; mutter, mutter, mutter, unchecked, throughout the court. Matilda sat clutching at the sleeve of Thomas's overcoat. 'What on earth does this mean, now? It's all too terrifying, what does it *mean*. . . .?'

'They're both trying to protect each other, that's all.'

'How could she have seen Tedward? Tedward was in the car at that time, with Rosie; we know that.'

'Of course she didn't see Tedward; he's trying to stop her talking, trying to stop her giving herself away.'

Matilda s grip intensified on his coat-sleeve. 'Giving herself away . . .? Thomas you don't think . . .?'

'My darling Matilda, somebody killed this man. Why do you think I went to prison, why do you think I kept mum about the car, why do you think I went through all that hell. . . .? When you went up to tell her that Raoul had been killed—she had her wig on again, *did*n't she? You told me so yourself. Not pinned on properly, she couldn't do that: but perched on. Why?—if she'd just been sitting reading in bed.'

Mutter, mutter, mutter; whisper, whisper, whisper. 'And I did think it was odd, Thomas, that she shouldn't have heard anything from her room; her hearing's so good.'

'He probably did go out to look for the huh-ha. And she went out just as she says; and looked over and saw him there, and took the mallet and crept down. . . .'

'But the mallet was in the desk downstairs.'

'The mallet was either in the desk downstairs *or it was in the chest on the landing*—I told the police that, half a dozen times. So there's only one thing left, there's only one possible way of escape. . . .'

'Because, Thomas, she couldn't have thought that he was Rosie's lover, she *could*n't have. Rosie'd told her some frightful tarradiddle about a strong, silent young fisherman, sweeping her off her feet. . . . And, I mean, anyone could see, even from upstairs looking down on his bald patch, one could see that Raoul couldn't have carried Rosie down to the water's edge in the moonlight, let alone ravaging her in the boat afterwards. . . .'

Shush, shush, shush! went the ushers all over the court; the prisoner had retired defeated, into a fretful silence, anxious, agonized, alert, the witness was on her feet pushing aside the cup of water. 'No more to drink!' cried old Mrs. Evans, starting up in the witness-box in outraged virtue. 'No more of your golden wines to take the memories from my mind and the ache from my heart! They desert you,' she confided to Mr. Justice Rivett, who sat electrified, gripping the arms of his chair, 'and then they stand you a couple of champagne cocktails and think everything's going to be just as it was.' She added, as she had added to Matilda on the day of Raoul Vernet's death, that these Frenchified Arabs were always the worst. 'The worst of the West imposed upon the worst of the East.' She smiled up at him brilliantly. 'Quite an epigram! But difficult to say.' Especially with false teeth, she added frankly.

Mr. Justice Rivett thought that it would be best if the witness would now retire; but Mrs. Evans had no intention of retiring until she had had her say, and a witness giving evidence cannot, against his own will, be removed from the witness-box. Very well, then, if witness would come back to the night of the murder . . . She had looked over the banister? And she had seen . . .

'I saw a mirage,' said Mrs. Evans. 'A mirage. I saw a great sandstorm and in the stinging swirl of the sand I saw the Avenger with uplifted arm, I saw the sign of the lily upon his breast and the legend on his banner, Avenger of the Innocent. But it was a mirage. I looked again and there was nobody there but the dusky one, the evil one, the betrayer, the seducer. . . .' She quoted again: 'He has broken his English Lily and left her there, weeping, on the golden sands.' She looked up at the Judge. 'Only of course I was on the stairs, really.' She added: 'But Madonna Lily was a Tiger Lily now; and—one blow from the tiger's claw . . .' There was a chair behind her in the witness-box and she sat down on it with a bump; to the policewoman

244

in attendance behind the box, she said, 'Have I been talking nonsense again?' in a puzzled voice.

Sir William gave up. He made a little bow to Counsel for the defence and himself sat down.

The Judge made a just-a-minute sign to Mr. Dragon. He sat for a long moment, silent, at his great desk, his face in his hands. He lifted off his little wig with the sticking-out, upward-curling pig's tail of a tail and passed his hand over his own scanty hair and replaced the wig again. He addressed himself to the jury. He thought he should remind them that no witness could be asked in court to give evidence that might incriminate himself. He thought the jury would agree that certainly nobody had invited the present witness to give the evidence they had just heard from her. Their present concern, however, was with the prisoner in the dock and nobody else; the truth or falsity of the witness's statement would doubtless be checked later by the proper authorities. But the man in the dock was entitled to a fair trial—and that meant a complete trial, and his lordship felt that they should just pursue this difficult matter to as rapid a conclusion as possible, after which, since Mrs. Evans was the last witness to be called for the prosecution, Counsel for the defence might or might not decide to put his client in the witness-box in his own defence—*in his own defence*, repeated his lordship, frowning over at the prisoner in the dock. Now—Mr. Dragon, matters must be left to your discretion and of course I shall assist you in any way possible in the conduct of this—I think we must agree— extremely, er, shall we say difficult situation. . . . Mrs. Evans, don't you think, in your own interests, it would be better if you remained seated? This must be most trying to you. . . .

But Mrs. Evans was making positively her last public appearance and she would do it in style. It was true that she was exhausted: exhausted with the physical effort of standing so long, of speaking so much, of keeping her poor wits clear, of keeping at bay the real dottiness which, as she had long ago confided to Cockie, was apt to impose itself upon the pretended dottiness with which she had brightened the boredom of her lonely room; but she tottered to her aching feet and, clinging rather desperately to the ledge of the box, faced the court once again. And please not to worry about all that business of incriminating herself, said Mrs. Evans. 'I don't know quite what I've been saying, I get these dotty patches you know; but if I said that I killed that poor Frenchman, then I think that may be true. Poor thing—he'd never done me any harm, or any of us any harm; but I think I got him muddled up with some book. He was dark and swarthy, you know, and I think I suddenly saw him in my imagination, wrapped in a burnous or whatever they call those things, and the fog swirling about him was a sandstorm and I'd recently been—well, I'd got into one of my muddles, you know and sort of mixed myself up. . . .' And across the court she said to Sir William: 'I *told* you not to dismiss Robert Hichens so lightly.'

'No questions,' said James Dragon, suddenly sitting down.

'No questions,' said Sir William, simply teeming with questions he could not put because this was his witness and he must not cross-examine her. He looked up, however, expectantly at the Judge.

And the Judge did not fail him. 'Very well—the witness may go. But—just before you go, Mrs. Evans: would you remind us of what you told the jury when you first came into the witness-box—about your right arm.'

Old Mrs. Evans had done her bit and she was all ready to depart. Her big black handbag was hitched by its straps over her left arm, in her right hand she clutched her gloves, rolled nervously into a ball. She turned back. She lifted a white, exhausted face to his lordship; shaken and near to tears, she lowered her eyes and so stood, staring, staring, staring at the little black, rolled-up ball of gloves in her hand. Then she leaned forward and dropped it neatly, over the edge of the box. 'Hit it!' she said, craning over to look at some invisible mark on the floor below. 'But then I'm a pretty good shot. I keep in practice—I'm always throwing things.' And she gave her last little bow and her last little, gallant, watery smile, and leaning heavily on the police-woman's arm, crept out of the witness-box.

Counsel for the defence was not looking towards the witness-box. He got slowly to his feet, a little piece of paper in his hand. He said: 'My lord—I have here a note from the prisoner. He advises me that he wishes to change his plea to one of—Guilty.'

CHAPTER EIGHTEEN

Your name is Edwin Robert Edwards?

Yes.

You are a qualified medical practitioner?

Yes.

Dr. Edwards, you were on intimate terms with the family at Maida Vale?

Yes.

And with Dr. Evans' young sister, Rose Evans?

Yes.

Rose Evans is now dead, isn't she?

Yes. Yes she is. Yes, Rosie's dead.

But Rosie came and leaned on the witness-box before him, resting her plump white arms on the ledge, looking up into his face, putting out a hand to him that fell away into dust and ashes when he took it in his own; and said that she was too utterly *mis.* to see him there in that horrid little pulpit thing and to think that it was ackcherly her, Rosie, let's face it, that had put him there and all because she'd been such a basket in Geneva; only, honestly, how could he have thought for one minute that that frowsty old Raoul Vernet had been one of her boy friends? Yes, yes, of course it was true that one of them had been old, quite old and terribly experienced and all that, filling one up with oceans of champagne and leering away like anything, fondly imagining that he was seducing one—but still, when one said old, about thirty something, or perhaps even forty, but

248

not practically an octogenarian not to mention being bald on top! 'But of course, Tedward, I suppose you didn't really have time to see. . . .?'

'Dr. Edwards, had you ever in your life set eyes on this man, Raoul Vernet?'

'No,' said Tedward. 'Not till that day he died.'

'Or heard his name?'

'No. Not till that day he died.'

'Can you recollect when you first heard it?'

'Matilda Evans mentioned it to me that morning. She said he'd flown over from Geneva and he wanted to see her. She said she thought he felt bad about Rosie and wanted to talk it over, I knew—at least I understood—that Rosie had been seduced by a middle-aged man, a well-to-do, middle-aged man. . . .' He shrugged. 'After that she went upstairs and left me to see myself out. I wrote a message to get Thomas Evans out of the house that evening and I went—taking the gun and the mallet as I passed through the hall. . . .'

And the shade of Rosie was there again, plump white arms folded along the ledge of the witness-box, saying how clever of clever old Tedward to think it all out so quickly, to plan it so cleverly, *clever* old Tedward Bear! He mumbled that it had all been vague in his mind, a far-off, sporting chance, a chance that the coming fog might offer, he couldn't yet see how. A chance to avenge—a chance to avenge, he cried out suddenly and loudly, looking down into her innocent upturned big blue eyes, seeing himself again as he had seemed to himself at that moment, as he had seemed to a shocked and astonished old woman peering down, trembling, from the shadows on the stair, having heard his car draw up at the door and footsteps in the hall—a knight in shining armour, an avenger, with uplifted arm and the sign of the broken lily upon his breast. 'She told me

249

she knew; she told me long ago that she knew, she tried to tell me again just now, she knew and she wanted to suffer instead of me. She knew that I had made a mistake, but . . .' She had thought of him as he had thought of himself—as an Avenger; Avenger of the Innocent. . . . Avenger of the Innocent!—of the slut who had trampled his lilies of illusion into ugly little fragments and handed them out to every casual, ravening passer-by. 'I killed an innocent man for you, Rosie,' he said, into the electrified silence of the court. 'I murdered him—I, a doctor, I murdered him.' Grotesquely shaking, his hand fumbled for her hand, felt along the ledge of the box for hands that were not there, for hands that seemed to be there but tumbled away to ash as he grasped at them. He lifted his weary head; somewhere out there in the far distance, there was a splash of scarlet that for two long days had been a symbol of something called Justice, of something called Retribution. 'She's gone,' he explained to the scarlet splash. 'She's dead.' That was justice too, that was retribution too. 'They found out about the telephone trick,' he said. 'They worked out how it had been done. You see—I had to have an alibi, I worked it so that she was with me, so that she'd come back to the house with me. . . . But the police found out the trick. I thought I was finished. I wanted her to know about it and why I had done it; I believed in her then, you see. I wanted to explain it all to her before they hauled me away. I told her everything. And then . . .' He put up his shaking hands to his face. 'I found the police had got it wrong after all; they thought I'd left her in the car and come in and killed him and gone back to her. And that was true—but they'd got it all wrong, they'd missed the essential point, they didn't know after all. But *she* knew now.' And he looked down again into the upturned plump, white, non-existent face and said: 'And you never could keep a secret, Rosie, could you?'

Yet Rosie had kept one secret. By telling half a dozen secrets, she had kept one secret from them all: by telling half a dozen secrets of Rosie, the innocent flower, betrayed by this man or that, she had kept the vile secret of Rosie herself the betrayer, of Rosie who had sold her innocence wholesale for a glass of champagne, for a sail on the lake, for an adventure in a student's flat. . . . Rosie, betraying, suddenly herself betrayed by her confidante: Melissa with her white face and dark, obscene round hole of a mouth as he would see it for ever, screaming out Rosie's ugly little secrets, screaming out that his love was no broken lily but a strumpet, a strumpet that would soon become a trumpet, a strumpet trumpeting forth the truth of his mistaken vengeance as he had confided it all to her. 'A joke,' he said, raising bleared eyes to the splash of scarlet on the bench; or was the scarlet there, now?—had not something happened in between, was not this some small, dim room, was there not a dusty, disinfectant smell that seemed vilely familiar?—vilely familiar, and yet comfortingly familiar, something remembered, something inescapable, something that held security, held freedom from responsibility, freedom from the necessity to try any more, to explain any more, to care any more. . . . 'A joke,' he repeated to that splash of scarlet receded away into the distance for ever, leaving him high and dry on the shores of God knew what blear-eyed, babbling lunacy. 'A joke!' But there had been no joking then. Tenderly helping her upstairs to her bedroom, the whispered words of advice, get hold of some headed note-paper, copy out the prescription I gave you, go to different chemists and don't tell a soul, don't tell a soul. . . . 'Why should I have died for her?' he asked the bare walls of the little cell, 'knowing what I now—at last—knew? Why should I let her live to tell them all the truth?' For her he had killed a man—a man who proved to have been utterly guiltless, concerned only with her protection and care; for her he had seen his friend suffer in his place, for her he had listened to an old woman telling him in parables that she would sacrifice her freedom for his life. All of them protecting Rosie, all thinking only of Rosie, suffering for one another, suspecting one another and yet without a thought of blame for one another—because of their faith in her. 'A slut!' he cried aloud. A slut, a cheat, as false as hell, as false as hell with her guileless confidences and her candid eyes. . . .

The door of the cell opened and somebody came in; somebody alive and wholesome with something not alive that tried to creep in too through the open door. But the door was closed, barring her out. He raised his head, his hands still covering his face, bleared eyes peering out through bars of fingers. 'Cockie? Is it you?'

'Yes,' said Cockie. 'You know me, now? That's good.'

'What's happened to the court? Wasn't I in court?'

'You sort of—passed out, you know. Just for a bit. So they brought you back here.'

'I did tell them about it?' said Tedward, anxiously.

'Yes, you told them. That was what you wanted?'

'I had to tell them it wasn't her, really. But then the judge said hewouldn't accept my saying "guilty". Didn't he?'

'Rather a lot of people had said so by then,' said Cockie, quizzically smiling. 'The thing was—you got yourself into the witness-box. There, you could say what you liked.' He mumbled that he was 'sorry about it all'.

For a moment the old, kindly habit of reassurance and friendliness reasserted itself. 'Don't worry about me. And tell the others not to worry. I'm all right. I'm fine.' He gave a travesty of his old smile. 'You knew, did you—all the time?'

'I only guessed. And not at first. But I couldn't get over

your taking Rosie through that nice warm room into the other one. Why?—if not to fix that telephone thing?'

'So you let her "confess"? You sent the old woman into that little box—to drive me into saving her?'

'I didn't send her; I just let her go. I didn't let them tell her there was no need to save you; that was all. I knew what she'd say; and—you or another—I knew that if she said it, the truth would come out.'

'You could have waited,' said Tedward, wearily.

'No,' said Cockie. 'That's what I kept saying to Charlesworth. We couldn't wait. In a very little while you'd have been acquitted, you'd have been a free man; and all the truth in the world after that would not have prevailed.'

Tedward stilled for a moment his restless hands. 'Do you think that the truth really mattered so much?'

'Yes,' said Cockie. 'It's something sacred. If you're a doctor—you have only one idea, to preserve life. If you're a policeman, ditto; to preserve the truth.'

The bleared grey eyes began to wander again, the restless hands itched and trembled on the little table, the haggard face jerked uncontrollably. 'Have I been . . . Have they . . .? I can't remember anything in the court . . .' And the face was there again and the ash-grey hands. 'Is Rosie here?'

'No,' said Cockrill steadily. 'Rosie's dead.'

'If they kill me,' said Tedward, 'Rosie will be there. Wherever I go, whatever happens to you when you die, Rosie will be there.' And he suddenly started up at the little table and stood there shuddering and shaking and cried out that they must not hang him, he did not want to die. . . .

'They won't hang you,' said Cockie. 'There's no question of your dying. You'll go somewhere—quiet; and forget all this and your mind will be peaceful again. . . .'

But Tedward went to the bars of the cell and thrust through his hands and caught at the ashen hands and held them close. 'Don't tell them, Rosie—keep it a secret for ever, don't let them find out the truth and condemn me to die. Don't tell a soul, Rosie, don't tell a soul. . . .'

Don't tell a soul, Rosie, that I stopped the car and got out to 'try to find out where we were' . . . Don't tell a soul how long it seemed to you, sitting waiting there until I came back. . . .

Other Mystery and Suspense Titles
Available from Carroll & Graf

The Third Arm—by Kenneth Royce
An intriguing plot places a band of world-notorious terrorists in a confused and vulnerable London in this literate and astonishing thriller that will enthrall fans of John LeCarre and Graham Greene.

$3.50

Channel Assault—by Kenneth Royce
A treacherous plot to negotiate a secret "peace" treaty with Hitler and assassinate Winston Churchill brings together a British doctor, his mistress and an American OSS agent in this novel which combines the realism of historical fiction with the gut grip of a thriller.

$3.50

Deadline—by Thomas B. Dewey
The Chicago private detective known only as "Mac" in a last minute fight against the corruption of a one-man dominated small town.

$3.50

The House of the Arrow—by A.E.W. Mason
An imaginative, well-crafted plot featuring a prominent London law firm, a famous French detective and a very difficult mystery to solve.

$3.50

Murder for Pleasure—by Howard Haycraft
A time-honored history of the mystery genre from A.C. Doyle to Raymond Chandler that will delight the general reader and fan alike.

$10.95

The Red Right Hand—by Joel Townsley Rogers
The chilling story of a young couple on their way to be married who pick up an ominous hitchhiker and are involved in a strange accident is a tale of sheer terror.

$3.50

A Sad Song Singing—by Thomas B. Dewey
Masterful suspense and an unusual mystery set "Mac" against Chicago's shadowy world of entertainers and caberets.

$3.50

The Shrewsdale Exit—by John Buell
Brutal highway terrorism destroys a man's family in this poignant and suspenseful tale of innocence confronted by irrational violence.

$3.50

Available at Fine Bookstores Everywhere
or
Order Direct from the Publisher:
Carroll & Graf Publishers, Inc.
260 Fifth Avenue
New York, New York 10001
Add $1.25 per title for postage and handling.
N.Y. State Residents please add 8¼% sales tax.

Fantasy and Science Fiction Titles
Available from Carroll & Graf

Citadel of Fear—by Francis Stevens
A masterpiece of the fantastic, a classic allegory set in Tlapallan, lost city of an ancient race.

$3.50

Om, The Secret of Ahbor Valley—by Talbot Mundy
Set in India in the 1920's this wonderful tale of adventure and mysticism can be fairly called a cross between *Raiders of the Lost Ark* and *Kim*.

$3.95

The House on the Borderland—by William Hope Hodgson
Renowned as one of the greatest cosmic fantasy tales in the English language, this novel is a work of pure imagination which sustains an overpowering level of wonder and mounting horror. It will appeal equally to fans of fantasy, horror and science-fiction.

$3.25

Available at Fine Bookstores Everywhere
or
Order Direct from the Publisher:
Carroll & Graf Publishers, Inc.
260 Fifth Avenue
New York, New York 10001
Add $1.25 per title for postage and handling.
N.Y. State Residents please add 8¼% sales tax.